Academy Gothic

by James Tate Hill

Southeast Missouri State University Press | 2015

Academy Gothic by James Tate Hill

Copyright 2015: James Tate Hill

Softcover: 978-0-9903530-8-9

First published in 2015 by
Southeast Missouri State University Press
One University Plaza, MS 2650
Cape Girardeau, MO 63701
www6.semo.edu/universitypress

Cover Design: Lori Jackson Hill

Library of Congress Cataloging-in-Publication Data

Hill, James Tate.
  Academy gothic / by James Tate Hill.
    pages cm
  ISBN 978-0-9903530-8-9 (pbk.)
  I. Title.
  PS3608.I4295A33 2015
  813'.6--dc23
                          2015006224

Academy Gothic

For Lori

Acknowledgements

Without Susan Swartwout's belief in this book, it might still be academy_gothic.docx. Thank you, Susan, for your vision and hard work in bringing my novel into the world. Many thanks to the late Wedel Nilsen, whose generosity and love of literature live on in the Nilsen Prize. This novel's astute first readers were Matt Armstrong and Paul Crenshaw, writers and friends of the highest order. Carrie Walker, Luke Epplin, and Karen Meadows also made smart, invaluable contributions. Three characters in *Academy Gothic* first appeared in a short story published in issue 9 of *Monkeybicycle*, a literary magazine for which I am now fortunate to serve as fiction editor. Thank you to Shya Scanlon, Laura Carney, and Steven Seighman for editing and publishing that story and for welcoming me into the *Monkeybicycle* family. I wrote and revised this novel at The Green Bean, Cheesecakes by Alex, Coffeeology, Tate Street Coffee, and Scuppernong Books; the friendly staff and caffeinated beverages of these Greensboro establishments improved many a morning. I learned so much from my professors and peers at UNC Greensboro, Hollins University, West Virginia University, and West Virginia Wesleyan College. A child whose parents never question what makes him happy is the luckiest kid in the world, and those are the parents I have. Lastly and most of all, thank you, Lori, for your brilliant cover design, your unwavering support, your love. You give meaning to whatever I write.

1

TWO YELLOW STREAMERS FORMED an equals sign in the dean's door frame. No one told me it was his birthday. The news might have been in one of the e-mails I deleted without opening. With the constant threat of staff eliminations, it seemed like a good idea to check the door for a card and add my signature. I got a few inches from his door. My eyesight is bad. Legally blind is one way to put it. It's not how I like to put it.

Beneath the name plate of Randall "Scoot" Simkins, PhD, there was only the homemade poster telling visitors, "This door is actually open (metaphorically)! Come back soon!" I didn't like metaphors. I knocked twice above the top streamer.

"Dean Simkins? It's Tate Cowlishaw. I came to wish you a happy birthday."

The dean and my colleagues were upstairs at our daily meeting for which I was ten minutes late. I reached between the streamers, opening the door in the literal sense. Campus theft and vandalism had been on the rise, and Simkins adjourned every meeting with a reminder to lock our office doors. Only two of us had office doors. The knob turned. That he treated his own words with the same indifference as his faculty made me a little sad.

I said his name again, waited three seconds, and limboed inside. The odor of rotten eggs overwhelmed the urine and black mold that were Parshall College's unofficial scents. One time, a colleague brought me into her classroom to examine the sulfurous aroma, to determine if it was one of the ghosts some blamed for the school's decline. The visually impaired have certain skills, like knowing when another person is in the room with us, that lend us a certain credibility in matters of the supernatural. I had placed an ear against two walls of the classroom and nodded ambiguously.

Three steps into Simkins's office, something crunched under my shoe. The carpet held shards of plastic the size of fingernails. Some were wet. I sniffed my finger, found the source of the stench, and coughed my way to the window.

"Dr. Cowlishaw," whispered someone on the ground outside the broken window.

I had an MBA, not a doctorate, but didn't correct students who conferred on me the additional degree.

"There he is." I recommend this greeting, even to the fully sighted, when you have no idea who you're talking to. From where I stood, I made out a blue coat, one arm waving beneath the leafless tree. To be precise, I have central blind spots, leaving the rim of my peripheral vision my only useful eyesight.

"Why are you in Simkins's office?" whispered the voice I now recognized as Wade Biggins. Wade's time at Parshall more than doubled my own five years. His inane, mostly sincere questions derailed many a lecture and class discussion. Some students had come to regard him with ironic reverence, the faculty with something between fear and existential heartburn.

"It's the dean's birthday, Wade. I'm decorating his office." I leaned in close to the shattered pane and placed a finger across my lips. Fixing the broken windows, we had voted last year, would only encourage more vandalism.

"Make sure he gets my present," Wade said.

"Will do. What did you get him?"

"Stink bomb!" he shouted before running away.

Footsteps in the ceiling reminded me why I was here. Between the dean's computer monitor and a chipped Parshall mug filled with pennies sat the memo holder on which Simkins impaled coupons for fast food. I freed the one on top and got out my magnifier, the 22X loupe that makes some reading possible. Free six-inch sub with the purchase of a six-inch sub. I slid it in my back pocket. They didn't pay me much.

I lifted the lid of the glass candy dish he kept filled with circus peanuts. The smell was vaguely floral, vaguely astringent. I gave one a squeeze and put it back. Stiff as they were, they might have been the same ones Simkins offered me five years ago along with my job. A Post-it in the center of his desk read "a Butter." The birthday card was nowhere to be found.

A heavier set of footsteps thudded overhead, possibly in the stairwell. Fearing they were those of my lumbering dean, I crouched behind the black file cabinet. My knees were exposed. I crawled under the desk, from which vantage it became clear the footsteps didn't belong to Scoot Simkins. Scoot's feet, along with the rest of him, lay on the floor behind his chair.

The footsteps faded. I said hello, a feeble uppercut at the overgrown silence. I knew what I'd find, or wouldn't find, before I checked his cold wrist. Like I said, I know when I'm alone in a room.

"Happy birthday," I said.

The dean's flaccid body was firmer than it had any right to be. That Randall "Scoot" Simkins had left the world on the same date he entered it lent a degree of nobility to his life. He meant well, his faculty would say at his funeral. One of us might believe it. The dean had no wife or children, and I tried to think of anyone who might miss him. Most faculty, myself included, often joked of ways we might take revenge on the man who increased our work load at the same steady rate he cut our salaries. Just last week someone proposed training a fire hose on a certain orifice with which our dean shared so many characteristics.

Something glinted in the corner of my eye. Everything I see is in the corner of my eye. Simkins's hand curled around an old-school, all-metal stapler. A shadow darker than most shadows ran from Simkins's head to the wall. I touched it the way I do when things seem like an optical illusion. The shadow was sticky.

I brought my face a few inches from the dean's. It was one of only a few good looks at him I'd ever had. A few looks are all you need. Most of the time voices tell you everything you need to know, but Simkins wasn't saying much.

His hair smelled of women's shampoo. He must have had a coupon. Scoot had the jowly face of an offensive lineman, the pretense of toughness undermined by features so soft they might have been drawn in crayon. A wattle the size of a generous meatball made its home beneath his stubbly chin. I pulled on it. Scoot's head crackled a little as it left the carpet. If I weren't looking for them I wouldn't have seen the three spots on the top of his head, a little darker than the rest of his blood-dark hair. The spots were equal in size, slightly bigger than the tip of my smallest finger. I pushed down on the stapler in the dean's hand, confirming staples were all it held. I would have been impressed if he had shot himself three times in the top of the head. It would have been the first and last time he had ever impressed me.

I was a little dazed. I might have stood up too quickly. I might have had an aversion to dead bodies. I called off the search for the birthday card in light of what I had already found. More footsteps in the ceiling reminded me where I was supposed to be, where Dean Simkins was supposed to be. Slowly I opened the door, my hand brushing against the birthday streamers, which weren't made of paper but tightly stretched plastic. Letter by letter I read the words, which did not spell happy birthday.

"POLICE LINE DO NOT CROSS."

2

IN THE STAIRWELL, I opened the face of my watch and felt the minute hand. Seventeen minutes late. Londell Bakker's soft baritone barely carried into the hall. Two years ago, during the flu scare that never reached Grayford, we voted Londell third in command behind Simkins and his assistant dean, Delilah Bibb. Rounding the last aisle of desks, I passed Delilah's wheelchair. She was the only one crying, as far as I could hear.

"Tate, I don't know if you saw the police car outside." Londell handed me a copy of the agenda, which I scrutinized with my eyes in a left to right facsimile of reading. Most of my colleagues knew the extent of my impairment, but I rarely passed up a chance to seem normal.

"Don't say it," said Delilah Bibb in a dim voice. "I can't hear this again."

Silence lasted ten seconds while the room honored her request.

"Write it down for him." This came from Duncan Musgrove, the five-times-married, four-times-divorced professor of the course formerly called Biology—in the latest curriculum, it had been repackaged as "Scientific Skills."

"Will he be able to read it?" asked Benjamin Tweel.

"I think he will," I said.

Tweel's wife, Mollie DuFrange, in whose bed I awoke regularly while the two of them were taking a break three years ago, passed me half a sheet of paper. Knowing what it would say and not being fond of reading in front of an audience, I slid my loupe across the tiny words and said, "How did he die?"

Delilah wept. The rest of us—eleven if we were all there—didn't make a sound. Outside the building, a car door closed.

"I'm sure our students, like us, will want some time to grieve." Londell Bakker was a half-black, half-Scandinavian professor of what we called "Societal Studies," with dreams of becoming a stand-up comedian. Nothing he had ever said onstage was as funny as the thought of our students, or the faculty minus Delilah Bibb, shedding a tear for someone who insulted our intelligence more frequently than we thought was legal.

A tiny breeze rattled the aluminum blinds. A door creaked on the first floor. Someone started up the stairs. None of my colleagues seemed worried. I followed their lead. Not worrying had come naturally since I turned sixteen, the age my optic nerves announced their early retirement. Because danger might forever lurk beyond my meager sightline, I had to decide whether to worry constantly or never at all. The latter seemed like less trouble.

The hard-soled shoes clicked into the classroom. "Good morning," said our darkly clad guest speaker. "Maybe not for what's 'is name, I guess. Anyway, I won't keep you as long as I understand he would have." He laughed in the deeply satisfied way that doesn't invite you to join in.

Duncan Musgrove joined in. "I like this guy," Duncan said.

"Excuse me, officer." Delilah located her voice beneath a sob.

"Detective," he corrected her. "Detective Stashauer."

"Detective," said Londell. "What can you tell us about the cause of death?"

"We'll let you know what we know when we know it. In the meantime, I'll let you fine educators tend to your *pressing* matters while I give your dean a lift to the morgue." Detective Stashauer approached Mollie's desk and picked up what must have been the agenda. "Think, pair, share ideas for Conference on Interdisciplinary Assessment." The words were stretched by his expanding smile.

"Well," Londell said when the detective's footsteps reached the stairs. He spoke in a low, defeated voice, which is to say his natural voice. "In light of recent events, Delilah, perhaps we can table some of these items on the agenda. Yes, Duncan."

Duncan Musgrove stood up from his desk. His head wasn't much higher than when he was sitting. In his voice like scratched glass, he said, "Am I going to have to be the asshole?"

Silence seemed to serve as a yes.

"Our jobs, goddammit. What's going to happen to our jobs?"

As much as we resented Scoot Simkins for the power he held over us, his talent for ruining days with never-ending meetings, and his passion for paperwork, he also had been our advocate to the school's trustees, the secretive group who authorized our paychecks. Small as the paychecks were, there were always adjuncts, numerous graduates from the state university across town, willing to work for even less.

"I'll let you know what I know when I know more than you know," Londell said. "At present, I'm just a man holding the same sheet of paper you see in front of you. Delilah, any thoughts?" Londell clicked his tongue, what sounded like the *William Tell Overture*. "I'll take that as a no. Oh, I almost forgot. Carly has some good news."

Co-coordinator of the writing course with Mollie DuFrange, Carly Worth was a nervous blonde who spoke at meetings more sparingly than I did. She cleared her throat. "I sold my novel," she said, sounding embarrassed.

"A novel?" said Mollie, who was a poet. "What's it about?"

Carly cleared her throat again. "Vampires."

Carly's was a pretty voice, something you'd keep on a high shelf so kids couldn't break it.

"Hmmm," Mollie said, one part "that's interesting" and two parts "go to hell."

"Congratulations," I said and clapped slowly, giving others the chance to join in. No one did.

To honor the memory of our late dean, we decided to, in the words of Delilah Bibb, "put our students first." My own students, as usual, expressed their disappointment upon seeing me enter Suddreth Hall. I wasn't much of a teacher, as Simkins liked to tell me during my annual reviews, and I didn't disagree. I was a box checker and gatekeeper of the industrial complex. I taught financial literacy and rudimentary math, courses deemed practical enough to remain in the curriculum, which Simkins revised each fall after returning from another conference on the depressed campus of a small Midwestern college.

Past the fog of urine stretching around the corner from the men's room, Carly Worth said my name. "It's Carly," she added in that soft, far-right-side-of-the-piano voice.

"I see that," I said. I knew it was her as soon as she spoke. Friendly gestures, like people I knew telling me who they were, always struck me as condescending. This might have been why I had few friends.

"Thank you," she said. "For congratulating me earlier."

"I assume this is your last semester with us," I said. "Published authors don't have to teach at mediocre colleges."

Carly shushed me as a pair of students filed past us into her classroom.

"They know it's a mediocre school," I said. "Ask them."

Carly got close enough for me to see her smile if I glanced a foot above her head. It's nice sometimes to see such things, however briefly, before returning to the art of feigned eye contact. Her mouth was very close to my ear, presumably to tell me something, when the student seated closest to the door started laughing.

"Dr. Cowlishaw. How did Simkins like his present?"

Wade Biggins was not what we used to call "college material." At this point, neither were most of his peers. He had an unhealthy penchant for mischief, a mild form of autism, possibly undiagnosed, and a future no brighter than a sock drawer slammed tight-shut. Even so, the odds that he had killed the dean seemed remote. One would have to progress from stink bombs to bullets, it seemed, and not the other way around.

"I don't think he'll need the gift receipt, Wade."

Carly led me away from the door. She continued to smile. She continued to smell like sweet, expensive perfume. She said, "I've been wanting to ask you this for some time. I'm doing research for my next novel. When are you going on your rounds again?"

In addition to teaching duties, I was also required to patrol the campus twice a month, performing what could nominally be referred to as rituals. When Simkins felt a meeting had not lasted long enough, he called on me for an update on the college's paranormal health, and I would describe what I had "encountered" on my most recent tour. With no teaching experience prior to this job, my hire came directly at the behest of F. Randolph Parshall, trustee and grandson of the school founder. In his expert, possibly senile assessment, I had a singular ability to detect and communicate with apparitions, the displeasure of whom, Parshall believed, was causing the decline of our quaint school.

"In light of our dean's untimely demise," I said, "I should probably go tonight."

"Can you have company? I mean, do the ghosts mind?"

"I'll introduce you. Wear something low-cut," I said. "They like that."

Carly had a laugh that made me want to cancel class. Many

things had this effect on me. She said she'd call me and disappeared inside her classroom.

"Does this count for a grade, Dr. Cowlishaw?" One of the Ashleys wanted to know.

I was passing out the exams and bubble sheets Simkins had placed in our boxes the week before. Nearly half of all instructional time consisted of tests to obtain data, longitudinal studies Simkins used to measure the efficacy of whatever we were or weren't doing.

"I took this in another class," said one of the Brittanys.

"Just do the best you can," I said in response to both questions.

Ten minutes had gone by when someone knocked on the classroom door. I carried one of the tests to the door. The individual made no efforts to come in. He was the size and shape of a twelve-year-old boy. He gave the exam a once-over and handed it to the much taller figure to his right.

"Are you Cowlishaw?" asked the short one.

"I am. Who are you looking for?" I stepped aside to invite them in.

"Can we have a word with you in the hallway?" asked the taller one, whose voice I recognized as Detective Stashauer. He placed the exam in what sounded like a Ziploc bag.

I left open the door of my classroom. Detective Stashauer closed it. He asked, "What were you doing in the dean's office this morning?"

I turned the truth over in my mind. I didn't like how it felt. Before I could think of an alternative, I felt the taller detective's hands around my arms. He spun me around, held my cheek against the wall. His partner, I presumed, in a gentler but no less decisive manner, fitted my wrists with cold metal.

3

ETECTIVE STASHAUER DRANK SODA from a
can. The interrogation room was quiet enough to hear
the bubbles pop. "I hear you like ghosts," he said, his
tone suggesting he was not a fan, possibly of ghosts, possibly of me.

I sipped coffee that tasted like a charred potato. A fragrant box
of donuts was open on the table. No one had offered me one.

I fixed my gaze on the wall just below the ceiling. "No, it's okay.
They know I didn't kill you. Absolutely. Students first," I said.

"What are you looking at?" Stashauer asked. "Who are you
talking to?"

"Oh, I'm sorry. Dean Simkins's ghost is with us. Would you like
to ask him anything?"

Stashauer got up from the table and leaned over me. "Fuck you
and your ghost."

"He isn't my ghost," I said.

Stashauer's partner, the very short man, scribbled everything I
said on a yellow legal pad.

"They ought to get you a tape recorder," I said.

The very short officer, whose name had not come up, asked
about the coupon they had removed from my back pocket. He had
the high, pubescent voice particular to adults shorter than four feet.

"I stole it from the dean's desk," I said. "Around seven-thirty,
not long after you were there. My fingerprints, which I'm assuming
you matched to those on file as part of the myriad burglary investigations—you haven't made any headway on those, I take it—can
also be found on the police tape on Simkins's doorway. From the

hardness of his body, I'd say the time of death was well before seven-thirty, but you probably don't need me to tell you that."

"I like the way you talk," said the short detective. He wrote something on a second legal pad.

"Does that mean I can leave?"

Detective Stashauer picked up the coffee I had touched only once. He held the cup under my chin, lifted it to eye-level and a little higher. I felt, saw, smelled, and tasted it in that order. The shorter detective called Stashauer by his first name, if his first name was Rick. The two left the small room in order of height, tallest first.

Five minutes went by. I pulled the box of donuts toward me and surveyed the contents: three iced, two glazed, two powdered and filled. I stuck my finger in one of the filled and came away with apple. I tried the other.

"If you're done finger banging my donuts," said Stashauer from the doorway, "Officer Delafield is going to escort you to a holding cell."

Delafield was not his partner, but a black officer wearing Aqua Velva and a tan uniform two sizes too big for his stocky frame. "What's that on your finger?" asked Delafield.

I tasted it. "Swiss chocolate." My second guesses were always better than my first.

For a moment, I felt dangerous and vaguely important in my tiny cell, nothing but a sink and a toilet with no seat. Then I felt nostalgic for the thin white room with the donuts and terrible coffee.

I considered shouting my innocence, but outrage didn't come naturally to me. "Aren't you an impervious one," Mollie DuFrange liked to tell me, in the days when she liked to tell me things. She wanted me to talk about my eyes. When I did, she was disappointed that they didn't fill with tears. In my experience, things are what they are, good or bad, regardless of how you feel about them.

I got used to the concrete floor. After a few hours, the strobe effect of the buzzing light no longer nauseated me. I imagined getting used to a trial and the bad breath of a nervous, court-appointed attorney. Before I could convict myself, a set of footsteps too soft to be Delafield's approached the cell. Keys jangled in the hand of Stashauer's partner. The lock was level with his forehead.

"I take it my story checked out."

"Our bad," he said.

The short detective led me down the hall past the interrogation room. The hall opened into the larger room with desks and ringing phones. I could have found my way to the front door and told him so. New places are sometimes difficult, but I'm an excellent retracer of steps. Stashauer joined us by the door, offering me a ride home with all the cheer of a man who has lost a bet.

The motel where I lived was less than a mile away. "I'll walk," I said.

Stashauer put a hand on my shoulder. "Stand outside with me for a moment."

I looked behind me. "Where did your partner go? I like you better when he's here."

Stashauer chewed a mouthful of gum. He handed me a stick, the kind wrapped in foil that loses its flavor in a hurry. I put on my sunglasses for a more discreet look at the detective. It's a shame only blind people get to wear sunglasses indoors.

Stashauer had curly hair that evoked adult films of another era. "Let me offer my condolences for the loss of your dean," he said. "Happens to a lot of cops. Stress of the job and whatnot. It's not my bag, but I don't begrudge a man for shooting himself in the head."

Stashauer waited for me to say something. I chewed the spearmint gum. I was a peppermint guy.

"They tell me you don't see very well," he said.

"When I see three bullet wounds, I don't think suicide."

"If you saw what you think you saw, you'd be our prime suspect. Do you want to be a suspect, professor?"

I was not a professor, but what they called a lecturer. I didn't correct him. He seemed to like his own conclusions, and because I had no attachment to my own, I shook the detective's hand and started walking.

On the corner of Market and Gray, a black man waiting for the bus said, "It's a nice evening, isn't it?"

I spat my gum into a trash can. "A little too nice."

4

THREE AND A HALF HOURS EAST of the coast, two hours west of the mountains, Grayford, North Carolina, wasn't a place people lived as much as waited for a reason to leave. For the textile industry, the reason came twenty years ago in the form of Chinese children with a tolerance for long hours and low wages. For the half-dozen call centers near the airport, the reason was the English-speaking population of South Asia with similar feelings to the Chinese about labor and pay. I had lived in Grayford for three years when the bank that had paid me to move here expressed their disapproval of how I gave away their money. I wasn't giving enough of it to the poor and unemployed, who made no convincing arguments for how they might pay back their loans. My own argument for why I should keep my job—that it's a slow, tedious, occasionally embarrassing process for a man with bad eyes to learn his way around a new town—didn't strike my employer as persuasive. By then my grandmother had found a nursing home in Grayford to be near me. Six months later, she was dead and I was a college instructor.

The Gray Knight was the last motel in Grayford where you could get a room by the hour, night, or week. Some people are fond of houses and apartments. I'm fond of not purchasing furniture and towels. Downtown Grayford is the only part of town friendly to pedestrians, and a 15x18 motel room is the only real estate I can afford.

Edward jumped down from the window and led me to his dish. He kept meowing while I filled it with food.

"You and me both, pal."

I found a box of pizza in the mini-fridge. I had just taken my second bite when the phone rang. The answering machine did its job after the first ring. This meant there were messages. The current caller didn't leave one. According to the machine, this was a pattern that began at 10:32 this morning. At 12:14, cutting through the dense fog of hang-ups, came a voice no one ever described as a beacon of light.

"Mr. Cowlishaw, this is Interim Dean Bibb. Please pick up the phone." She had recovered nicely from her grief. "I know you're there. Your phone has been busy all morning." She paused again and gave a terse sigh. "I passed by your classroom and noticed you weren't there. This kind of shirking cannot continue. I hope—"

I hit delete and listened to some more hang-ups. They ceased at 1:30, resuming around the time I was released from the Grayford jail. They make talking phones that read you the numbers of missed calls, but I try not to dwell on what I miss.

I pulled off my coffee-stained shirt and threw it in the pile for housekeeping. I waited for the shower to get warm. The phone rang. I turned off the water and listened. The machine waited four rings. The voice wasn't one I had heard in my room in three years.

Mollie DuFrange said my name and paused. She told me once that poetry was the best words in the best order, but her silence seemed less a search for words than hesitation. "I noticed you weren't in class and got worried. I just wanted to make sure you were okay." After another pause, she added, "Sorry about the hang-ups."

I had no idea she still cared. I would remove that from the list of things I didn't know. It was a long list. The other items wouldn't get lonely.

Darkness had overtaken the shadows by the time I got to campus. Carly and I had agreed to meet at the fountain that had been drained for the winter sometime in the 90s and was never refilled. Carly's blonde hair was visible from twenty feet away. For this reason, I preferred blondes in the moonlight, brunettes in the midday sun. She threw what sounded like a pocketful of coins into the marble basin.

"That's a lot of wishes," I said.

"I hope to sell a lot of books." Her tight jeans were more flattering than the ankle-length skirts she wore inside the classroom. "What's in the bag?"

I showed her the mortar and pestle, four sandwich bags of different colored sugar, and what a used bookstore employee told me was a Russian thesaurus. They were meaningless props, but perhaps no less so than the papers my colleagues presented at out-of-town symposiums.

"What does that do?" she asked as I sprinkled blue sugar on the fire escape of Parshall's only remaining dorm.

I wished for Carly's novel more originality than I mustered for the story of Agnes Fairmont, a 1920s freshman who hanged herself after her boyfriend ended their passionate affair. "She gets out of sorts from time to time. It's likely her appearances coincide with a current student going through a bad break-up."

"Have you ever seen her?"

"I've sensed her," I lied. "It's a common misconception that you can see ghosts. Anyone who says they've seen a ghost hasn't actually seen one."

I led her up the crumbling steps to the former theater, made up a tale of twins who had hanged themselves above the proscenium arch before a play in which one was cast and the other was not. I scattered a few pinches of sugar by the entrance.

"I see you're using red this time."

I wasn't used to questions. Dean Simkins had not requested any explanations the single time he accompanied me on my rounds. This was four years ago, the first and last time I had been on my rounds. "Red helps when resentment was involved. Is any of this helpful?"

"I'm enjoying myself," she said and started down the steps without me.

I followed her to the massive oak tree between the library and Furley Hall. Carly gazed at the second-floor window of our former dean. I stood in the spot from which Wade Biggins had delivered his thoughtful gift.

"What do you think happened to him, Tate?"

I considered the possibility, not for the first time, that Simkins had taken his own life. He was a miserable son of a bitch, though I never got the impression that he realized it. What I didn't know about ballistics could have filled Simkins's file cabinet, but common sense held that a man doesn't get off three rounds in his own head, let alone in his crown.

"It doesn't matter what I think."

Carly looked at me. "Didn't you see him? Isn't that why they took you to the police station?"

"Let's just say the cops and I didn't see the same thing."

"What did you see?"

"I saw a dead man who didn't choose to be that way."

Carly shivered in the low-cut camisole I noticed for the first time. Her shampoo smelled like an otherworldly peach. She tilted her head onto my shoulder, and I dropped my bag of nonsense in the high grass.

"How soon," she asked, taking a few steps toward Furley Hall, "before a ghost haunts the building where it died?"

"Sometimes years," I said, trying to change her mind as she reached for the door. "Some don't return at all, especially if no hanging was involved."

No lights were on. The windows were stingy with moonlight. Carly started up the stairs. We were on the landing between the first and second floor when a muffled banging began in the inner wall. Carly grabbed my arm. I directed her to the far left, where the creaks were less pronounced. The semester I taught on the third floor, I learned how to walk undetected past the office of my dean, who liked to ask about tasks I had not completed.

The banging had an irregular pattern, ruling out plumbing or the heat. The sound of metal seemed to rule out the animal kingdom. A scraping took over as we reached the second floor. I looked at Carly. She mouthed something I couldn't understand.

I wasn't sure how many murderers returned to the scene of the crime. Whoever was scraping and rattling in an empty building with the lights off might object to company. Heavy breathing followed the next round of banging. Then came the litany of expletives familiar to any student who's taken a science course at Parshall College.

Carly flipped on the light switch. "Duncan? What are you doing here?"

"What am I doing here? What the fuck are you doing here?" Duncan's short arm reached past me and angrily returned the lights to their off position. Duncan did everything a little angrily.

"Did you kill Dean Simkins?" Carly's tone was more complimentary than accusatory.

"I didn't goddamn kill anybody." Duncan assumed a threatening stance, the top of his head coming only to Carly's shoulders. "Why are you two here? Maybe you offed him."

"We heard scary noises," I said. "Maybe you can protect us."

Duncan swung his paunch in my direction. He had the dusty

breath of a man who hasn't eaten since breakfast. "I'm not in the mood for your bullshit, Cowlishaw."

In spite of his background in Biology, Duncan did not possess the cool, objective temperament of a scientist. He liked science, he once told me, because he liked being right and liked even more to prove it. He was a fireball of nerves, fueled by debt and the constant paranoia of losing his job. I had spent enough time with him, though, to see the man to whom five different women had vowed their eternal love. My first semester, in a bad thunderstorm, he saw me walking and stopped to offer a ride. When I waved him off, he pushed open the passenger door and said, "Get in the goddamn car, Cowlishaw. You're going to catch pneumonia, and you don't have health insurance."

He went back to Simkins's door, threw the tool he was using into a plastic toolbox. Instead of expletives, he made a clucking sound consistent with sobs. He fell back against the wall, sank to the floor, and hugged his knees.

"He was going to fire me," Duncan said.

"So you did kill him?" I asked.

Duncan blew his nose and wiped his hand on the carpet. "I didn't kill him, dammit. I don't kill people. Neither do I fire people two years before they're set to receive their pension just because they're the only one who was hired when they still offered pension and health insurance and didn't make you buy your own paper for the copy machine."

"As a professor of scientific skills," I said, "you're probably aware that breaking into Simkins's office isn't the most empirical evidence of your innocence."

"I just want my file, Cowlishaw. Whoever gets his job, whether it's Bibb or somebody from the outside, doesn't need to know about my pension. And yeah, okay, if there's an investigation going on, maybe I'd rather nobody know I had a motive for killing the son of a bitch."

His sobs resumed, and Carly knelt beside him. She petted his black and white hair. Duncan dyed it at the beginning of each semester, and over the next few months we watched him age in fast-forward as the gray returned.

"I don't know about your pension," Carly said, "but Tate says there isn't going to be an investigation."

"How the hell does he know?"

I offered Duncan my hand and struggled to pull him to his feet.

"That detective from our meeting," I said, "seems to have his heart set on calling it a suicide."

"Good. That's one less thing to worry about," Duncan said.

"Unless whoever killed Simkins isn't done killing people."

"You just said he killed himself."

"The detective says suicide. I saw the body, and it wasn't suicide."

Duncan grabbed my shirt collar and pulled me level with his eyes. "What the fuck do you know, Cowlishaw? You're no detective. Let him do his job, and let me keep mine."

Carly pinned some of her hair behind an ear. "Duncan's probably right, Tate. Maybe you don't know what you saw."

"Yeah, Cowlishaw. How many fingers am I holding up?"

"Am I the only one who sees that?" I asked, pointing to the wall. For the last few seconds, flashing blue lights from the classroom window did the Charleston above our heads. "My guess is the cops, but maybe you want to ask them what they think it is."

"I'm not going anywhere," Duncan said. "I goddamn work here."

Carly was already on the stairs. I struggled to catch up. Outside, I lost her footsteps under a siren and Duncan's renewed banging. I said her name, listened for mine. I returned to the oak tree, finding nothing but the bag of props with which I had arrived.

5

EVEN AT ITS PEAK ENROLLMENT in the 1960s, when Parshall College conferred degrees on four hundred students per year, the school had a reputation as a "pay your fees, get your Cs" diploma mill for the upper class. Annually ranked atop the category of Worst Value by *U.S. News and World Report*, Parshall's enrollment decreased for thirty-eight consecutive years as most applicants who were accepted found plenty of reasons to attend more affordable schools. Nevertheless, the number of applications increased each year as a college degree became the inalienable right and requirement of every American. Enter an enterprising administrator named Randall "Scoot" Simkins, who relaxed admission standards to accommodate the needs of the modern student. As it turned out, these needs were right in line with the financial needs of the school's trustees.

For a few years, Simkins's lower admission requirements helped to slow the bleeding. Tourniquets, of course, cause their own problems. Students got less and less bright. Admissions still threw a few scholarships to high achievers to keep up appearances, the hundred dollar bill wrapped around a roll of singles. Give us your poor, your tired, your huddled minds, and maybe our graduates couldn't get or keep jobs for which they had no business applying. The checks of Mr. and Mrs. Biggins still cleared the bursar's office.

It was Delilah Bibb who had spearheaded Simkins's newest initiative, an interdisciplinary curriculum designed in opposition to the traditional liberal arts model. A lifelong educator whose own discipline was education itself, Delilah had merely found a more palatable name for the shit burger Simkins had served the student body by eliminating majors four years earlier. Instead of a degree in Nursing or Business Administration, graduates now received degrees in collegiate studies. The move inspired some students. They purchased cans of spray paint by the gross. Rocks flew through windows. Feces made regular appearances outside of bathrooms. None of the students transferred to other schools. If they had anywhere else to go, they wouldn't be at Parshall.

"The problem is not our students," Delilah Bibb told us in an emergency meeting twenty-four hours after our dean went on eternal sabbatical. "If you want to honor our late dean, give these students the hard work and innovation they deserve."

Delilah sat up tall in her wheelchair, her orange hair a bit higher than usual against the yellow wall. I added a few inches to her height, which I had always estimated at five-nine.

"If your students are not winning Nobels and Pulitzers and serving on the bench of the Supreme Court, perhaps it's time for you, the faculty, to look in the mirror."

Duncan Musgrove, who had apparently avoided jail time, took care to ensure the word "cunt" went no further than a one-desk radius. Behind him sat Mollie DuFrange, who had greeted me without mentioning her message on my answering machine. Carly Worth came in late and didn't greet anyone.

"Soft skills," Delilah intoned as she wrote on the lower portion of the chalkboard. "Reading comprehension, critical thinking, written and oral communication. These are the skills our students need to succeed, skills that translate across disciplines. You each have your specialties." She said this word with a European accent and a chuckle. "Everyone needs hobbies, of course, but what good do your particular academic interests do our students?"

"No disrespect, Delilah," said Londell Bakker, "but isn't this—"

"Dean Bibb."

Londell sniffed the new title, deciding whether or not he wanted to taste it. "Okay, Dean Bibb. Isn't this what we've been doing?"

"Thank you." This was Benjamin Tweel, whose academic specialty was the study of space tourism, a burgeoning industry, as he liked to refer to it.

I moved my pen whenever my colleagues spoke, a substitute for active participation in our meetings. Any transcription of actual words was strictly coincidental. Benjamin Tweel craned his neck to see what I was writing. I covered my paper. "No cheating," I said.

"No disrespect to our late dean . . ." Delilah paused to compose herself. "What we were doing was unfocused and disorganized. Our students have no use for seventeenth-century poetry or the digestive system of a katydid any more than we want to know which songs make them want to get up and shake their *groove things*. I will meet with all of you individually, starting today, to discuss how you can adapt your current syllabi and lesson plans. Until then, why don't we break into pods and brainstorm formative assessments for the upcoming symposium in Duluth. Think, pair, share."

No one moved. Delilah clapped her hands two times, and we slowly turned our desks to face each other.

"Incidentally," Delilah added, "I have received the police report, and they have ruled Dean Simkins's death a suicide. With regard to our personal safety, there is no cause for concern."

After the ceiling collapsed in Ragsdale Hall, lecturers and adjuncts relocated to cubicles in the campus's retired swimming pool. Blue and white tiles remained on the walls. The heating system ran like a freight train in the ceiling. No heat came out. The scent of ant spray, a headache-inducing blend of citrus and glue, lingered in the air. The ants lingered in the bathroom and along the walls.

At my desk, I reached around the framed photo of an attractive couple I had never met and turned on the outdated desktop no one bothered to steal. In my first year, stopping by my office to introduce himself, Duncan Musgrove asked why I didn't have any pictures of family. In truth, I had little use for pictures, but I told him the other truth, that my parents had died in a plane crash when I was two.

"A goddamn orphan," Duncan said. "Now if you'd just tell people you were blind, they might actually like you."

The next day he gave me the 5x7 wedding photo of the couple in their late twenties. "If anyone asks, Cowlishaw, tell people these are your parents. When you have a family, people think twice about firing you."

Between the photo and the computer mouse I never used, I noticed a handwritten note large enough to read without my magnifier. "Sorry you went home alone," it read. "Meet me outside Simkins's office tonight at ten? Carly."

It was my first clue, other than her head on my shoulder under the oak tree, that she had been interested in more than ghosts. I donned my earphones and opened my e-mail. Special software reads me what is on the screen. I sent a note to Carly proposing a few venues more romantic than the second floor of Furley Hall.

Of the seventeen unread messages in my inbox, sixteen were from students wanting to know if class had been cancelled. Most were from yesterday. The other was from Delilah Bibb, the schedule of individual conference times. Mine was to begin five minutes ago.

I climbed the stairs to the third floor of Furley, where the meeting had adjourned half an hour ago. Delilah was too prideful, too nonchalant about her disability, ever to take an office on the first floor. The scent of pumpkin pie mingled with the aroma of water damage. Delilah's scented candles didn't so much freshen the air as trick you into taking a deep breath.

"Tate Cowlishaw. Late as always."

I sat in the chair beside her desk, situated against the wall.

She clicked her mouse and then her tongue. "One of the matters on which Dean Simkins and I disagreed very strongly was that of your qualifications to be working here."

I tried to hold eye contact, but her eyes were small, and there was a glare from the window.

"You're not a scholar, you're not much of a teacher, and let's be frank, Mr. Cowlishaw, the whole ghost thing never struck me as a viable method of revitalizing the college. In his most honest moments, I'm certain Dean Simkins would have acknowledged the absurdity of supernatural possibilities."

"Many scholars of the paranormal would say honest moments are those in which we are the most open-minded."

Delilah sighed through her nose. "I don't even know what that's supposed to mean. Let's save some time, shall we, and skip to the part where I say your contract will not be renewed for next year."

I crossed my legs at the ankles. "As you may or may not be aware," I said, "I was hired on the high recommendation of F. Randolph Parshall."

Delilah brushed something from the arm of her pale blouse. "According to the faculty handbook, which I'd wager you have not read, the dean has complete discretion on matters of personnel." Her cold fingers rested on the back of my hand. "All due respect, Mr. Cowlishaw, I've observed you in the classroom. I don't think teaching is your calling."

It wasn't the teaching but the paychecks, paltry as they were, of which I had grown so fond. Incessant meetings notwithstanding, teaching provided a good bit of down time in which to wonder what else people might pay me to do.

"Did you see it coming?" I asked.

She had just blown out the pumpkin pie candle, the smoke drifting my way. "Excuse me?"

"You knew Scoot better than we did. You must have recognized some of the troubles he referenced in his suicide note."

Delilah's hand was on the folded wheelchair behind her. She let go of it. In a quieter voice, she said, "There was no note, according to the report."

"I suppose when the depression is that profound, they don't bother."

Delilah swiveled her chair toward the window. "He wasn't depressed. He had just called me that evening. He had questions about PowerPoint. He was terrible with the simplest things."

"But deep down, you must have sensed a sadness in his confusion."

"NO, dammit. He was giddy. He had this stupid idea for a presentation based on that game show with all the briefcases." Delilah wept into her hand.

"I should tell you that I saw the body," I said.

Delilah plucked a tissue from her window sill. She tried to say something and had to try a second time. "So did I."

"Really? What did you see?"

She pulled in a series of jagged breaths before her voice caught. "I saw the sleeve of the Oxford shirt I gave him for his birthday. It had mint stripes. I was bringing him a scone. I assumed he was asleep on the floor. He slept in his office sometimes. I yelled at him to wake up. I laughed at him. He didn't move. Then my heart dropped into my stomach. Maybe I should have gone to him. I know CPR. I just sat there, frozen in the hallway. I don't know when I would have moved if the policeman hadn't arrived."

"After you called them," I said.

I thought she shook her head. Non-verbal responders don't know how rude they are to the visually impaired.

"I assume you didn't get a look at the bullet wounds on Scoot's head. CPR doesn't help those much." I let the wick on that one burn for a little while. Then I told her what I had seen.

Delilah shuffled through papers. "The police report doesn't mention a gun."

"Maybe they didn't find one. Maybe they didn't look. I looked. I found a stapler in his hand and three bullet wounds in the top of his head. Seemed like an odd place to shoot one's self, but Scoot never liked to do things the easy way, did he?"

Delilah left that one alone.

"Are ghosts going to keep kids from coming to Parshall, Dean Bibb? I doubt it. Is a new curriculum going to attract more applicants? Probably not. But one thing you can be sure about: schools where people get away with murdering deans don't show up in the Princeton Guide."

"What are you saying, Mr. Cowlishaw?"

"I'm offering to find out who murdered Dean Simkins."

She handed me what must have been the police report. I didn't take it.

"If the police think he killed himself, Mr. Cowlishaw—"

"What do you think?"

She said nothing. I smiled and got up to leave. I was halfway to the stairs when she told me to come back.

"Suppose you find something. What do you get out of it?"

"My contract is renewed."

Delilah overdid it with her laugh. "Why not? I'll renew your contract for next year."

"Indefinitely," I said.

Delilah took a deep breath, which didn't become another laugh. "I want updates," she said.

6

SOMEONE IN DARK CLOTHING waited outside my eleven o'clock class. I got close enough to discern a trench coat and shorts, the flasher look Wade Biggins sported on warmer days. He sucked a loud, snotty breath through his nose.

"It was just a stink bomb, Dr. Cowlishaw. The guy at the store yesterday laughed when I asked if they could kill people."

"I was in his office, Wade. I'm not dead."

Wade Biggins covered his eyes. "Maybe Dean Simkins was allergic."

"Dean Simkins was allergic to a lot of things, Wade. At the top of the list was exercise, generosity, table manners, and respect for other people's time. But I'm certain that stink bombs were not on the list."

"Really? Do you promise?" The thirty-year-old's delivery evoked a little boy asking dad to check under the bed for monsters.

"I promise, Wade, as sincerely as my promise that if you keep attending all your classes and hand in some pages with your name on them from time to time, you'll have your diploma before you know it."

Wade stood up straight, his guilty conviction overturned, his unfulfilled dreams ready once more to be extinguished in the natural way. His thick, bare legs carried him across the hall to Londell's classroom.

My own class was empty but for one dark-haired student in the second desk of the third aisle. Students who arrive on time always sit in the same seat, but it had been a few years since I had bothered to learn who sat where.

"Where is everybody?" I asked.

"People thought you were in jail," said Islanda Purvis, one of the last recipients of the Parshall Presidential Scholarship. In recent years, the college had not attracted many applicants who met the minimum test scores or grade point average to qualify.

I wrote "class cancelled" on the chalkboard in my customary large letters. "We wouldn't want your classmates to get behind," I said.

Islanda Purvis unzipped a large backpack, slid the textbook I had not yet used inside it, and said good-bye to me as harshly as any woman whose lipstick I had not tasted. She was a quiet student who had not missed a question on any of my quizzes or exams. This was Financial Basics, hardly a difficult course, and the question she asked me when she turned in her exams, "Is this all?" managed to communicate her disappointment with her choice of college and her college's choice of me.

"I could assign you a paper," I said. "Do you want to write a paper?"

"Are you going to read it?"

My usual method of grading the pair of one-page papers I assigned each term was to put a check mark beside the student's name and either a plus or a minus, depending on how far from the bottom the last line ended. "I always do."

Islanda sat back down.

"In one page," I wrote, "discuss how you would fix a failing business."

Islanda asked what kind of business.

"Be creative," I said, an answer which usually prevented further questions.

"I knew you didn't kill him," said Islanda on her way to the door.

I held her gaze, or pretended to.

"Where I'm from, Mr. Cowlishaw, when people shoot people, it's either because they're mad or they want something. I've never seen you get mad, and you don't seem like you want anything bad enough to shoot somebody for it."

"Thank you, I think." She was already in the hall when I asked, "Who told you he was shot?"

"I heard it. I'm an R.A. in the dorm. I was on my last rounds a little after two in the morning. I could have stayed in Baltimore if I wanted to be around this mess. This school is nothing like

34

I thought it would be. The brochures showed these rolling hills and this student throwing a Frisbee to his professor. They ought to show a toilet with the last three years of my life floating in the bowl."

"Those brochures," I said, "might be a little outdated."

I sat in the empty room, thinking of mad people and those who wanted something. Duncan Musgrove fit the former, Delilah Bibb the latter. Duncan's anger seemed to have escalated in the days since Simkins's demise. Delilah's inherited promotion didn't seem like a prize, but tedium is in the eye of the beholder. What most people wanted badly enough to kill for, according to movies and old mysteries, was money, presumably more than Simkins had in his wallet. Simkins never struck me as a man in debt to the leg breakers, or a man involved in nefarious business, but I couldn't rule it out. Stashauer certainly fit the profile of a cop on the take.

By 9:18, no other students had arrived. I erased the paper assignment and wrote "Mr. Cowlishaw's" above "class cancelled." Halfway to the door, I went back to pluralize class.

"You are home early," said Sundeep when I stopped in the office of the Gray Knight to pick up my laundry. Because their family remained in India, my landlords tended to know when their long-term residents were home. They told me I was their favorite, perhaps because I was the only one whose job didn't pay in cash.

"One of your shirts had a stain," said Jaysaree, Sundeep's wife, whose thick accent had not dissipated in her decade in America. "Do not worry. I will find a way to remove it."

Jaysaree set down the laundry basket to hug me. She did this when she hadn't seen me in a few hours. Sundeep draped his long, thin arm across my back, the way tennis players sometimes do while shaking hands after a match. Before dreams of a more stable life led him and his wife to the doorstep of a seedy motel in North Carolina, he played tennis professionally throughout the 90s. He had lost to all the greats.

"Sundeep said a girl named Carly called you while he was cleaning." Jaysaree said this with a teasing lilt. "Does she like Malai Kofta, Tate? We are having Malai Kofta tomorrow night."

I thanked Jaysaree for the clean clothes and made my way to the door.

"I will get that stain out," she shouted as the door closed.

Edward greeted me at the door, looking like he wanted to go

outside. I gave him the opportunity. He never took it. He thought it looked like a lot of trouble out there. He was a smart cat.

I pushed play on the answering machine. Carly cleared her throat. "Tate? I got your e-mail. I'm kind of confused. What note are you talking about? I was planning to work on a short story later, but maybe another time, okay?"

I took the note out of my pocket. The large black letters became smudges in my blind spots. I held it close enough to smell what I had thought to be her perfume, a scent I now recognized as the bittersweet ink of a felt-tip pen. Maybe she had changed her mind.

I opened my laptop and searched online for Simkins's obituary. In terms of evidence, those bullet holes were the best thing I had going for me. It might be useful to know when exclusive access to them would belong to worms. Grayford's only paper, *The Chanticleer*, had posted the notice yesterday afternoon.

"Randall 'Scoot' Simkins, cherished Dean of Collegiate Studies at Parshall College, passed away Monday. He was fifty-five. Simkins is survived by the faculty and students of the school, who will miss his wisdom and leadership. In lieu of flowers, donations may be made in the dean's name to Parshall College's Annual Fund."

I called the number for the person in charge of obituaries.

"This is Hoopel," said a boy barely old enough to deliver papers, let alone write for one.

"I'm calling to report an error in one of your obituaries."

Hoopel sighed. "Which one?"

I told him. Hoopel put me on hold. When he returned, he sounded pleased to tell me there was no error.

"You didn't ask what the error was."

"I didn't write it," he said.

"Then put your father on, or whoever did your work for you."

"We don't write most of them. People send them to us as they want them to appear." Suppressed anger leaked from the corners of his words, a sound familiar to anyone who has sat in on a faculty meeting at a mediocre college. It made me like Hoopel a little more, which wasn't much.

"I'd like to know who sent this one in. They gave you some bad information."

"I'll look it up and get back to you. What's the error?"

"First off, it says he passed away. That phrase doesn't generally encompass murder, does it?"

"Excuse me?"

"You heard me, Hoopel. Reporters are supposed to be good listeners."

"I'm not a reporter." The disgust with which he said this seemed general and not necessarily aimed at me.

"It also says he was cherished, another error. And I doubt he'll be missed, but I'll have to get back to you on that one."

"Wait a second. We haven't covered any murders this week. Who is this?"

"I'm a concerned member of the faculty. There's also an omission. It should say there's a memorial service and public viewing tomorrow afternoon." I gave Hoopel the details as I thought of them, not sure if their publication on *The Chanticleer*'s website would make them come true. "When can you get that correction up?"

He was typing. After a minute, he said, "It's up now. Sorry, but I can't put anything about a murder until there's a story to corroborate it."

"Maybe you ought to go find news instead of waiting for people to e-mail it to you."

Hoopel gave me what for. I gave him a dial tone. I stared one more time at the note Carly claimed not to have written. I kept staring until I realized there was no one in the room to convince I was reading it. "So much effort for such tiny lies," Mollie used to say whenever I pretended I could see. Considering the falsehoods found in police reports and the local paper, maybe I should trade up to bigger lies.

I switched off the lights and closed my eyes. My blind spots lingered behind my eyelids, tiny shapes waltzing to and fro like a broken kaleidoscope. Only in occasional dreams do they go away. Within minutes, I fell into the recurring dream in which I'm driving a car. It's my favorite next to the one where I read a book without earphones, and the one where I return the smile of a beautiful woman from across a bar. There was a phone inside the car, but I couldn't find it. The voice that answered was mine, but not mine.

"Tate, are you there? Pick up, man. I need you."

I turned the light on and reached for the phone. "Londell. What's going on?"

He was out of breath. "Thank God you're there. I need bodies, man."

"What kind of bodies?"

"I'm at the club. It's open mic night. I need five people at my table or they won't let me go onstage. Can you make it? I'll pay your cover."

Gazing at the note on my nightstand, the large words completely disappeared. I said I had no plans.

7

WALKING AT NIGHT, traffic lights are visible against the dark sky. I can cross streets when nothing is coming rather than waiting for cars to stop. With its awning of twinkling lights, I could spot Oral Tradition's without counting doors. In six years, the space had used the same name as a gay dance club, a cigar store, and now a coffee shop and bar with a stage no larger than a table for four. Last year the acerbic British judge from the televised talent show, or someone who looked like him, stopped in for a drink, delaying the café's inevitable demise; ditto the disappointment of Grayford's amateur talent pool.

The heavyset hostess ran a finger down an open book. "Looks like your cover's been covered." She laughed at the joke she thought she had made.

"At which table will I find my party?"

The hostess looked behind her at the darkened room. "I guess you can look around."

"Why didn't I think of that?"

I stood in the back for a few minutes, waiting to be seen. When no one said my name, I made my way to the bar. Most bars are built against walls, making them easy to find. The level of crowd noise suggested the room was less than a third full. A dim spotlight illuminated the wall behind the stage. I wasn't sure if the show had started. I asked a bartender in a vest what he had on tap, and he gestured to the wall behind him.

"Which would you recommend?"

"I don't drink beer," he said.

"You're not very useful, are you?"

The fellow in the vest found a customer who didn't ask so many questions.

Someone took the stage to a smattering of applause. A second bartender seemed friendlier than the first. It might have been her cocktail dress. I find them very friendly. Not wanting to play the same game, I forewent the beer and ordered an Americano.

I looked at the ceiling while the bartender's back was turned. She had lovely shoulders, a dark tattoo on the left one. Unfortunately there are only a handful of ways to get a good look at a girl's face. Some of them you regret.

A guitar started playing. I turned in my stool toward the stage. A female's voice filled the room like shower steam. She sounded like a brunette with chin-length hair she didn't like to wash every day. The lyrics referenced a beach and a hotel, looking for someone who was gone, gone. I could hear dark brown eyes and a smile just a little bit naughty. I'm not always right about such things. I don't always care.

"The girl singing," I said to my barista-bartender. "Who does she remind you of?"

She studied the stage. "Sort of a Mexican Garbo."

The song ended. Everyone clapped. The heavyset hostess went, "Woo."

The barista-bartender set both elbows on the bar. "People say I look like Kim Novak."

Staring into her eyes, I had a view of her smiling mouth and her breasts pushed together. I had no complaints with the view, but there's something more appealing about what you can't see. "Do me a favor, Kim."

"What's that?"

"Find out what Mexican Garbo's drinking and send her another on my tab."

The barista-bartender blew a lukewarm breath into my face and walked to the other end of the bar. I sipped my watery Americano with tasting notes of sneaker and hard water. In my experience, cafés that are also bars aren't much of either.

"I'm going to read from a one-act play in progress," the next amateur said nervously into the microphone. "I don't know. Maybe it's a screenplay."

The familiar voice was high around the edges and deep in the middle. Voices you've never heard before can seem familiar, not unlike the faces of total strangers.

"Thanks for the martini," said another, even more familiar voice behind me.

"Filthy and dry, if I remembered correctly."

Mollie DuFrange sat on the stool to my right. "You always had a great memory."

Perhaps the barista-bartender, from a few feet away, could see the difference between Mexican and half-Asian. As for Garbo, I would have gone with Joan Fontaine. I was right about the eyes and hair. The smile knew how to be naughty when it wanted to be.

"My memory must be slipping," I said. "I don't remember you ever singing."

"I've been taking lessons. Maybe I'll busk for quarters since poetry doesn't seem to have a place in the new curriculum."

"Is Dean Bibb in attendance?" I glanced over Mollie's shoulder at the crowd, giving me a better view of Mollie herself. She had on a white blouse with the sleeves rolled up, the top couple of buttons undone. Red neon from behind the bar twinkled in the leather pants I hadn't seen on her in a few years.

"No, she isn't." Mollie hopped down from the barstool. "Londell's been waiting for you, you know. You could have put aside your hubris for two seconds and asked the hostess to lead you to the table of the tall, freckled mulatto."

"I find things in my own time."

"How did that work out yesterday morning?"

I reached for my coffee. "Thank you for the phone call. I didn't realize you still cared."

Mollie brought her face within an inch of mine, balancing herself with a hand on my thigh, her martini on my knee. "Don't tell Ben I called."

She held her uncomfortable pose until I found it very comfortable. She was offering her face for me to see. Her smile tried to be naughty, but had too much on its mind.

The light musk of her hair, which she washed every third day, lingered briefly as she returned to a table near the stage. I picked out Tweel's voice and made my way over, wondering what the last two minutes had meant, the same confusion I felt after reading one of her poems.

The playwright was still onstage. "Suspect: They ought to get you a tape recorder. Detective: Where did that coupon come from? Suspect: I stole it from the dean's desk not long after you were there. I assume you have my fingerprints on file from the myriad burglary investigations. I assume you're no closer to solving any of them." A little puff of the playwright's breath hit the microphone. "That's not the ending, but I guess that's where it ends right now. Thanks for putting up with me. My name's Thayer."

I pulled out the empty chair between Benjamin Tweel and one of the panhandlers Londell occasionally rounded up to meet his quota, promising them free vodka. Thayer sat down at the table to our left. Londell slapped his hand on his way to the stage.

"Didn't expect to see you here, Cowlishaw." Benjamin Tweel rarely bothered to look at me when he spoke.

"How's outer space?" I asked.

"Closer than you realize."

I got up to change seats, letting Tweel have the last word. He needed it more than I did. I sat beside the short detective who had stolen my lines. Londell asked us to imagine Jack Nicholson as a Depression-era prostitute. Thayer laughed along with everyone at his table. I didn't hear his partner's distinctive guffaw.

"I'd be interested in how the play turns out," I said.

Thayer looked at me.

"Does your partner write the endings, or is it a collaborative process?"

Londell took the mic out of its stand. "This next one's for my colleagues in the audience. This is our late dean as played by the late great Redd Foxx." He sat down on the stage. He breathed heavily into the microphone. "I'm comin', Elizabeth! This is the big one!"

"Are you watching, Thayer? A heart attack. Your erroneous conclusions are impacting the future of comedy."

"What the hell are you talking about?"

I told him what I was talking about. He kept his eyes on the stage.

"Seemed like the autopsy results came back pretty fast. A few hours, was it? Is that pretty typical for a suspected homicide?"

"I'm no coroner. I never even saw the body." Thayer raised his voice, but his anger didn't seem directed at me. "I'm trying to enjoy myself, Cowlishaw. Why don't you do the same?"

I had nothing else to say. His ignorance seemed sincere. So did Carly when she claimed not to have written the note on my desk. I hoped I sounded half as sincere as I complimented Londell on his new material and apologized for not sticking around.

Two doors down, kids stood in line to get in the former art

museum that had reopened as a dance club. Orange cones in front of the old theater reminded people not to wait around for the box office to open. I made a left at the public library, which had converted the first floor into a coffee shop. They had talked of doing the same to the second and third floors. Presently, someone in flannel had converted the front steps into a bedroom.

A block from campus, a growling dog propped his front paws on the top of a picket fence, making himself a head taller than me. I scratched behind his ears. When everything is unknown, you don't startle easily. They say fear is useful, that the little hairs on your neck alert you to the presence of danger. My little hairs hadn't gotten off the couch in years.

Campus was quiet. The days of movie nights on the quad and Spring Sing talent shows were in the distant past. Fewer than fifty students still opted for the overpriced, underfurnished dorms. At a quarter of nine, the windows of Furley Hall remained dark. I waited under the oak tree until five after. The note's author, if he or she still wanted me inside, must already be there.

I opened the front door one inch at a time. Inside, a few creaks overhead were not necessarily footsteps. I took the quieter side of the stairs. When I reached the landing between the first and second floor, a sound like an out-of-tune cello moved from one side of the ceiling to the other. What might have been a drop of water came down hard on the step in front of me.

From just inside the doorway that opened to the second floor, I listened for the cello's next overture. There were only the eggshell moans beneath my own feet. I could sense someone in the hall or classroom. In spite of the abiding faith of F. Randolph Parshall, this was the extent of my extrasensory perception, the magic beans I had received in exchange for my optic nerves.

I took inventory of the shadows: three diagonal and one round. I was thinking of round objects that were not someone's head when the shadow shifted.

There was nothing within reach that I could use as a weapon. I thought of the keys in my pocket. I didn't think much of them. I wasn't wearing a belt. In one swift move, I leapt into the hall and swung at the shadow. I swung again. I generated quite a breeze. Beside the elevator, my leg tangled with something hard and soft in the proportion of a body. Losing my balance, I grabbed it, pulling both of us to the floor. I landed on the bottom. Her perfume had a citrus base with notes of cardamom, peach, and mildew. That last one might have been the carpet.

"I thought you didn't write the note," I said.

Carly's earring grazed my cheek. "I didn't. I wanted to know who was using my name to leave messages on your desk."

Our bodies remained stacked on the floor. The weight of an attractive woman isn't one you hurry to remove.

"I've been texting you all evening," she said.

"I think you need a cell phone to receive text messages."

"You don't have a cell phone? Who doesn't have a cell phone?"

"People who know better."

We helped each other to our feet.

"So why are you here?" she asked.

"I was invited. I'm trying to find out by whom."

Her head turned in both directions. She walked into the stairwell and returned. "Do you think someone else is in the building?"

"If so, they're trying hard to make us think otherwise." I took a few steps into the condemned classroom with water damage. Detecting the presence of multiple people was more than my modest gifts could handle.

"I don't like my name on that note, Tate. I don't like it at all. Besides Duncan, who else knew we were here last night?"

"I'm sure no one saw you leave, fast as you were moving."

Carly let out a breath. She leaned forward. Her lips offered me more than an apology. They were sticky with gloss.

"I was hoping you'd say that," I said.

A smile flashed on her face and disappeared. "Duncan," she said. "He was the only one."

"Unless someone was behind door number one." I gestured to Simkins's office, the only closed door besides the restroom and a closet.

"Delilah's office is upstairs. Maybe she heard us." Carly's voice gathered some anger. "Has it occurred to you that she's the only one benefitting from Simkins's death?"

"The thought crossed my mind. Then she said I could keep my job if I find out who murdered him."

Carly was on her way to Simkins's door and spun around. "What? When was this?"

"This morning. After she tried to fire me."

"Maybe, Tate, she's staying one pace ahead of you."

Carly made sure no one was hiding in the unisex bathroom. I did the same with the closet used by janitors when the college still employed them. Together we checked the first floor and then the third. Delilah's office was quiet. The lights were off. Carly tried the doorknob, but it didn't turn.

I placed my ear against the door, heard nothing. "She isn't here."

Carly led the way down the stairs, stopping on the second floor. "I don't even know why you'd want to keep working here. You should come with me to New York."

Nothing in her voice suggested she was kidding.

"Why don't you?" she asked when I hadn't responded.

I stood behind her by Simkins's door. "I might wait until our second kiss before I commit to an out-of-state move."

She pushed me gently against the door. Her lips pushed a little less gently against mine. Our tongues finished the job. It was a long job, but I didn't mind the work.

"I'm probably being too forward," she said.

I tried to think of a clever line. It's hard to do after you've been kissed. It's even harder when the person who kissed you must have been crying during said kiss because you can taste a tear on your lip.

She covered her eyes and turned her back to me. "I'm sorry, Tate. I just don't know how to be around people anymore. With people."

"The kiss was a good start."

"You don't understand. For years, I've focused on nothing, worried about nothing but my writing, and all this craziness with Simkins and that note, which I swear to God, Tate, I didn't write."

She buried her face in her arm against the wall, in the same corner where Duncan Musgrove had wept the night before. After a handful of tears, Carly stepped back from the wall. She twisted the doorknob. The door opened. Her head turned in my direction. It stayed that way while she grabbed my hand and led us forward into the dean's office.

Moonlight from the window made it a little brighter than the hall. Carly turned the light on. I turned it off, but not before noticing something different about the room.

"His file cabinet's gone," Carly said, sounding more surprised than I was to find the desk had been relieved of its contents. Carly pulled on the top drawer, unlocked and empty. She opened the other drawers. All of them opened with the speed of weightlessness.

"Looking for something in particular?" I asked.

"My file. Don't you want to see yours?"

I sat down in Simkins's chair. "I can guess what it says. Does not volunteer for committee work. Does not volunteer for non-committee work. May or may not possess abilities to communicate with malicious spirits who may or may not be causing the rapid decline of the college. On the front page, if not on the folder itself, it likely says F. Randolph Parshall likes this guy."

Carly flung open one of the tall wooden cabinets, three of which comprised the entire wall to the left of the door. "I had a meeting with Simkins scheduled for yesterday morning. He wouldn't tell me what it was about. 'A very important matter' was all he said."

"He's dead and you're going to New York. Whatever it was, I don't think it matters now."

Unable to see the blood stain, I crouched on the floor. My hand couldn't find it either. A square of carpet was gone. Somehow I doubted its new home was the forensics lab of the Grayford Police Department.

"Things can follow you, Tate, if people want them to. Do you know what Delilah asked me in my meeting this afternoon? 'Ms. Worth,' she said, 'would you characterize yourself as a risk taker?' I said of course, that every writer has to take risks, and she replied in that contrived Victorian accent—you know she was born here in Grayford—that she wasn't talking about writing. Then we just sat there for like two minutes, waiting for each other to say something. Finally, she started typing. Another minute went by and she looked over at me and said, 'Parshall College won't require your services next fall.' I mean, to hell with this place. I wasn't coming back any-way."

I opened the wooden cabinets she had already examined. The shelves contained boxes of broken chalk, five keyboards from old desktops, a hard drive without a monitor, stacks upon stacks of bubble sheets used to measure whether or not our students were achieving their learning objectives, sometimes whether or not the tests were measuring what they were intended to measure. The cabinets were a shrine to obsolescence, not unlike Simkins himself and the school he had so effectively steered into the ground.

"What if Delilah did kill him, Tate. What do you—"

Carly's conjecture was interrupted by a loud bang. Our heads turned toward the office door, now closed. I turned the knob, but the door wouldn't open. I knocked on the center of the door. The echo was much louder on the other side, the sound of a hammer against thick wood.

8

I GRABBED CARLY'S WRIST. She had been knocking for over a minute. "Someone wants us in here, sweetheart. More noise isn't going to change their mind."

She broke free of my grasp and returned to the door, slapping and pounding. "Let us out!"

"So what's it really about?"

"What's what about?"

"This new novel of yours that isn't about ghosts. That was only your excuse to make your way into Simkins's office and retrieve your file."

Carly leaned toward me so gradually I didn't notice until her breath warmed my lips. I held her at bay before she could warm them further.

Her eyes closed. "Please don't hate me."

"You're not making the alternative very easy."

"I wasn't sure I could trust you." Her eyes were black smudges in the center of my blind spots. "Somebody's been following me, Tate. Since yesterday afternoon. A black car was behind me on the way home. This morning it was waiting for me when I left my house."

It sounded outlandish, as most things do after someone has lied to you. It wasn't the lie itself that concerned me, but my inability to catch it. In my experience, blind spots get bigger, not smaller.

"Why would someone want to follow you?" I asked.

"I'm the one who found the body. Maybe they think I saw something I shouldn't have."

"Delilah said she found him."

"That's interesting. I'm the one who called 911."

I recalled Delilah's version in which the police arrived before she had the chance to call them. I wondered why I hadn't been followed, finding what I had found. Then I glanced at the door. Maybe I had been. Whether or not Carly was supposed to be here I couldn't say.

Carly sat down against the door, hugged her knees, and began to sob.

I said, "Delilah's going to be the first one in tomorrow. I wouldn't expect our presence here to enhance her opinion of us. Why don't you calm down, get out that cell phone of yours, and call someone to let us out of here."

"I don't have it. It's in my car."

"So much for that idea."

I felt the Phillips head screws in the door's hinges. The paper clips on the stacks of bubble sheets were no help. I double-checked the desk drawers for some kind of makeshift tool. On the floor, I noticed that whoever took the computer had left the cords. I carried one of the old towers and a keyboard from the cabinet to the desk.

"There's no monitor," Carly said.

The tower booted up with a grand sigh. She stood behind me as I typed. There was nothing to watch, save the yellow light on the hard drive. It flashed whenever I hit Enter.

"Tate, what are you doing?"

"Sending an e-mail."

"How do you know what you're typing?"

"I try to press the right buttons."

People with limited vision remember how to get places we've been before without our eyes. On my own computer, the screen reader told me what I was looking at, but even without it, maybe because I didn't trust what I was told, I knew how many taps of the TAB key got me from one part of the screen to another.

"What now?" Carly asked after I hit what I hoped was the send button.

"We wait."

She sat on the corner of the desk where Simkins had kept his coupons. She aimed her voice at the floor. "This is my fault. I never should have lied to you. I'm so sorry."

I remained skeptical of what she told me. She slid forward on the desk, pushing aside the keyboard. Her legs dangled on either side of my lap.

"Werewolves," she whispered in my ear. "That's what my novel's about."

I brought my lips to her ear, but not for whispering.

I wasn't sure how much time had gone by when the hard knock came. My hands had better things to feel than the face of my watch.

"Tate, are you in there?"

"We're in here."

The doorknob rattled before hitting the floor, rolling to a stop in front of the desk. "The door has been nailed shut," Sundeep said.

I thought of Duncan Musgrove's toolbox.

"Stand away from the door," Sundeep said.

I pulled Carly down to the floor with me and gave Sundeep the go ahead. She looked at me as I covered her ears. She started to say something when the first bullet hit the door, its echo circling the ceiling like a trapped bird. He fired four more and kicked open the door.

"Carly, meet Sundeep Gogenini: the three-hundred-eighty-sixth best tennis player in the world circa 1997. Sundeep, meet Carly Worth, future bestselling author of spine-tingling tales of vampires and werewolves."

"Seventy-first in doubles," Sundeep sheepishly added, extending his hand.

"My book won't be out for a while," Carly said.

I carried the computer back to the cabinet. Nothing could be done about the door. If anyone asked, I could accurately say we weren't the only ones up here.

"Now maybe you will get a cell phone," Sundeep said as we descended the stairs.

"Life seems so much simpler without one."

"Men who find dead bodies do not live simple lives."

My landlord unlocked the passenger side of his Civic. Carly unlocked the passenger door of the white sedan next to it.

"I can drive Tate home," she said.

"But he lives where I live," Sundeep said.

Carly cleared her throat in that ineffably sexy way. "I meant my home."

I walked around Carly's car to the passenger side.

Sundeep laughed. "Nicely done, Tate Cowlishaw."

Carly checked for black cars at every turn and traffic light. I noticed no headlights in the rearview. It was just us when we pulled into the driveway of her rented bungalow in the gentrified neighborhood behind the old Civic Center. It was just us, fumbling with clothes and light switches in the cluttered living room, just us against the wall outside her bedroom.

9

WHEN I OPENED MY EYES, Carly was putting on a white robe that covered nothing but the essentials. Outside, the birds were still clearing their throats. The sky behind her curtains was hardly blue, but there are worse things than being awakened before dawn by a beautiful woman offering to cook you eggs.

I asked Carly if I could use her cell phone and tried to guess which buttons were which. On regular phones, there's always a bump on the five. Cell phones didn't even have buttons anymore. Carly saw my confusion and placed the call for me. They made cell phones for the visually impaired. My problem with most technology is philosophical. If change were the same thing as improvement, Randall "Scoot" Simkins and his penchant for "Innovation" might still be alive, chairing a presidential task force on higher education.

I stepped onto the front porch and dialed my own number for messages. Still in my socks, I walked to the end of her driveway to check the color of two cars parked across the street: light blue and burgundy. They might have been silver and mahogany—colors aren't my specialty—but I could tell they were not black.

"First message: seven forty-two P.M. This is Hoopel at *The Chanticleer.* Randall Simkins's obituary was e-mailed to us yesterday afternoon by someone in the Trustees' Office. I've made the corrections you asked me to, but maybe you should talk to the trustees if you want to be mad at somebody."

As the message ended, a vehicle parked far enough down the street that I couldn't see it. I waited for the engine to cut off, or the car to drive away. I stepped onto the driveway and kept waiting. The engine kept running.

Carly opened the door to tell me breakfast was on the table.

"That running car," I said, pointing in its general direction. "What color is it?"

Carly cinched her robe and stepped off the porch. "That's it. Tate, that's the car." She climbed the porch steps too quickly. One of her house shoes flew into the front door. She was breathless. "Tate, what should we do?"

"As long as he knows where we are, we know where he is."

"Or she."

We went inside. At the kitchen table, I searched furtively for a knife before realizing my toast was already buttered. Carly watched the car out the window above the sink.

"Do you have one of those lists of supplemental faculty assignments?" I asked.

"Somewhere. Why?"

In recent years, Parshall's administrative offices had been reduced to several cubicles in the swimming pool. Many were no longer occupied. Last year Simkins began delegating former staff duties to faculty. An adjunct with a bachelor's degree in Psychology, for example, became director of counseling services.

"I want to know who's responsible for the Trustees' Office."

I followed Carly into the living room. Every surface was covered with stacks of paper and magazines. She located the list on the seat of a wingback chair.

"There is no Trustees' Office. Maybe Simkins handled it."

"Not unless he wrote his own obituary."

We had our daily meeting at 7:30, meaning I didn't have to ask Carly for a ride to campus. I don't like asking for rides. She hung her robe on the back of her bedroom door, reminding me what she looked like without it on. I hadn't forgotten, but I appreciated the reminder.

While Carly showered, I splashed water on my face in the half-bath. A thin coat of dust covered the edge of the sink. Hard water had left a ring around the basin. Perfume bottles in various stages of empty comprised an entire shelf of her medicine cabinet. I recognized two of them from Carly's neck. The clear contents of a plastic bottle had a vaguely bitter, almost salty odor I thought I recognized, but couldn't say from where. It wasn't the travel-size mouthwash I had hoped it might be. I made sure the tube of minty paste wasn't liniment and used a finger to brush my teeth.

I had a seat on the floral print sofa, shoving aside several books the size of Parshall student handbooks when they still printed them. I got out my magnifier. The titles could have been the names of rock formations or mythological beasts. They were literary journals, one of which I had seen, in a more orderly pile, on the nightstand of Mollie DuFrange. On the end table sat three bundles of paper-clipped pages, one of them titled "Elegy for Childhood Quilt." I read a few sentences while Carly dried her hair. With twelve-point font, I'm good for about forty words per minute. I didn't make it to the parts with vampires or werewolves.

"The black car's gone," Carly said, grabbing her keys.

She checked the rearview every few seconds, driving what felt like fifty through a twenty-five. She parked crookedly outside the former dorm turned sandwich shop turned space for lease. The sandwich shop had provided jobs for a lot of Parshall alumni. They sold a lot of sandwiches in the first year. The second year people realized they were only sandwiches, and there was nothing special in the way our graduates made them.

Carly stopped walking before we reached the library. She was looking at her phone. "Delilah says the meeting's cancelled."

Delilah Bibb, like her predecessor, enjoyed meetings the way most people enjoyed sunny, seventy-five-degree days. Her first as interim dean yesterday morning had seemed no different. "Does she say why?"

"No."

We continued to the swimming pool. Dim, varicose light above our cubicles gave the impression of imminent rain on the sunniest days. The air was reminiscent of a basement that regularly flooded. Those who kept long office hours often complained of headaches, one of the many reasons why I limited my time here.

Duncan Musgrove stood on the balls of his feet and blocked our path. "Do either of you motherfuckers know how to fix a paper jam?"

"Ask Tweel," I said. Our colleague's scholarly interest in space travel had caused Simkins to appoint him the director and sole representative of the college's tech support. His expertise, as far as I could tell, was limited to turning off a computer, waiting thirty seconds, and turning it back on.

Duncan didn't glance toward Tweel's cubicle, from which were audible the voices of public radio, as clear as bottled water and about as compelling. Duncan said, "I'm asking you, Cowlishaw."

"That doesn't seem to be working, does it?"

Duncan squared his compact body in front of me. His fists might have been clenched. Carly squeezed between us. Duncan held his position, his coffee breath sailing toward me above Carly's shoulder. The public radio hosts fawned over their guests, who had just yodeled.

"Why don't you leave things alone," Duncan snarled.

"Are we still talking about the copy machine, Duncan?"

Carly's back was pressing harder against me, not of its own volition. I turned my foot sideways to keep from moving. Carly said Duncan's name. She sang it softly like a lullaby. His left hand hooked past her, not softly at all. The punch was rather slow, or I was fast. I grabbed his wrist and stepped sideways, holding on as I moved behind him. His wrist was small. My fingers met. His right arm swung back and forth. My knee helped him forward against the copy machine.

"Where were you last night around nine?" I asked.

Duncan moaned like a set of old brakes. I held his left arm in a chicken wing until his right behaved itself.

"None of your goddamn business."

This wasn't the most exculpatory answer. It was, however, the same answer he gave if you asked what he was doing for lunch. When he started crying, I backed away.

Carly waited at my cubicle. "Do you think it was him?"

"If so, he'd rather not say."

"Maybe he'd like to tell the police."

"Maybe the police would like to know what we were doing in Simkins's office last night."

Carly sighed in my face and ducked into her own cube.

I scanned my desk for handwritten invitations. Finding none, I put on my headphones and checked my e-mail. Four were from students, one from Delilah cancelling the meeting. I selected the lot of them and pressed delete. A man who responds to e-mail is a man who receives more e-mail. The important questions tend to be asked more than once.

From the other side of my cube came the tinny laughter of a live audience filtered through computer speakers. A comedian explained the similarities between camping and homelessness. Applause gave way to a light tapping on the metal part of my cubicle. Londell Bakker rested his chin atop the thin wall. He wasn't easy to see, his face a shade lighter than the beige partition.

I offered him a seat on the lawn chair beside my desk. Simkins ordered them in bulk after the last of the hand-me-down furniture from the state university disappeared.

"So you liked the new material?" Londell asked.

"*Saturday Night Live* ought to be calling in no time," I said.

Twice a year since age eighteen, Londell had sent a tape of his impressions to the show's producers. He worked tirelessly on his material, polishing and revising. Thus far, his efforts had gotten him a series of postcards from Rockefeller Plaza, acknowledging receipt of his package.

"That pocket-sized playwright," I said. "The one who read last night. What's his story?"

"Thayer? He's got a degree in theater. He became a cop for the emotional experience."

"Must be a great actor. He isn't much of a cop."

"We all have things we'd rather be doing," Londell said.

"Let me know when you post last night's set online. I'll give you more detailed feedback."

Londell began a sigh and abandoned it somewhere in the middle. "Who knows when I'll get the time. Bibb's got me organizing data for the accreditation people. They're coming tomorrow."

"Is that why she cancelled the meeting?"

"I don't think so. She told me she wasn't feeling well. Looked like she had seen a ghost."

"She told me she didn't believe in ghosts. Hey, maybe you would know where I might find the Trustees' Office."

Londell refolded the lawn chair and leaned it against my cubicle wall. "There is no Trustees' Office."

"Are you sure about that?"

"I believe the whole point of being a trustee is not having to work in an office."

"Who are the other trustees, besides Parshall?"

"My guess is a bunch of old white guys. Don't quote me on that."

I reached for my rotary phone, whose obsolescence, like that of my refurbished desktop computer, seemed to protect it from thieves. I called Hoopel at *The Chanticleer*. He sounded no closer to puberty on his voicemail.

"This is Tate Cowlishaw, the guy you gave some bad information. There's no such place as the Trustees' Office. Maybe you could do a little investigative reporting instead of cutting and pasting fabricated e-mails."

Carly's head appeared above the partition separating our cubes. "Have you heard anything about a memorial service today at two? A student wants to know if classes are cancelled for it."

Londell stood up inside his cue. "What memorial service?"

"I noticed that in the obituary," I said. "I figured Delilah would have you working on the program."

Londell loosened his tie and punched the felt-covered wall between us. "Goddamn him. Even in death, that fat bastard finds new ways to waste my time."

"You've got a PhD," said Carly. "Why don't you teach somewhere else?"

Londell let out a laugh about as loud and sincere as someone in the audience on amateur night. "That's rich, Miss Worth. Mind if I use that in my act?"

10

I PUT A NOTE ON THE CHALKBOARD cancelling the day's classes in light of the memorial service. I would have cancelled them anyway, but it was nice to have a reason. With no class, no meeting, and no Trustees' Office, I walked the tree-lined mile of sidewalk to the corner of Ruffner and Spruce, where the trees gave way to cracked asphalt and failing businesses. I heard my name as I passed the office of the Gray Knight and kept walking.

"Tate, come here," said Jaysaree. "Sundeep has something for you."

"I don't think I need anything."

Jaysaree grabbed my wrist and pulled me back to the office.

Sundeep came around the counter. "Hold out your hand, Tate Cowlishaw."

My landlord placed a flat object in my hand no heavier than an empty wallet.

"Welcome to the 1990s. Jaysaree and I have added you to our plan. Do not use too many minutes talking to your girlfriend."

Jaysaree threw her arms around me. "Sundeep says she will come to dinner tonight?"

"I'm not sure that's been decided," I said.

Sundeep flipped open the phone. He made me feel the buttons and quizzed me. "You will like it," Sundeep said.

I disagreed.

"Your shirt will be ready this afternoon," Jaysaree shouted as I made my way to the door.

I walked through the parking lot behind the cars. There were only two. Much busier were the hours after work when husbands and wives met the wives and husbands to whom they were not married. They rarely left their rooms to take in the majesty of the dry cleaner and the video store that no longer rented videos. The Gogeninis never rented the rooms near mine. For these reasons, among others, I didn't like the sound of a man's cough before I turned the corner to my room.

I leaned back against the graffiti. "Revolution is the opiate of the intellectual," someone had painted in giant blue letters. Beside these words someone had written "Jesus' dick" with an arrow pointing to an unadorned portion of wall. A light breeze carried cigarette smoke my way. The only person I knew who smoked was Duncan Musgrove, who claimed he had quit two years ago. Another cough came with a tail of a high, nasal voice. Duncan spoke through his nose, but his coughs were heavy with decades of disappointment and phlegm.

I could think of no positive scenarios involving strangers waiting by my door. I took a casual step around the corner, followed by a pair of less casual ones. My visitor wore a red shirt and khakis. He was several inches shorter than me. I noticed all this as I wrapped an arm around his narrow waist and pushed him face-first into my door.

I pulled out my new phone whose rounded corner must not have felt much like a gun because my visitor grabbed my wrist and spun around. Cell phones make a bleak sound when they hit concrete, a sound made bleaker when it precedes a set of knuckles striking one's jaw.

I made my own fist. I was a little behind in this game. He moved from side to side. I took a swing. He took two. Mine found air. His found both sides of my jaw. Something too dark and large to be his fist moved swiftly into my blind spot, my head twisting further past my shoulder than it ever had any desire to go, giving me a helpful view of the car on which I was about to land.

"I'm not Cowlishaw," said the visitor to whom I had spoken only on the phone.

"That makes one of us, Hoopel."

"How do you know my name?" His wide, youthful cheeks got bigger in my peripheral field.

"How do you know where I live?"

"Mr. Cowlishaw? Why did you attack me?"

"Technically," I said, "you threw the first punch. If you're eager to write my obituary, you might not want to be the cause of death. Conflict of interest, I would think."

Hoopel helped me to my feet. Blood rushed to my face, reminding me which parts hurt.

"Are you going to tell me why you're here, Hoopel?"

"I've found some information. About the Trustees' Office."

"I didn't know obituary writers made house calls."

"I don't want to be an obituary writer, okay?" He raised his hand—to hit me, I assumed, until I saw he was handing me my cell phone. He puffed out his little boy cheeks with a big, calming sigh. "You were right, okay? My ex-girlfriend said the same thing. I'm never going to be a reporter if I don't take initiative."

I unlocked my door and invited him in. Edward hopped down from the window sill. He ran to his dish and let out a full-throated meow.

"I'm okay, Edward. Thank you for asking." I felt guilty for leaving him alone all night and opened a can of the good stuff. "Where did you learn to fight, Hoopel?"

"I kickbox. I've never been in a fight out of the ring, though. That was pretty cool."

"Congratulations." The loss dropped my record to one and one on the morning. In hindsight, my win over Duncan felt less impressive.

I offered my guest some of the rum I had bought for eggnog last Christmas.

"It's eleven in the morning, Mr. Cowlishaw."

"Don't be rude, Hoopel." I unwrapped one of my daily plastic cups by the sink and poured him two fingers. For myself I ran some tap water. It was eleven in the morning.

I sat across from him at the small table I used for stacking mail and entertaining aspiring reporters. The rum made him cough worse than his cigarettes, which he probably smoked to add years to his voice.

"Let's hear this information, Hoopel. People are dying for you to get back to work."

He set his drink on the window sill. "You might be interested to know," he said, "that your college does not have a trustees' office." He savored these words more than he had my rum.

"That doesn't surprise me, Hoopel. Possibly because I told you that about an hour ago."

"But I confirmed it."

"Now you're a fact checker, Hoopel. That sounds like a demotion."

"You're not very nice."

"Says the man who kicks me in the face outside my own home."

Edward returned to the window and sniffed the rum. Hoopel stood up and fished in his pocket. He handed me a sheet of paper from a spiral note pad. I handed it back to him after a cursory glance.

Hoopel sat back down. "Well?"

"Well what?" Sooner or later he'd let me know what the note said.

"Trusteesoffice123@hotmail.com? I don't think this e-mail account is even affiliated with the college." He sounded hurt that I hadn't drawn the same conclusion.

"Let me see that again." I gave it another glance and slid it into my pocket.

Hoopel handed me another sheet of paper. "Trying to find a list of trustees, I came across an obituary for Marlon Letrobe. He's dead, of course, but his great-great-grandson was the only surviving relative. Maybe he took over as a trustee? I found a phone number with a Massachusetts area code."

I stored the second sheet beside the first. I might have a pocketful of nothing, but it was more than I had five minutes ago. "Anything else, Hoopel?"

Silence lasted long enough that I assumed he had shaken his head. I went over to the metal rod I called a closet and selected a white dress shirt.

"Where are you going?"

"Never used to question anything, Hoopel, and now you can't stop asking questions." I got down my wingtips and one of my two ties, the one with stripes. "I need to see our interim dean, make sure she's aware of that memorial service you wrote about so eloquently."

11

STAR FALLS WAS A SPRAWLING SUBURB of rolling hills easily mistaken for golf courses. Its residents were the sort who owned pianos and horses, if not quite wealthy enough to use the seasons as verbs. Delilah's refusal to volunteer her capacious estate for last year's holiday party had earned her a public rebuke from Dean Simkins. We held it instead in the front office of the Gray Knight after I drew the shortest straw.

"How much do you professors make?" Hoopel asked as we pulled into Delilah's quarter-mile driveway.

"Less than whoever mows her lawn," I said. "It's family money, from what I understand."

I thanked him for the lift and closed the door. I hated asking for rides, but Hoopel owed me one. I had given him a sense of initiative. He rolled down the window.

"What now, Mr. Cowlishaw?"

I pointed to the house, another hundred feet down the circular driveway. "I'm going to go there, and you're going to go alphabetize dead people."

Hoopel's window remained down. "Give me something else to look for. I want to find things, Mr. Cowlishaw."

I rested my arms on his open window. "Okay. See what you can find out about Detective Rick Stashauer of the Grayford Police Department."

Hoopel revved the engine of what I only now noticed was a station wagon. "Yes, sir."

"Dig deep, Hoopel. Don't bring me anything I could have Googled myself."

"Yes, sir," he said again and reached through the window to shake my hand.

The driveway culminated in a half-circle in front of a house I had heard Delilah describe apologetically to Londell as "plantation-style." A birdbath on an island of bleached gravel lent the place a semi-rustic charm. A garage looked wide enough for two cars. Square bushes with bright flowers lined the sloping walkway leading to the front door. On the porch, between a pair of rocking chairs, sat a glass table under which someone had left a potted plant. The envelope on a plastic trident was unsealed. I stood between the windows and door and got out my magnifier.

What I took to be a sunflower decorated the front of the card. The typed message inside read, "You are a wonderful human being." The sender had not included a name. I returned the card to its envelope, licked the adhesive, and sealed it. I picked up the plant and rang the doorbell.

The door opened sharply. Whoever stood before me was not Delilah, as Delilah was not in the habit of standing. "More fucking flowers? My mom doesn't even know this many people."

"This one's a plant, actually."

Juliet Bibb had bright orange hair like her mother, but very little of it. On closer inspection, she had a crew cut. She took the plant, pushed past me, and let it fly from the edge of the porch. The pot shattered on one of the stones around the birdbath.

"I like it there. It adds color," I said.

Delilah's only child shoved me out of the way and went back inside. I got my foot inside the door before it closed.

"I'm here to see your mother, actually."

"God, why?" Juliet Bibb stopped wrestling with the door, walked down a long hallway, and slammed a door.

"Stop slamming doors," said Delilah in a wan voice unfamiliar, or perhaps overly familiar, with protest. She rolled into the living room from the opposite hallway. "Mr. Cowlishaw, shouldn't you be in class?"

"Should is a subjective word."

I waited for her to call me clever in that special way that meant "asshole." Instead, she wheeled into a larger room with white sofas and an abundance of natural light. I followed, passing an upright piano and the balance of the flowers with which her daughter seemed to have a problem. We came to a stop in a small, warm room with skylights and glass walls.

"Lovely view," I said.

For a long time she said nothing. When at last she faced me, Delilah Bibb said, "What can you see, Mr. Cowlishaw?"

People who ask this aren't interested in the answer. They can see that for themselves. They want to know what you can't see. I saw a brown surface with dark outlines, beyond it a green blur. "I see your wrought-iron furniture," I said, "on the deck overlooking your manicured lawn."

"How do you know the furniture is wrought iron? What makes you think, since I know you can't see it, that my lawn is manicured?"

"I draw conclusions based on high probability."

"You make assumptions," she said, opening what I had not assumed was a French door. She rolled down a little ramp onto the wooden deck.

I followed her outside. If she was trying to get away from me, I liked my chances. I stood beside her at the table and chairs. Delilah's cold fingers grabbed my hand and put it on the edge of the table. Next she guided my hand to the back of a chair. They were grainy with rust. Chips of paint came off on my fingers.

"Does that feel like wrought iron, Mr. Cowlishaw?"

I lifted the chair, no heavier than a skillet.

"I paid sixty dollars for the set at a big-box department store. I haven't had my lawn mowed since last August. You assume, because I have money, that I concern myself with nice things. The money, by the way, belonged to my parents. They are both dead, so now it belongs to me."

Delilah rolled to the edge of the deck. There was a cranking sound. Something small and white became level with her face. She rattled a bag and filled what I concluded to be a birdhouse with five seconds worth of seed.

"And what assumptions did you make about my daughter?" Delilah asked.

A plastic clip fell on the deck. I traced the sound, picked it up, and handed it to her. "She doesn't seem to like flowers or plants."

"Did she seem tired to you?" Delilah spoke without looking at me, restoring the birdhouse to its former height.

Juliet Bibb might have thrown like a girl, but not a tired one. "I thought she had spunk. Why?"

"She is having what her doctors call a good day." Delilah filled a birdhouse on the other side of the deck. "Some days she doesn't get out of bed."

"I believe I've had that."

"Don't be clever, Mr. Cowlishaw. My daughter is very ill. Last month she had to cut short her freshman year at the College of William and Mary. Her personality has changed. The language she uses..." Delilah trailed off, leaving the birdhouse at eye level.

"Should I assume, since she's having a good day, that Juliet is not the reason you cancelled today's meeting?"

"Mind your own business, Mr. Cowlishaw." Delilah aimed her chair at the house.

I grabbed one of the handles on the back of her chair.

"Londell said something had spooked you."

"Dr. Bakker thought wrong." She pushed in vain against the wheels. "Let go of me!"

"Making Londell do your work for you? That doesn't sound like the Delilah Bibb I know."

Grunting, she gave the wheels another ineffective shove.

"What are you so afraid of, Interim Dean Bibb?"

"No. I will not. I refuse to cry."

For over a minute she shook her head. Her refusal was loud and wet. She wiped her face and pulled a pair of uneven breaths into her lungs. Whether it was guilt or fear I couldn't tell, similar as they often sound.

"This is all too much." Her voice was high with fresh tears. She swallowed them and said, "I've had opportunities over the years. Several times I applied for positions at other schools. I turned down a couple of offers. Juliet was always my excuse, but there were other reasons. I have a confession, Mr. Cowlishaw."

A long pause allowed me to ponder the implications. A murder confession would negate our deal, but if Londell was next in line, I would probably keep my job.

"I have never been," she began and repeated the words twice more. "Much of a leader."

Behind us, a bird went into one of the houses, scattering seeds across the deck.

"That's disappointing to hear," I said.

Delilah sniffled. "No one is more disappointed than I."

That ghost she had seen sounded like the specter of self-doubt. Because my skills at giving pep talks were about as effective as colored sugar, I let go of her chair.

"You know, I was hoping for a different confession."

She swiftly maneuvered her chair to face me. "Excuse me?"

"Thus far, Delilah, you're the only one who's profited from Dean Simkins's death."

"How dare you?"

"It looks a little suspicious, taking a personal day hours before the memorial service."

"What memorial service?"

"The one in the obituary. Didn't you organize it?"

Her metal foot rest touched my ankle. "No, I did not."

"There I go making assumptions again. Maybe it was the trustees," I said, following her through the French door into the sun room. "I don't know why they wouldn't have informed you. I hope that doesn't speak to a lack of confidence in you as Interim Dean."

"They can go to hell if they think I can't do a better job than Scoot."

Anyone with a disability is familiar with self-doubt, but the doubts of others are a taste one never fully acquires. Delilah snagged a set of keys from a waist-high hook on the living room wall. Juliet Bibb emerged from the kitchen with plenty of energy.

"I poured your boiling water down the sink, Mother. Maybe next time you want your cinnamon apple tea, you'll take the fucking kettle off the fucking stove. It's been making that piercing sound for like ten minutes, Mother."

"I need to go back to campus, sweetheart. Try not to watch any television."

"Who is this, Mother? Did you meet him on your online dating service? I know you're on one. I think it's disgusting."

"I'm just the plant delivery man," I said. "I'll bill you for damages to my delivery."

Juliet stepped between me and her mother's chair. "I don't like you. I think you're snide."

"I think I'm charming. You're not the first to disagree."

"I'm going with you, Mother. I don't want to stay here."

Judging from the scream and where Juliet was standing, Delilah ran over her daughter's toes. "Go get some rest. I have a memorial service to attend."

Juliet followed us into the garage. "Memorial service? For the dead dean?"

There were two cars. Delilah made her way between them.

"My mother killed him, you know. Snide man, did you hear me? She killed my father, too. She killed my grandparents and one of my teachers and two Guatemalans who were painting our house, and she made me dig the graves in our backyard." Juliet's voice got louder, competing with the opening garage door. "She killed my boyfriend because she's an asexual freak who wants the rest of the world to be as miserable as she is."

Delilah unlocked the dark sedan. I opened the passenger side. The paint seemed fresher and a little darker on the door. I could feel the uneven patches where it began.

"Don't you dare take my car, Mother. I have plans."

"I heard you making them, sweetheart. That's why I'm taking your car."

"I can't drive yours with your fucking hand controls!"

"I know." Delilah leaned under the dashboard and attached something to the pedals.

"Goddamn you!" Juliet shouted before slamming another door.

I took my time getting in, continuing to study the paint job. "Nice car. What color would you call this?"

Delilah backed out of the garage without turning her head. "You're not good with colors, are you, Mr. Cowlishaw?"

"Not all of them."

"I'd call it black," she said.

12

"IN LIGHT OF HER FORTHCOMING NOVEL,"
I said, "I'm curious why Carly Worth's contract isn't
being renewed for next year."

Delilah turned down the country song on the radio. I had figured her for classical or adult contemporary. "Where did you hear
that?"

I told her where.

"I wasn't aware the two of you were friendly. If I had known
your objectivity was going to be compromised, I would not have
agreed to our arrangement."

"She said you seemed suspicious of her. Should I be?"

"It's a personnel matter, Mr. Cowlishaw. Human resources
would frown on my sharing confidential information."

"Human resources? You mean the tattooed fellow Simkins
moved to the front cubicle because he scared away thieves? I believe
he went back to bartending six months ago. At the very least it
would be helpful to get a look at Simkins's files."

"Yes, it would. I don't have them. As I understand it, they were
not in his office when the authorities found him." Delilah pulled
a lever for the brakes before an upcoming curve. She was not a
woman who took risks, or so her driving seemed to suggest.

"So you killed all those people," I said.

"My daughter's condition," Delilah began, pausing to let emo-
tion subside, "has caused her to become very hurtful."

"Kids say the darnedest things." I stared at her car stereo,
watching her hands manipulate the gas and brakes, pushing for the
former, pulling for the latter. "You're very dexterous," I said.

"I can't use my feet, so I'm good with my hands. I'm sure your ears and nose have compensated accordingly."

"How are you with a hammer?"

"Excuse me?"

"Nothing."

At the entrance to the college, Delilah took the high speed bump one inch at a time, so slowly you could hardly feel it. She parked in the spot furthest from the one marked handicapped. She didn't thank me for opening her door. She might have been insulted, as I was when someone placed my hand on something they wished to show me.

I had scheduled the service inside the Boss Hog's Rib Shack Theater, the only venue suitable for a large crowd, not that I expected one. Previously the theater had been known as the Simple Kneads Bakery Theater, and before that the Shane Schiffman's Hyundai Theater. The wealthy donors of yesteryear who had paid to have buildings named in their honor were long gone, along with their original donations, and Simkins decided to sell new names to local businesses. Bids got lower each year. Boss Hog's Rib Shack had closed a year and a half ago, but no other businesses had yet made an offer.

The air in the lobby was dusty and stale. The building had, like all the buildings on Parshall's campus, a funereal stillness even on days we weren't memorializing late deans. The theater had three sections of floor seating and a balcony condemned by inspectors in the 1980s. Only during graduation, when the building filled to half its capacity of four hundred, was the theater anything but a muse for faculty who made up ghost stories. The lack of attendees in any of the rows I passed seemed fitting for a man without friends or family.

Halfway down the center aisle, Delilah extended her hand to a mourner. "It's so wonderful of you to pay your respects. What is your name, sweetheart?"

The girl gasped, possibly upon contact with Delilah's icy fingers.

"We'll have a portion in the service when you, or anyone else," Delilah said, speaking to the empty seats around her, "can come onstage and share stories of how the dean impacted your life."

The girl zipped her backpack and moved toward the far aisle. "The power went off in the library. I just came here to finish my paper."

I sat down a few rows behind my fellow faculty. Chatter was minimal, but I heard the whispering voices of Mollie and her husband, and the heavy, tobacco-strained lungs of Duncan Musgrove. From a few rows away, I smelled the cheddar funk of the adjunct who never bathed, whom I had mistaken last night for a homeless man seated at our table. Someone whispered my name. I pretended not to hear it, my way of requesting another verbal flare in the darkness.

"Over here," Carly whispered.

I followed the echo to the second row in which she sat alone. The walk permitted me a rough head count, a few more than the sum of faculty. Carly got close enough to kiss my cheek, but pulled away.

"What happened to your face?"

"A world-class kickboxer roughed me up over some information."

She put a hand to her mouth and lowered it slowly. "What kind of information?"

I handed her the slips of paper from my pocket. I couldn't help scrutinizing her reaction.

"Who is Theodore Skipwith?"

"Not sure. He might be a trustee. He might have written Simkins's obituary, literally if not figuratively. By the way, I found a black car. I rode here in it. I don't know if it's the one you've been seeing, but the driver," I said, nodding to Delilah as she rolled past us down the aisle, "doesn't seem to like you."

Carly's hand moved mouthward again.

Delilah asked Londell to adjust the microphone. She had called from the car and asked him to hook up the sound equipment he kept in his trunk for occasional unpaid sets at the Irish pub.

"Just talk to us like we're human beings," said Duncan Musgrove. "You don't need a goddamn microphone to talk to fifteen people."

Londell returned to his seat. A few rows behind me, an unfamiliar throat of unknown gender politely cleared itself. The building yawned as old buildings do, our little breaths pushing rudely against the ceiling and walls.

"Can we begin with a round of applause?" Delilah asked.

We complied only gradually, our slow clap never reaching the crescendo of its cinematic counterpart.

"Thank you," Delilah said in the tone we used to thank students for the work they handed us. "And I'm going to thank you on behalf of our late dean, who never got the chance to thank you—thank us—as completely as he would have liked. Perhaps this is fitting since you certainly never thanked him for the life blood he poured, quite literally, into this institution."

The microphone split the last word of each sentence into myriad, shrinking versions of itself in the high ceiling. Eventually, they went away. Delilah didn't. For thirteen minutes, my furtive thumb tracked the minute hand while she praised Caesar, cataloguing Dean Simkins's contributions to the academy, the majority of which began, "He attended the conference of."

"Certainly he could be aloof." She paused to let her word and all its clones complete their laps above our heads. "At times, yes, he could be a hard man to please."

Good as my hearing is, I couldn't have been the only one who heard Duncan Musgrove's competing eulogy one aisle over. "Sisyphus," he seemed to say in a voice slightly lower than an airport announcement. "For twenty years that motherfucker strapped another boulder on my back. Pretests and posttests, committees and subcommittees, assessment of assessments, workshops and conferences and peer reviews, never passing up a chance to tell us our jobs were on the line, and what happens to the boulder when you get to the mountain top? It rolls down the other side."

Delilah paused. "I'm sorry, Dr. Musgrove. Did you have something you wanted to share?"

"I'm not doing this." Duncan was in the aisle, pushing his short arms through the sleeves of his ill-fitting sport coat. "The rest of you can sit here in Hell and pretend it's getting a little toasty, but sooner or later," he said, making his way to the exit, "you're all going to burn to death."

The doors opened and closed. Delilah waited for the fresh air to dissipate.

"Well," said our interim dean with what sounded like a suppressed smile, "Dr. Musgrove will be sorry to have left us prematurely. My vision, many of you will find, is rather incompatible with our late dean's."

"She's so guilty," Carly whispered.

I didn't disagree. At the same time, I didn't understand why a guilty woman would let me investigate, going so far as to point a finger at Carly when she could more easily join the chorus of law enforcement calling the dean's death a suicide.

"Dean Simkins worked very hard for a very long time." Delilah left that one in the air for a while, let it collect on our shoulders like falling ash. "As his former assistant, I will not dispute his efforts. As his successor, I cannot defend his results. Let us mourn the loss of the man, but we can best honor his memory by succeeding where he so consistently failed."

Delilah asked who wished to come forward and share a favorite memory of the dean. Her voice oscillated from one aisle to the other, her eyes, I imagined, doing the same. None of us moved.

"Let's hear from everyone," she decided. "Ms. DuFrange, why don't you begin? What will you miss most about our fallen leader?"

We waited to hear if Mollie was going to take our answer. There weren't many answers to go around.

"What I'll miss most about Dean Simkins," she began and paused like a student who had not studied the material. "What I'll miss most is how he thought poetry had a home in the academy. Just last month he encouraged me to develop a new poetry course for upper classmen who—"

"Thank you, Ms. DuFrange. Dr. Tweel, you may be seated. You may all remain seated. If no one has any objections, let us transition from the memorial service to more pressing matters."

Delilah was unsnapping her briefcase when a seat several rows behind me bounced a few times, returning to its upright position.

"Interim Dean Bibb, if I might say a few words." The man whose earlier cough I had not recognized stepped into the aisle. He had a languid Southern accent, the kind very fond of vowels and indifferent to other people's time.

"Are you one of the trustees?" Delilah asked with equal parts hope and fear.

"No, ma'am."

"In that case, as you must have heard, we're about to move on, but I thank you, on behalf of the late dean, for coming to pay your respects."

The man took a step forward, bringing him even with the row where Carly and I were sitting. "If I might be so bold, Interim Dean Bibb, as to offer some advice to you and your faculty." The man took his time with the word interim.

"Should I know who you are?" asked Delilah.

The man made his way forward five feet. Another five remained between him and the interim dean. He was tall and thin with unexpectedly broad shoulders. The entire body was unexpected. The voice didn't match the frame. Some don't. He extended his hand to Delilah Bibb and held it there as he came forward those final five feet.

"I do apologize for the apparent confusion," he said. "I spoke very briefly with Interim Associate Dean Bakker a little while ago, but you and I have not met. I'm Dr. Jefferson Totten. Jefferson suits me fine if you don't mind dispensing with such formalities. I'm your liaison to the accreditation board." He liked the taste of liaison as much as he did interim. "We aren't scheduled to meet until tomorrow, but when I heard about your loss—our loss—and Dr. Bakker—Londell, right?—mentioned this service, I hopped right on the interstate. Interim Dean Bibb, you aren't going to leave me hanging, as the kids say?"

I aimed my gaze onstage, where an actor's face might have been. Beneath my blind spot, Jefferson Totten moved his arm from side to side. He had an ornate, colorful laugh, a wide spray of flower petals falling slowly to the floor.

"There you go. Now give it a good pump. That's it. Now we're friends." He scattered some more petals on the floor. "May I borrow this for a moment?"

Delilah rolled backward and sideways, positioning herself in the aisle just behind the first row. Jefferson Totten doubled over to reach the microphone. More petals. Londell got up to help.

"Thank you, Londell. And thank all of you for your attention. I promise to keep this brief. For the last nine years, Scoot and I worked together very closely and very effectively to keep the winning team of this fine, fine college in the good graces of the accreditation board. Speak freely, Dean Bibb. No need to raise your hand."

"I'm sure we'll talk with specificity in tomorrow's review, but the faculty and I are very excited to share some of our formative assessments, which Dean Simkins had been putting together for the annual Liberal Arts in Transition conference in Temecula next fall, and—"

Jefferson Totten had raised his own hand. "Assessments are fine, Dean Bibb. At some point, I suppose one needs to measure what one has done or not done. The board requires a certain amount of fanfare in that regard. Per your central mission, however, I occasionally reminded Scoot that, as my granddaddy used to say, you can't put pounds on the pig by weighing it. Sooner or later, darlin', you're going to have to feed the pig."

13

D R. TOTTEN MADE HIS WAY UP THE AISLE, offering condolences with every handshake.

"He'll be back tomorrow," Delilah said when he was gone. "Prepare for classroom visits. Prepare your students for potential interviews. Please, please prepare."

She spoke to Londell in acronyms I was grateful not to understand. Her demeanor was less authoritative, a little frantic, a bird returning to its nest to find a larger bird.

The rest of us congregated in the lobby. It was tradition, or unbreakable habit, to endure each other's presence for a few more minutes, express outrage over new tasks we had been assigned. From my colleagues' anger I could gauge how many reminders I would receive when my task went uncompleted.

"Meet the new boss," said Mollie. "Same as the old boss."

"In my country, we do not hold meetings while a dead man's ashes are onstage." This was Esther Yeboah, the Nigerian adjunct whose contributions to post-meeting discussions rarely involved her own opinions.

"In Nigeria," said Benjamin Tweel, "I suspect teaching is still a noble profession."

"What was that about a dead man's ashes?" I said.

"He must not have seen the urn," said Benjamin Tweel. He opened the door to the theater a couple of inches and peered inside. "Does anyone here," he said, "have the slightest confidence in Delilah Bibb?"

My gaze went idly from face to face. No one spoke.

"I believe we know how Duncan would vote," said Tweel.

"What kind of vote, honey?" Mollie opened the door for her own peek. Her tan skirt and lavender blazer nearly erased my memory of last night's tank top and leather pants. There always had been two Mollies, the one I liked and the one I didn't. In the months we were together, I tried pretending the bad Mollie, the one who said being with me was like swimming through concrete, was a bad cold she would eventually overcome.

"A vote of no confidence," said Tweel. "We could take it to the trustees, and maybe they can get someone in here who knows what they're doing."

A soft leather briefcase slapped the carpet by Tweel's feet. I traced its arc to the plump hips of Christine Katzen, Parshall's registrar. Those who came within a ten-foot radius of her cubicle received status updates on her digestive health, or how much more attractive everyone had found her in upstate New York. Today she simply pointed to her briefcase.

We looked at the briefcase. We gave up on it and looked at Christine Katzen. She bent down and picked up her briefcase. Again she slammed it against the carpet. It wasn't an impressive sound. I reached against the wall, where Benjamin Tweel had set his own briefcase.

"Try this one," I said. "It's the hard kind with sharp edges."

Tweel yanked it out of her hand.

Christine Katzen started to cry.

"Now see what you've done," I said.

Carly touched Christine Katzen's arm. Mollie touched her other arm. Her tears kept coming.

"Do you really think," the registrar said, holding together her words with obvious strain, "that anyone can save this school? Did you not hear the man praise the *effective* work of Randall Simkins?"

The unkempt adjunct whose name I could never remember said, "What I think that dude was saying..." The adjunct's theory receded, unformed, into the haze of his marijuana buzz.

Christine Katzen broke loose of Carly and Mollie, picked up her briefcase, and flung it into the bulletin board on which no events had been advertised in my years at the school. "The winning team?" she asked, steadying herself on a hard platform of anger. "Does anyone here think you're on the winning team? I'll tell you what I won last summer. We didn't have the money to hire the annual temps to play admissions counselor. Guess whose desk that steaming pile landed on?" She blew her nose. "It wasn't the extra work, mind you. I get paid by the hour. What was particularly enlightening—and by enlightening I mean soul-gouging—was seeing what absolute, bottom-of-the-barrel, empty-headed morons we accept into this school."

Benjamin Tweel passed a pen and a sheet of paper around the circle for us to sign our names. When it came to Christine Katzen, she simply glanced at it and gave it to me. I passed it to Esther Yeboah without signing it.

"If not new leadership, Miss Katzen," Mollie said, "what do you propose as a solution?"

"Don't you see? Don't any of you see?" She stepped inside the circle and turned to look each of us in the eyes. "Do you have any clue what I do every time the dean decides to overhaul the curriculum? I change the names of existing courses. I change the numbers. I change the descriptions and type it all up in a brand new catalog. That's the easy part. When I'm done, I get to revise the transcripts of every current student and send them each an e-mail detailing the new courses they now need to graduate. Many of them write back. Many of them stop by to see me when I'm not there and leave red plastic cups under my desk filled with their own feces." Christine Katzen sucked an elephantine breath into her nose. It whistled on the way out. "I can't eat fresh fruit anymore. God, how I miss watermelon. How I miss Rainier cherries. It's stress. The doctors said so. I'm still paying him for that wisdom because I don't have insurance."

"Neither do we," Tweel said. "If your job is so bad, why don't you quit?"

"Why don't you?" she retorted. "Why don't any of you?"

It wasn't a hard question to answer. The answer wasn't easy to say. The piece of paper came back to Christine Katzen. She tore it into a pair of oversized bookmarks and let them fall to the floor.

"It's time," said our registrar. "This place has been begging to die for two generations. For God's sake, if you have any sense of mercy, let this poor school rest in peace."

Benjamin Tweel held together the halves of his makeshift petition. "Technically, Miss Katzen, since you're not faculty, we don't really need your signature, but we thank you for your frank contributions to the discussion. Carly, I don't see your name on here."

Christine Katzen grabbed the torn halves and extracted a pen from her battered briefcase, adding her name with the flourish you'd find in a film whose climax hinges on a last second signature. She pushed the signed page into Tweel's chest. Her next shove found the exit door.

"I, Geraldine Christine Katzen," Tweel read to us, "resign effective immediately. Fair enough." He handed the half-sheet to Carly.

"Ben, I'm not even going to be here next year."

"That's right, honey. Carly is going to be a famous author. I've not gotten a chance to congratulate you." Mollie hung a lilt on her words as jolly as Christmas lights and twice as gaudy. "You know, Carly, I've been looking for your short story in the *River Creek Review*, the one you said had gotten accepted there last year. When is that coming out, anyway?"

The adjuncts, seeing nothing at stake for themselves in the conversation, wandered the way of Christine Katzen. They were the cockroaches of the Academy, admirable for the unwanted scraps on which they survived. Some had other jobs. Some sent their paltry salaries home to family in the third world. Some dedicated nights and weekends to classic rock cover bands and appreciated an employer with leniency on matters of personal hygiene. None of them, I was inclined to believe, expected enough out of Parshall College to point a gun at their boss.

"The editor and I couldn't agree on revisions," Carly said.

"That's too bad. What about *Cavern Rock*?" Mollie asked. "When is that one due out?"

"I'd be glad, Mollie, to print you a copy of any of my stories. I didn't know you enjoyed fiction."

"Sorry, Carly. I'm afraid I only read published work. What is the release date on that novel?"

"Next year. I'll have the publisher send you an advance copy as soon as they're available," Carly shouted on her way out the door.

"She didn't sign, did she?" Mollie asked.

"Maybe if you had kept sweet-talking her," I said.

Tweel put the pen in my hand. "You can see to sign your name, can't you?"

My handwriting isn't the bee's knees, but I wrote Tweel a message large enough for him to read. Tweel studied the two words and shook his head.

Mollie glanced at my penmanship and sighed. "She's not going to rehire you, Tate." She said my name with a shot of pity chased with contempt.

"I suspect she'll have a hard time firing anyone from a correctional facility," I said.

"Jesus, not this again." Tweel took a dramatic step away from us and paced a quick lap around the lobby.

"Suppose he was murdered," Mollie said. "And suppose Delilah did it. Suppose she goes to prison because you have managed, against all reason and probability, to find enough evidence for the state to convict her of murder. Someone is going to replace her. Don't you want a say in who that is? Some candidates might not see the value of an MBA with quote-unquote paranormal talents."

"I'd like to think a college has a home for someone who solves the murder of its dean. That shows critical thinking, Mollie. No doubt your husband's scholarship on the subject of space tourism will impress any dean looking for teachers with experience relevant to the modern student."

Tweel put his hands on my chest. He gave me a shove that wouldn't have opened an automatic door. I didn't mean to smile. He stepped back and gave it another try, putting all hundred and forty pounds into it. My smile, along with the air in my lungs, went away when my back hit the wall.

"I've never liked you, Cowlishaw."

"I'll file that under surprising revelations." I got most of that out without coughing.

Tweel got close enough to let me smell the hummus he had eaten for lunch. I had forgotten how much his gaunt cheeks resembled those of a British supermodel.

"You don't belong in the academy," he said. "You're a terrible teacher. You're sure as hell not a scholar."

"He means you're being selfish, Tate. Think of the students. Think of your colleagues."

Tweel stayed put, continuing to brief me on the contents of his lunch. I reached between us for the lapel of his tweed blazer, held on tight, and traded him places.

I backed away casually, thinking we were even. He thought otherwise. He sent a hard left into my right cheek. My teeth scraped in places that didn't normally touch. I stared Benjamin Tweel in the eyes, a vain act and an act of vanity. It seemed less so in idle moments of conversation. Tweel was done talking. If I had aimed my gaze at the ceiling, I might have noticed the left hand making a return trip to its recent destination. The pair of punches knocked me off balance. Gravity finished the job.

He was still pissed, if the force with which he pushed open the front door was any indication. Mollie knelt over me. Her hair was a black curtain between my face and the ceiling.

"I'm sorry, Tate. I don't know what's gotten into him."

"It felt like anger. I think Duncan has it, too."

Mollie's hand lay in the center of my chest. Her face got closer to mine, her hair scattering across my neck. Her eyes were closed. I closed mine. Her lips made themselves comfortable against my cheek.

"He did hit me twice," I said.

A white smile streaked below my blind spot. I held her gaze. Close as we were, eye contact let me see the rest of her face. It was a face worth seeing, worth remembering: enormous eyes above a tiny nose and a mouth that did everything well. She kissed my cheek a second time. She pressed a finger against the center of my lips and kissed it, our lips coming together at the edges.

"Carly isn't who you think she is," Mollie said, as low as a voice can get before becoming a whisper.

"Who is she?"

"Bad news."

"And what are you?"

"I'm married."

"I've never liked that about you."

Mollie's laugh was short but full of meaning, like one of her poems. Voices became audible behind the doors to the theater. Mollie's head turned. She stood up and collected the torn sheet of signatures her husband had left behind.

I propped myself on my elbows. "Tell Ben I hope his hand feels better."

Mollie was halfway to the door. "Remember what I told you about Carly."

"I have a good memory," I said.

Mollie tested it by lingering in the foyer. In our months together, she told me the extra seconds by the door were spent waving to me and hoping one day I would see her and wave back. I waved to her, as I used to do once she told me what she was waiting for.

I had not gotten up when the door to the theater clanged against the side of Delilah Bibb's wheelchair. Londell could have held it for her. I was certain she hadn't asked him. She paused beside my legs, which blocked her direct path to the exit.

"Could you please move, Mr. Cowlishaw?"

I crossed my legs at the ankles. "I thought you said there wasn't a will."

"There wasn't. Please move."

"How did you know to have him cremated?"

A few feet behind her, Londell set down what must have been the speakers and microphone.

"I didn't."

"Who did?"

"I don't like the tone of these questions. In fact, Mr. Cowlishaw, I don't see any productive reason to let you continue your little investigation. This college needs to look ahead, not backward. Henceforth, our deal is off the table."

Delilah reversed her chair a few feet and skirted the wall, squeezing past the soles of my shoes. I sometimes wondered which was worse, bad eyes or bad legs. People in wheelchairs could still drive. I could climb stairs. I could walk wherever I wanted, though I might not know where I ended up. I could hide my blind spots, if not as well as I sometimes believed. There was no way to hide a wheelchair. Sometimes I envied that. It tires you, hiding things. If Delilah didn't know this yet, she would eventually.

Londell joined me on the floor. His long sigh sounded like an old joke that no longer got laughs. "I just spent the last ten minutes helping Bibb decide whether the PowerPoint slide describing our efforts to enhance reading comprehension should feature a photograph of an open book or a shelf of books."

"What happens if this presentation doesn't go well?" I asked.

"Maybe they ask us to make another presentation. Maybe the trustees get someone who can guide the school into a smaller iceberg."

"FYI, Space Boy's planning his own revolt. Expect him to ask for your Hancock on a ripped sheet of paper."

Londell flung a high-pitched laugh at the ceiling. "Tell him to watch our presentation. He might be inclined to let failure take its natural course."

"Maybe Tweel's angling for a promotion. Is he qualified to be dean?"

"You're buddies with F. Randolph Parshall. Ask him."

"He isn't the only trustee." I fished in my pocket for the memos from Hoopel. "Does the name Theodore Skipwith ring a bell?"

Londell held it in front of his face for a few seconds. "Never heard of him," he said.

"Any idea how many there are?" I asked.

"Skipwiths?"

"Trustees."

"I don't have any idea. I'm just the lowly assistant to the interim dean," he said in the trenchant baritone of Morgan Freeman. He was sifting through the contents of his wallet. "If you really think Simkins was murdered, why don't you give this guy a call."

All four of our knees cracked as we stood up.

"Who's this?"

"Guy we were talking about. Thayer." Londell handed me a business card. "I heard a rumor that the police handle crimes."

"A black man tells me to go to the police," I said.

"Half-black."

I stuck the card in my wallet. I asked Londell for a pen and wrote my new phone number on the back of my Café Club discount card for the coffee roaster that had moved to a part of town without sidewalks. I told him to give me a call if Delilah saw any more ghosts.

I was almost outside when Londell called my name in his best Eddie Murphy. "You don't think that bitch would kill me, do you?"

I said to give me a call if that happened, too.

14

T HE ACCIDENTAL STUDENT MOURNER was right about the library's lack of electricity. I walked through the non-functioning metal detectors, past the unmanned circulation desk. The white-haired reference librarian partial to corduroy jumpers had either retired or resigned, whichever didn't include benefits and pension. The tall fellow with the gray pony-tail, with whom I made pleasant small talk about the movies I used to check out, now worked at the video store across from the Gray Knight that no longer rented videos. A sign on the circulation desk encouraged students wishing to check out books to sign their names on the first page of a three-ring binder. At a faculty meeting I hadn't attended, I had been selected to verify that borrowed books had come back, but never got around to it.

Passing through the stacks, I pulled one of the dusty artifacts from the shelves. It had a light blue, possibly gray cover. The edges had been worn to downy fur. I breathed its scent like the hair of an ex-girlfriend. The usefulness of books, like that of cars, had diminished greatly a few months after I turned sixteen. To judge by their perseverance on the shelves of a library unguarded and unlocked, their usefulness to others had also diminished.

In the far corner of the first floor was a small, carpeted room where I sometimes showed my classes films with a business theme—*Wall Street* and *Trading Places* usually went over well. Room-darkening blinds covered all six windows. I closed the door behind me, a small amount of late afternoon light filtering through the narrow rectangle of pebbled glass. Sitting in a desk in the front row, I felt the momentary lightheadedness one occasionally feels in old buildings. Believers in the supernatural say spirits are passing through you. More likely it was toxins in materials no longer used in the construction of newer buildings.

I held my magnifier against Thayer's business card. The small, bubbly serif required some guess work. Even with a 22X magnifier, I don't so much read as piece together words and sentences through deductive reasoning. Thayer was his last name. His first name seemed to be Hammond. "ACTOR," he had chosen for the line where you told people what you did. I slid my loupe past the stock image of tragedy and comedy masks in the card's center. I had made it to the third number, an eight or a six. I also couldn't decide what kind of help he might provide, wary as I was of his partner's influence. I returned the card to my wallet.

Hoopel's handwriting was large and neat. I typed Skipwith's number into my phone. It had the raised bump on the five, but I wasn't a fan of the tiny buttons, of pressing them tenuously with my fingernail instead of my thumb. The sound as well was inferior to the cord-tethered receiver on my nightstand. Static enveloped the voice of the young woman who didn't say Skipwith's name when she answered. She had the good cheer of a receptionist who likes her boss but not her job, or the other way around.

"Ted there?" I asked.

Her silence didn't foreshadow the click of my call being transferred. "Do you mean Theo?"

"Of course. Theo."

Still no click.

"Whom should I say is calling?"

"Tell him Simkins. First name Dean."

She said she'd see if he was available. The click sounded skeptical. Outside, the conversation of two birds was muted by unbroken window panes. The library had incurred far less vandalism than the buildings with classrooms and faculty offices. Somewhere beyond the stacks, less muted than the birds, came the hiccupy laugh of a flirty debutante.

"Who is this?" said someone other than the receptionist. He sounded no older than forty-five, possibly as young as his early thirties. The seriousness of people who work around money has a way of aging a voice.

"That got your attention, didn't it?" At the last second I had decided on a Southern accent. I had spoken with one, or so my grandmother told me, well into elementary school. Years of hard work had covered it with a lovely, non-regional coating of white paint, but it was still there when I needed it. I never needed it.

"May I help you?" Skipwith's harsh tone sloughed away the pretty parts from the word help.

"I suppose you can start by telling me what's going on at that overpriced institution where I sent my son more than ten years ago."

"Your son is an alumnus?"

"He's a junior." I stretched my vowels until they snapped. "What my boy tells me, he's further from his diploma than he was last year. How is it, in Christ's good name, that a college can move a student backwards?"

Skipwith didn't tell me how it was. He was too busy typing on his computer.

"Whoever murdered that Simkins fellow was probably tired of writing forty-four thousand dollar checks each September and seeing no return on their investment."

"The way I understand it—I'm sorry, I didn't catch your real name."

"Biggins. Francis W. Biggins."

"Well, Mr. Biggins, the way I understand it, the dean took his own life. I don't have the details, but I'm sure it was very tragic. These things usually are." Skipwith had all the patience of a janitor the day before his retirement.

The sound of the chuckling girl returned. I stood by the door and held the phone at my side. The laughter got quieter, more closely resembling a furry, ugly-faced creature a zookeeper brings on a late night talk show.

I returned the phone to my ear. "Call it a suicide if you like. That's all in the past. Day trader like yourself, you must be a man with his eye on the future."

Skipwith's sigh would have blown out a candle across the room. "Yes, sir."

"This Bibb woman who's taking over, my son's had her for a few classes. His descriptions don't paint a picture I'd like to hang in the living room. Do you believe, Mr. Skipwith, that the future of Parshall College rests in the lap of this Bibb woman?"

Silence on a cell phone sounds a lot like a line that has gone dead.

"You there, Skipwith? I heard a rumor that the trustees might

84

have conspired with this Bibb woman to put an end to Dean Simkins. What do you know about that?"

Skipwith blew out another candle. "I'm going to level with you, sir, in the hopes of returning to my regular job, the one that pays actual money. I'm one of three trustees. In making decisions germane to the college, I receive one half of one vote. The other trustees have full votes. Therefore, Mr. Biggins, my opinion is not as important as that of the other trustees, which I'm sure you were able to discern unless you, too, are an alumnus of the diseased institution my great-great-great-uncle inflicted on higher education those many years ago. I'd just as soon cede my half-vote to someone like yourself, someone who seems to care about the students, or at least one of them, which is one more than I care about, but you'd be surprised how strict our legal system can be when it comes to wills and inquests and blah blah blah."

I sat down in the desk closest to the door. It was smaller than the one beside it, a gift from one of Grayford's middle schools. "Perhaps, Mr. Skipwith, you could tell me how to get in touch with those other trustees with their full votes and greater concern for the young minds of Parshall College."

"Love to, Mr. Biggins. Can't. Not since the reading of my great-great-great-uncle's will, prior to which I believed I was about to inherit something of actual value, have I set foot in that humid, beige city called Grayford. Mr. Biggins, can I give you some free advice on your son's future? Take that annual check and put it in a low-risk mutual fund."

"Why not some blue chips or a high-interest CD?" I knew a thing or two about finance, even if I never had money to invest.

The line was silent. This time it was dead. Somewhere beyond the classroom, the keening continued at a low volume. Ghosts who make loud noises aren't the ones you need to fear, I told people who cared enough to respond to Simkins's occasional e-mails offering up my services. It's the quieter sounds, the respectful tones that warrant consternation. Angry spirits use hushed tones to draw you closer. All my wisdom of the paranormal came from books by men with Eastern European names and advanced degrees from schools with the word Institute in their titles. Once in a while, I caught myself considering a passage more thoroughly than a reasonable man should, the way one checks a day-old horoscope for anything that sounds true.

A protracted squeal split into little beeps. The sound seemed to get further away, pulling me closer, as the experts say. Placing my ear against the wall of the classroom, I could hear it well enough to say it was human, or used to be. I remembered the utility closet in the back corner. I skipped the ear routine and gave a light knock. When no one answered, I went for the doorknob.

A bonfire of a scream engulfed the closet and classroom. The force of it, along with the darkness and a tangle of coaxial cable, sent me tottering into the metal cart with the VCR and projector. I grabbed the cart's middle shelf, but continued to fall.

"There she is," I said.

The closet was the size of a motel bathroom. On the deeper side, scantily illuminated by the twice filtered daylight from the open door, three breaths tried to decide if they wanted to become a second scream.

"Dr. Cowlishaw?" It was a young girl's voice, ruling out my first guess of a homeless squatter, a recurring problem in cooler months.

"You are aware you're in a closet," I said, not yet able to place the voice.

"I had to get out of my dorm, Dr. Cowlishaw." The screams hadn't cleared her voice of tears, which seemed to be starting up again.

Blood rushed to my face, most notably to the parts that had seen fists rush toward them. I freed my foot from a pile of cables. "The dorms are pretty small, aren't they? Nowhere near as comfortable as these storage closets."

She laughed slightly. It might have been a miniature sob. "I'm sorry I stopped coming to your class."

"You had plenty of company, Nikki." The crying had made Nikki Gladstone's husky voice difficult to identify.

"You shouldn't have passed me. I only took the first exam."

"You had the highest score in the class, Nikki."

"Really? I didn't even study."

I could hear the smile around her words and felt guilty for the lie. "Not really."

"How did I pass then? I didn't do any work."

"Do you remember the sub shop on campus? They punched a card each time you bought a sub. After six punches, you got a free one. Dean Simkins thought you had earned a free sub."

Nikki Gladstone was getting up. She stepped over me into the classroom. "I didn't like him," she said.

"I'll add you to the list."

She sat down in the desk closest to the window. She had on loose-fitting pants with a plaid pattern, possibly pajamas. I sat beside her in the second aisle. My pocket buzzed. I gave it a good swat that would have killed it if it weren't a phone.

"You wouldn't have been hiding in there, would you, Nikki?"

She crossed her arms. "Somebody broke into my room."

I told her I was sorry to hear it. I wasn't surprised to hear it, but this I didn't tell her.

"They stole my file cabinet." The cracks returned to her voice. "I keep all my papers in it. On a flash drive. My senior project," she said, her smoky voice reduced to a little wisp.

"Did you think it might be in here?"

Nikki shook her head with enough authority that I noticed without looking away. "I just had to get away from those people."

"Which people?"

"Other students. I'm just tired of it, Dr. Cowlishaw. It's just— I mean, a lot of us have vandalized stuff to vent our frustration. Some people steal things because, like, this place steals our money. But we never vandalized or stole each other's shit. A line's been crossed, you know?"

"That's all they took?"

"Yeah. They left my jewelry and laptop, but most of us—most of them—don't steal because we need money. It's not like anything on this campus beyond our rooms has any value."

"When was your file cabinet stolen?"

"Last night. Some jerk pulled the fire alarm and we had to wait outside until it got turned off. When I went back inside, it was gone."

In class, whenever I noticed damaged or stolen property, I generally laughed along with the students. I was only encouraging the culprits, but I wasn't much of a teacher and thought I should encourage my students any way I could. Instead of laughter, I offered Nikki Gladstone what I hoped was a believable look of concern. "Anyone else have anything stolen?"

"Islanda—she's the R.A.—she said I'm the only one. Maybe someone doesn't want me to pass my class. Some teachers grade on a curve, you know, and one high score can affect the grades of the whole class."

"What's your current grade in this class?"

"A low C."

"So much for that theory. Whose class is this?"

"Miss Worth's."

"I'll talk to her, see if I can't get you an extension." I was reaching into my pocket when Nikki threw her arms around me.

"You're the best, Dr. Cowlishaw. Seriously."

"You're grading on a generous curve, Nikki." I handed her the business card Londell had given me. "Give this fellow a call about your stolen property."

She held the card in front of her face. "You want me to call an actor?"

"He's also a detective. Tell him I referred you. Tell him your file cabinet's being held for ransom. The thespian in him will appreciate the drama."

15

I LINGERED BY THE LIBRARY'S EXIT to see who had called. Even magnified twenty-two times, the numbers on the screen were very small. I pushed a few buttons until the number of the missed call was highlighted and pushed send.

"I found some articles about that cop," Hoopel said, not bothering with hello. "Should I e-mail them to you?"

"Why don't you summarize them for me?"

He sounded as though he were climbing stairs. "Well, there's one about a wife who killed her husband. In the trial, Stashauer testified about the gun she used and the ballistics. There's another about a homeless man who stabbed another homeless man to death. Stashauer testified about the knife that was used, the fingerprints." He kept going. Afternoon dimmed in the sky.

"I don't mean to impugn your journalistic instincts, Hoopel, but this is every homicide in Grayford for the past ten years. Detectives testify at trials. It's part of their job."

"I thought you wanted a link between him and your dean's murder. I thought since these were all murders . . ." Hoopel's voice slumped over, wounded.

"That would be helpful. And if you find one, by all means, let me know. For now, we might have to start small. Do any of your articles describe our detective in terms other than ordinary?"

Hoopel grunted in concentration. It turned into a sigh. "Not really. Here's a notice of his divorce, but lots of people get divorced. He participated in a fundraiser. I guess a lot of people do that, too."

"How many fundraisers have you participated in, Hoopel?"

"None."

"Between us, that makes zero. What kind of fundraiser?"

"Some kind of annual event for the Grayford Food Bank. 'Will Read for Food,' it says on the flyer. It took place at the state college."

"See what else you can find about this event. What do you know about that divorce?"

"Just the date it was filed and the date it was granted. Sixteen months ago and four months ago, respectively." Hoopel was excited again. "State law says you have to wait a year. My parents almost got divorced when I was in sixth grade."

"No doubt your inquisitive spirit helped keep them together. What's her name?"

"My mom?"

"The former Mrs. Stashauer."

"Marianne Randallman."

"Why does that sound familiar?"

"You know, Mr. Cowlishaw," Hoopel began to sing. "If you get in a wreck, slip and break your neck, call Randallman Dudek, Attorneys at Law."

The ads were ubiquitous on local TV. Every six months, a new spot premiered with a new plot that always resolved with Lady Justice carrying a bag of money to a bad actor in a neck brace. Somewhere in the middle, Marianne Randallman and Mark Dudek recited their spiel about "the money you deserve." A few times I had been close enough to the TV to see their faces. Dudek had white hair and whiter teeth. He wore sweater vests and bore a resemblance to Andrew Jackson on the twenty dollar bill. Marianne Randallman wore short-sleeve blouses that showed off her toned arms. She had short red hair and the genial face of a second-grade teacher. That she or anyone had considered Stashauer worthy of marriage, and presumably love, gave me pause. So did his charity work. That he had redeemable qualities, traits that had to be set aside, suggested a man with motivation rather than an asshole who doles out threats and coffee stains without reason or prejudice.

"Maybe I could pay her a visit," said Hoopel. "I could say I got into an accident, then tell her I'm going through a divorce and see what she says."

I started walking with the phone against my ear, which felt a bit like walking with one eye closed. "You've got too honest a face, Hoopel. Besides that, you're much too valuable to our research department. Keep pounding that pavement."

"What pavement?"

"Keep typing," I said. "Go where your curiosity takes you."

"That's what my journalism professor used to tell us." Hoopel laughed. "I'll bet you're a great teacher, Mr. Cowlishaw."

"I'll bet you're a horrible gambler, Hoopel."

I slid the phone into my pocket and entered the swimming pool to the brittle, dissonant bells of a ringing desk phone. The caller had plenty of patience. I stopped counting after the eighth ring. We no longer had voicemail. Only a handful of desks still had a phone.

I followed the bells to the cubicle of Duncan Musgrove. Duncan was not there. The adjacent desks were also empty. I sat in Duncan's lawn chair and reached for the receiver, but it was no longer ringing.

The ceiling lights buzzed. I had the feeling that I wasn't alone in the pool. I had taken a pair of steps toward my own desk when the intrepid caller tried again.

"Musgrove," I answered, making no attempt at his abrasive voice.

"This isn't Duncan." The outraged voice belonged to a large woman, the flesh around her neck and throat padding her words.

"Okay, it isn't. Who's this?"

She responded without words, only tears. Lately I had this effect on women. "We have a little money," she said. "Not much, but it's yours if you promise not to hurt him."

"Janice," I said, remembering that Mrs. Musgrove's name rhymed with Denise and not the name with which it shared its spelling. When they were newlyweds, Duncan said how much he loved this alternate pronunciation, her exotic jewelry made of found objects, how she styled her hair into a corkscrew, this woman who weighed more than three hundred pounds and moved across a dance floor with what he called "a sinewy grace." For the past two years, however, after Janice dropped out of the physical therapy school whose tuition Duncan had paid, claiming a phobia of injured people, he had opted for the traditional pronunciation of his wife's name.

"Who is this? Is Duncan okay?"

"Janice, this is Tate Cowlishaw. I'm one of your husband's colleagues. Your husband left a faculty meeting about half an hour ago."

"I know that. He called me from this phone before he left. At most, if every light is red, it takes him eleven minutes to get home, door to door."

"He seemed upset. He probably went for a drink."

I set my magnifier on a memo pad beside the phone. "These thoughts are the intellectual property of Sir Duncan Musgrove, PhD" was printed at the top of each sheet.

"What do you mean he was upset?" Mrs. Musgrove's voice was talcum-soft, a twenty-nine-year-old trying to sound ten. The first time I met her, I thought she was putting me on.

"We had a wake for our dean. Duncan was disappointed not to be a pall bearer."

"Scoot Simkins? Duncan hated that man. I don't believe a word you're saying. Duncan's there, isn't he? Put him on."

I could feel the grooves of the prior memo. I couldn't tell what it said. White on white isn't the easiest to decipher. "Duncan isn't here," I said. "If he hasn't come home in twenty-three hours, give the police a call. I imagine he's at the bakery, ordering a small replica of your wedding cake."

Janice Musgrove was breathing heavily, like a very large woman who has just stood up. "I remember you," she said in her powdery voice. "The one with bad eyes."

"They're not so bad once you get to know them."

"I'm not crazy, Mr. Cowlishaw." She claimed this in a reasonable tone. The craziest ones have that talent. "I think someone has been threatening him."

I tried to picture Duncan in all his salty beligerence on the receiving end of threats. Having seen him crumpled on the floor outside Simkins's office, it wasn't as difficult as I thought it would be. Could his wife have mistaken guilt for fear?

"Lately I've seen less and less of my husband." She spoke with strain, her words in the back of a drawer just out of reach. "He used to stick his head in the bedroom and ask if I wanted to watch one of his old detective movies. I used to say yes. He would sit in the rocking chair in the corner while I lay on the bed. At some point in the movie, he would reach across the nightstand and hold my hand. Do you know how hard that was, Mr. Cowlishaw, knowing he was leaving our bedroom to return to his other home? Most days he came home just to get the mail."

"Perhaps he stopped to say hello to this other woman." I felt my watch. The value of my time, trading so low for so many years, had experienced a sharp uptick in light of recent events.

"That's the thing. There is no other woman. He told me so. Last night he came into the bedroom. He lay on the edge of the bed, sobbing into his old pillow. He said he wanted to help me get out of bed. Let's get out of this house, he said, out of this town."

"He might have been lying. Cheating spouses have been known to do that."

"Duncan doesn't believe in lying," said Janice. "He says scientists don't have to."

"What time was this when he got into bed with you?"

"Late. A little after two."

The timing didn't clear him from nailing shut the door of Simkins's office. "Why do you believe he was being threatened?"

"This morning, while he was making me pancakes, he got a phone call. At one point I heard him say, 'Don't you dare come near her. Do what you want with me, but don't you dare touch her.' I asked who he was talking to. Greedy assholes was what he said."

"I'm sure he's fine. If I see him, I'll let him know you're looking for him."

"Mr. Cowlishaw?"

"Yes?"

"Tell him I love him."

I returned the phone to its cradle. The locomotive in the ceiling that kept the pool a toasty sixty-three finally kicked off. When I got to my cubicle, a blonde who smelled and kissed like Carly Worth stood up from my desk.

"I didn't hear you come in," she said.

My computer monitor was on. I tried to decide how I felt about her using it. It seemed inappropriate and oddly endearing, like someone asking you to move with her to New York after a first kiss. Who was I to judge? I had answered Duncan's phone, and we hadn't even held hands.

Carly put her thumb on my chin and turned my face two inches in each direction. "Your bruises are multiplying."

"The first one was getting lonely. I sprang for the matching set."

Carly kissed my jaw very lightly, left then right. "I never knew Mollie hated me," she said. "Is it because we're together?"

I returned the recently used mouse to its home beside my empty paper clip holder. "Her jealousy sounded more professional in nature."

"Oh, I caught a student using your computer," she said.

"When was this?"

"A few minutes ago. I didn't catch their name."

A few times I had walked into my cubicle to find a student typing away, one of them writing a paper to my own class. I let him finish. It was the least I could do since I had no intention of reading the paper. I put in my earphones and minimized the browser on the screen. Carly leaned against the wobbly partition, watching me open a new browser. A search of "Hammond Thayer actor" yielded his personal website with video clips of selected work. I went with the first entry under musical theater, hit full screen, and unplugged my earphones to let Carly have a listen.

"What do you think of the short fellow?" I asked, hoping there weren't more than one.

"What is this, Tate?"

"*Godspell*, apparently."

I plugged my earphones in again and closed the page. My software began reading the browser I had minimized, an article about cremation.

Carly pulled out one of my earphones. "It was me, okay?"

I faced her while my left ear heard the temperature required to cremate a body.

"My Internet was down. I didn't think you'd mind."

The article described the weight of the ashes relative to the weight of the body before cremation. It didn't tell me who decides when and if to cremate the deceased, my own lingering question from the memorial service. Forty-eight hours seemed a quick turnaround for a man without a will.

Carly moved behind my chair. I aimed my gaze at the monitor where her reflection would be. She rested her chin on my head.

"This is so stupid," she said. "Promise you won't laugh." Her nervous breath sailed over my shoulder. "Seeing the urn onstage gave me an idea. Vampires turn to ash when they die, right? There's a scene in my novel when . . . anyway, I wanted to know how much ash there might be."

"I thought it was dust."

"Whatever. It's not like they're real, Tate. You can call it what you want."

"I suppose they could weigh whatever you want them to, since they're not real."

Carly laughed. "Maybe you should be a writer."

"I'd be terrible with the part where everything gets tied together."

She pulled out my chair, making room for herself on my lap.

Her cheek pressed against mine rather painfully. Her hair covered my face. Two women inside of an hour had blinded me with their hair. It suggested a pattern, but murder has a way of lending meaning to the ordinary.

I typed "Rosewall Glen Retirement Village" into the search bar.

"What's that?"

"Home of our esteemed trustee and grandson of our school's founder, F. Randolph Parshall. He should be able to clear up a few things."

"Do you need a ride?"

I hesitated, working through the calculus of whether or not to accept a favor. There are additional equations for favors from someone you've slept with and hope to sleep with again. Mollie and I had failed, I occasionally believed, because I had asked her for one too many rides to the supermarket.

"It's no big deal, Tate. I'd love to meet Dr. Parshall."

Ultimately, the only arithmetic that mattered was the current time, four thirty, and the end of visiting hours at Rosewall Glen, six o'clock.

Carly hooked her arm around mine as we approached the parking lot. Delilah's black sedan was gone. Two spaces down from where Carly was parked sat Duncan's tan VW bug. Duncan Musgrove was not a man who walked places. For years after elevators had stopped working, he continued to push their buttons and wait half a minute before resigning himself to the stairs.

I circled the Volkswagen. There were plenty of dents. The front fender resembled a pouty lip. The passenger side window was cracked. None of this suggested foul play. Duncan called them beauty marks. He told anyone who asked, and most who didn't, that he had bought his bug for two hundred dollars. "Fuck the bank," he liked to say. "They can keep my Saturn."

"Do you think he's working with Delilah?" Carly asked. I had filled her in on my conversation with the worried Mrs. Musgrove.

"Their exchange at today's meeting didn't suggest colleagues on the same page."

"Maybe that was for our benefit."

I opened the passenger door of Carly's car. Another vehicle started on the street a hundred feet away. A set of headlights shone in the rear windshield as soon as we pulled out of the parking lot. They held fast to our bumper through a pair of intersections and a detour into a gas station.

"Is somebody following us, Tate?"

"It seems that way."

Carly banged the steering wheel. "Damn her. I thought she had a presentation to prepare."

Carly sped up. Delilah, if it was her, did the same. Not until we pulled into the driveway of Rosewall Glen were there more than a few car lengths between us. We parked by the entrance, our traveling companion lingering by the front gate with the engine running. The black car's headlights brightened the woods as we made our way inside.

The receptionist lifted a guest book onto the counter with a heavy sigh. She handed me a pen. I feigned an incipient sneeze and handed the pen to Carly. Signing is easy. It's those little lines people like you to follow that make it next to impossible.

The receptionist read the names Carly had written. "Cowlishaw." The middle-aged black woman said my name as if it were a lovely fish she had eaten on her honeymoon. "You didn't know a Miss Katherine, did you?"

"She was my grandmother."

"I thought you looked familiar." The receptionist led us to the corner of the lobby where they hung seasonal decorations. She reached over a giant Easter basket to pull a frame off the wall. "Miss Katherine painted that."

I took the frame from her and held it at arm's length. Blue and orange were possibly involved. Carly stopped staring out the window long enough to turn the painting a hundred and eighty degrees in my hands. It didn't help.

"It's Grandfather Mountain," said the receptionist.

"So it is."

The receptionist returned it to the wall. "Funny you're here to see Parshall. As I recall, your grandmother couldn't stand that man."

"She liked him well enough," I said. "Particularly when he wasn't around."

The smell of bodies just this side of eternity got stronger past the double doors. The walls held artwork and crafts made by current residents. It reminded me of an elementary school. Carly paused halfway down the hallway to gag.

"You get used to it," I said.

People here remembered my grandmother so fondly because she got used to things with a wide smile. A retired art teacher from the public schools, she didn't have the money for a long stay in a place as fancy as Rosewall Glen, but decided to splurge when the doctors gave her less than six months. Its proximity to my new job at the Grayford bank was the primary selling point. When the doctors shortened her prognosis to three months, she began tipping the nurses and orderlies with fives and tens. After she died, one of the staff gave me an envelope filled with fives and tens. I tucked it under her arm inside the casket.

In the larger lobby without furniture or carpet, a pair of staff members spoke in raised voices, more aloof than angry. We crossed the room, passing a half-circle of wheelchairs in front of the giant television. I heard the voices of Barbara Stanwyck and Fred Mac-Murray. High as the volume was turned up, tourists on the Outer Banks might have heard them as well. The residents not interested in the movie faced the wall of windows overlooking the gardens.

"What does he look like?" Carly asked.

"White hair," I said. "He'll be the one in the wheelchair."

I moved out of the way of an elderly woman pushing the chair of someone she called mom. Near the nurse's stand, a young black man and a full-figured white woman bickered dispassionately. Their language made their loud, robotic voices sound even stranger.

"You're reading it like a brochure," said the rusted voice of F. Randolph Parshall, seated in the wheelchair directly in front of them. "Let the words come naturally, like conversation."

They tried again. He gave them one line apiece before cutting them off.

"Your resumes noted a background in the arts. I don't see it."

"I played clarinet in my high school marching band," said the young black man, sounding sincerely contrite.

"I could live without the clarinet," said Dr. Parshall. "What's your excuse, woman?"

"I'm a nurse, Dr. Parshall. You asked if I had ever been in a play, and I said yes. You didn't ask if I liked it." This voice was sharper than the dull blade she had used to recite Shakespeare. "And if you'll excuse me, sir, I'm late for my rounds."

I touched the nurse's arm when she came near us. "Excuse me. Is he in his right mind?"

"Dr. Parshall?" The nurse gave a fake laugh. "He's his usual self."

"Does he know where he is? I heard him say he hired you."

The nurse put a hand on her sizeable hip. "He hired most of us.

Dr. Parshall purchased Rosewall Glen a few years ago. The previous owners wanted to move someone into the room near his. He wanted it to remain empty."

She walked away, hand on hip. She must have meant his library, the room beside his filled with floor-to-ceiling bookshelves. I made my way behind Parshall's chair. I had been back only a few times since my grandmother left in the way most residents leave. He hadn't mentioned purchasing the place, but Parshall was never showy with his wealth, regarding his family money as a mildly favorable trait on par with good teeth.

"You ought to be playing that clarinet in an orchestra," Parshall told the black man in an orderly's blue uniform. "I suspect any symphony would require a bachelor's degree. I know a terrific institution right here in Grayford that would be lucky to have you."

The orderly noticed us waiting and shook our hands with gratitude. "Dr. Parshall, I believe your grandchildren are here to see you."

"I don't have any grandchildren."

The orderly had already made his escape. Carly and I stepped into the positions of the untrained actors. I extended my hand.

"Dr. Parshall, you're looking well."

"I look terrible. I take it your eyesight hasn't improved, Nick. How's your grandmother?"

"Dead," I said.

"I hope that hasn't stopped you from communicating with her. You of all people, Nick, ought to know better."

"Who's Nick?" Carly asked.

"I call this young man Nick," said Dr. Parshall, "after the esteemed Russian scholar of the paranormal, Nikolai Cherkasov. I guess you could call it a nickname." Parshall unfurled a raspy, winding laugh that luck prevented from becoming a cough. He reached for Carly's hand, which he kissed. "And who is this exquisite vision, Nick?"

"Carly Worth teaches writing at our fine institution."

"It's truly an honor to meet you, sir."

"The honor is completely and thoroughly mine, Ms. Worth. Are you a writer yourself?" His speech was labored, each word a heavy stone hoisted from the bottom of a well.

"I am."

"Carly just sold her first novel," I said.

Dr. Parshall placed his hand over his heart. The gesture caused the immediate arrival of two nurses and an orderly. They went away after checking his vitals.

"Perhaps my room will offer more privacy," he said.

I pushed his chair to the end of the hall. His was the last room on the left, across from the room my grandmother occupied in her brief residency. Being on the corner, theirs were the only rooms with two windows. Like all the others, Parshall's room consisted of a full-size bed, nightstand, an open wardrobe, and a chair with an ottoman. Carly and I helped Parshall into the chair without wheels and sat ourselves on the foot of his bed.

"Carly Worth," said Dr. Parshall and whistled through his teeth, which he liked to remind people were still his own. "It warms my heart to know the written word is alive at Parshall College."

"More alive than some things," I said. "I assume you've heard the bad news."

"What bad news?"

I shouldn't have been surprised he hadn't heard. Dean Simkins had been the only liaison between Dr. Parshall and the college's day-to-day operations. He might have come across the obituary, which people his age are wont to read, if *The Chanticleer* still existed as a print newspaper. I gave him the short version, the one that included bullets and left out my own suspicions.

Dr. Parshall stared at the moonlit colonnade of trees out his window, possibly his own reflection. "I take it you've spoken to Scoot."

"I tried contacting him," I lied. "He didn't pick up."

"It's possible he hasn't yet gotten where he's going."

"Spoken to who?" Carly asked.

"Whom," said Parshall. "Darling, I mean no offense to the realist tradition to which you doubtless belong, but this is a conversation for believers. If you'd like us to pause while you step into the hall, we'll gladly do so." Parshall threw his words a little harder at the top of the well. A few hit the edge and fell back down.

"Carly's a believer," I said. "Her novel is about vampires."

Parshall's hand covered his heart again. "Is this true?"

"It's true," she said in the same sheepish voice that had shared the news Monday morning.

Parshall offered her a sincere apology. The elderly have no reason to be insincere. Turning to me again, he said, "Goddammit, Nick. You were supposed to take care of this."

"Due respect, Dr. Parshall, I've never known ghosts to fire guns."

A big, derisive breath must have flared his sizeable nostrils. They were as wide as nickels, sometimes registering beside my blind spots like small eyes. "Spirits wield their influence in a variety of ways. I shouldn't have to tell you that."

As always, I declined the opportunity to deny my paranormal talents. The week we met, while showing me his library, I had heard a click in the ceiling, and his excitement—"You can hear it!"— prompted him to pull down a book from one of the lower shelves. He pointed to a passage, which I pretended to read.

"Do you think you could give it a try?" he had asked, and I had nodded, not sure what *trying* or *it* entailed.

The next day he declared his study ghost-free. In the coming weeks, I did him the courtesy of scanning his various tomes into my computer, converting the text to speech, and parroting their contents to him over bowls of rice pudding my grandmother made with assistance from the kitchen staff. The whole charade was for her benefit, I long presumed, an elaborate plan by Dr. Parshall to convince her, after so many refusals, to say yes to his standing proposal of marriage. She cited the twenty-year difference in their ages. Never mind how little time she had to live. Only when he asked me to close the door of his study, not wanting my grandmother to hear the finer details of his employment offer, did I realize it was only a charade to one of us.

I sat down in the wheelchair. "Maybe there's a book you can recommend, Dr. Parshall."

It sounded as though a piece of popcorn were caught in his throat. He kept making the sound without much vigor. Carly said his name, and the sound rolled to a stop.

"Tate, his eyes are closed."

I reached for his liver-spotted hand, as small as a child's. "Dr. Parshall, wake up."

Carly was in the hallway, yelling for help.

The nurse with a questionable background in performing arts took his pulse and blood pressure one more time. There were curse words, his and hers, and the sound of a motorized bed.

"He just needs some rest," she said, ushering us into the hallway. "Between you and the woman who was here earlier, he's had about all he can handle in a day."

"Which woman was this?" I asked. Dr. Parshall had no family to speak of, and I remembered no regular visitors from the time I came to Rosewall Glen on a daily basis.

"Some woman trying to save a nest of birds. She wanted him to sign a paper giving her group permission to rescue them from one of the buildings at the college."

"Do you remember her name?"

"It would be in the guest book. She had burnt orange hair. In my opinion, she could have used conditioner. I don't like to speak ill of someone in a wheelchair, but her clothes were several sizes too big. She looked like a little girl who raided her mother's closet."

"Did he sign it?" I asked the nurse.

"You'd have to ask him."

I opened his door. Parshall was already asleep. I shook him gently until he made a B sound.

"Dr. Parshall, do you remember the woman who was here to see you earlier?"

"What woman?" he said. Sleep had punched a lot of holes in his voice.

"She wanted you to sign something. Did you sign anything today?"

"Sign," he said in a glassy voice you could see right through.

"He has good days and bad days," said the nurse.

"When we have to separate them, the good isn't that good, is it?"

I sent my gaze upward to see the nurse shake her head with a flat smile.

"We can't blame them, Nick."

"Blame who?"

"We put our school on their land. Of course they're going to be mad."

"Whose land?" Years earlier, he had told me they were the ghosts of students denied admission. Then they were the ghosts of faculty denied tenure.

"I have a new theory." He thumped his hand on the arm of the chair, as though it had fallen asleep. "What if the college was built on the sacred land of Indians. What can we do to appease them, Nick?"

I noticed on his nightstand one of the green plastic containers used by the library for the blind for books on tape. I had told him about the service when his eyes could no longer manage large print. "What are you reading these days, Dr. Parshall?"

"A new writer. Talented fellow named Stephen King. That one's called *The Shining*."

"I've heard of him," I said, realizing where he had gotten his new theory.

"Dr. Parshall, maybe you would like to do a little reading before bed." The nurse insinuated herself between me and the chair. "Visiting hours are over. He needs his rest."

"Just one more thing. Dr. Parshall, I understand there are three trustees. I know you're one of them. One of the others wouldn't be Theodore Skipwith, would it?"

"That's right. Old Letrobe passed on, left his share to the Skipwith boy."

"And who's the third trustee?"

"That would be Ms. Freyman. Sarah Freyman."

"Does Ms. Freyman work out of the trustee's office?"

Parshall held out his arm as far as it would go, gesturing to the room. "When you reach our age, this is what an office looks like."

The nurse pulled my wrist in the direction of the hall. "Might Ms. Freyman have an assistant?"

Half a minute went by. I asked him again, a bit louder.

"No, Sarah was an only child."

"Not a sister, an assistant."

Dr. Parshall grabbed my hand. He pressed it between both of his. "Go purify the land, Nick. I give you my blessing. Ask Ms. Freyman to give you hers." He dictated her address to Carly. "Never mind the Skipwith boy. Too many generations separate him from the founders. He has no connection to the land."

We checked the guest book, not expecting the bird activist to have used her real name. At 10:30 this morning, in what Carly described as block letters, was the name of our interim Dean. Under the column where guests wrote whom they were there to see, in more block letters, she had written F. Randolph Parshall.

16

NO CARS, BLACK OR OTHERWISE, followed us to the Gray Knight. I counted only a pair of vehicles on our side of the building. The hourly customers didn't arrive until the bars closed.

"Why do you live in a motel?" Carly asked.

"I don't like making the bed."

The office was hazy with smoke and garlic. The Gogeninis had put a white table cloth on the card table against the wall. In the center of it, a single candle burned beside a bottle of red. The housekeeping cart was diagonal between the desk and the door to the Gogeninis' apartment.

"What a picky man," Sundeep said from behind the desk by way of acknowledging us. He picked up pillows scattered on the floor and stuffed them on a shelf under the counter. "For two hours, this man has run me ragged. There is a spot on his sheets. I change the sheets. The sheets are scratchy. I change the sheets. Thread count this, lumpy pillow that. Finally, I tell him, sir, if you want luxury accommodations, I recommend the suites across town named after the dead writer."

"Hope we're not too late for dinner," I said.

Sundeep bowed his head. "Forgive me. Welcome, Carly. Welcome, Tate."

He promised dinner would be out shortly and disappeared inside their apartment. I pulled out one of the card table chairs for Carly and took the seat beside her. I slid my hand along the table until my fingers found the base of a wine glass. I rested the neck of the wine bottle on the glass's lip and gave myself a generous, five-second pour. I gave Carly the standard three count.

It was an Italian pinot noir of which Sundeep had grown particularly fond in recent months. Notes of vanilla and red fruit gave way to subtle, nearly imperceptible hints of clove. Some wine drinkers say the pleasure comes less from the flavors themselves than the search and contemplation. Personally, I like finding what I'm looking for, even if it's gone in a matter of moments.

Jaysaree made us get up to hug her. She complimented Carly on the top she was wearing. She complimented me on Carly's face and figure.

The serving dishes of rice and Malai Kofta were still going around when Sundeep raised his glass. "To the first of many meals among the four of us."

Jaysaree put a hand on Carly's wrist. "We worry about Tate. He is too old to be playing in the field."

I complimented the food. The subject didn't change.

"Do you want children, Carly?"

Carly hummed the letter M for a long moment before letting it become "maybe."

"Do not wait, dear. Sundeep and I have been trying for some time. You cannot predict when the toughness will get going."

"Jaysaree, you are embarrassing us all," said her husband.

"Tate will not admit it," said Jaysaree, "but I believe he wants a big family. It is only natural for someone whose parents—"

"What's the status of that stained shirt?" I asked a little too loudly.

Jaysaree stopped talking. She pushed her chair away from the table and moved around the desk into their apartment. I feared I had offended her until she emerged a few seconds later. She held the shirt, folded inside a thin box, very close to my face.

"All gone," she said. "Get out your magnifier and look at the buffet."

"Feast your eyes," corrected her husband.

I did not get out my magnifier. I thanked her and set the box on the floor.

"I ran into your colleague while I was at the dry cleaners," Jaysaree said.

"Which colleague?" Carly asked.

"The red-haired woman in the wheelchair. The one with a face like . . ." Jaysaree's hand went around in a circle, trying to conjure the right comparison. "A newborn squirrel."

"Delilah Bibb," I said.

"That is her. She claimed not to remember me from the Christmas party, but I remembered her. Each time I brought out pakoras or samosas, she would ask me what was in it. She had brought her daughter and wanted to make sure she was not allergic."

Carly held her glass while Sundeep refilled it. "Delilah recommended that dry cleaner to me last year. They ruined a pair of my wool slacks."

"Cleaner Than Cleaners?" Jaysaree leaned back in her chair.

"Washed Up. Off Summitview."

"No, dear. They are far too expensive. I always go to Cleaner Than right across the street."

I ushered a mouthful of wine past my tongue, foregoing the search for clove. "This isn't exactly Delilah's neck of the woods."

"The owner, Mrs. Thopsamoot, said she had never been there before. Mrs. Thopsamoot wanted to know why I called her Miss Bibb. Apparently, this wasn't the name she had given her."

"How is Mrs. Thopsamoot with blood stains?" I asked.

The question floated in the air with the masala. At last the moaning door to the lobby punctuated the silence.

"Sure smells like Heaven in here. Your people don't call it Heaven, do you? How are the good people this evening?"

I connected the syrupy accent to its lumbering owner, whose acquaintance I had made at the end of the afternoon's memorial service.

Sundeep pushed a sigh through his nose. "What can I get you now, Mr. Totten?"

The accreditation representative took a few more steps toward our table. "Dr. Totten," he said, "but Jefferson is just fine. May I?" Standing between Carly and Jaysaree, Jefferson picked up the wine bottle and set it down with a click of his tongue. "Drink as you go. I used to be in that boat myself once upon a time. I'm working on a cellar these days. I don't know if this will mean anything to you good people, but I have a 1973 Chateau Gerard. Bordeaux, of course. I've never been as keen on Pinots. They just don't stand up against serious meats."

Sundeep stood up from the table. "What can I get you, Dr. Totten?"

Jefferson Totten seemed not to hear him. He bent down again, but didn't pick up the wine. I noticed gray sideburns as thick as outdated carpet. "You two look familiar. You didn't dine with my wife and me on an Alaskan cruise about a year and a half ago, did you?"

I weighed the benefits of telling him how he knew us. They didn't weigh very heavy. Carly had different scales. She told Totten where we had met.

Jefferson Totten gave us a double clap. "Lovely. Absolutely lovely. An absolute shame about Scoot." He set a large hand on each of our backs. "You know, I have been trying to learn a little bit about your interim dean all afternoon. All I've come across are papers and presentations." He tossed those words like a handful of sand into the ocean. "If I'm going to work with someone, I need to know if he or she is someone I can work with. I'm talking about somebody's essence. You can't type that into a search engine."

Sundeep, who had disappeared into their apartment, came back with two pillows. "My wife and I sleep on these in our own bed. Take them."

Totten waved him off. "The other pillows should be adequate. It's the air in the room. It's rather dry. Could I trouble you good people for a humidifier?"

Jaysaree said there was a vaporizer on the shelf above the washing machine. Totten said that would possibly work. Sundeep went to retrieve it.

"As I was saying," Totten resumed, "I like to know what kind of person I'm working with. Dean Simkins, you see, was a good man. A good, good man. We worked together just fine. Would the two of you say the same of Delilah Bibb?"

"Good at what?" I asked.

Jefferson Totten touched my shoulder with his fingertips. "In the most basic sense, would you say she does right by those around her?"

"At least one person," I said, "thinks she's a wonderful human being. She has a card to prove it."

Sundeep returned with the vaporizer in his arms.

"If you could just get that started for me," said Totten. "I do thank you."

Sundeep carried the vaporizer out of the lobby without a word.

"See there? That is a good man." Totten had a seat in the empty chair and touched Jaysaree's arm. "If I could make a recommendation for you to pass along to the owner of these accommodations. It would be a prudent investment to centralize the heating and cooling. The finer hotels have gone in that direction, particularly in Western Europe."

Jaysaree rested her hand on Totten's arm. "My husband and I

are the owners. And if I might ask, doctor, why isn't a man with such sophisticated taste not staying at one of these finer hotels?"

Jefferson Totten sat up straight. He inspected the folding chair in which he had sat and groaned disapprovingly. "Unfortunately I am in town for business and not pleasure. The fine folks in Raleigh handle my travel arrangements, and they are a decidedly impecunious breed."

17

AFTER DINNER, ON THE WAY to my room, Totten's voice was audible through the single-pane window of his meager accommodations. Carly paused behind the car outside his door.

"Look at this, Tate. He drives a Mercedes Benz. He has a wine cellar, takes Alaskan cruises, stays at the finer hotels of Western Europe." She kicked the rear fender of his luxury automobile.

"He does have a PhD," I said.

The click of high heels on asphalt curved around the building in our direction. The volume and interval of the footsteps told me she was tall and full-figured. The cloud of olive oil, in which Myrsini liked to bathe, reached us a few seconds before she did. Six-four in heels, she leaned down to kiss my cheek.

"Good evening, Tate Cowlishaw." Myrsini maintained a Greek accent as thick as moussaka, though she had lived in America since age nine. She would be a good match, at least in height, for Jefferson Totten, on whose door she began to knock.

"We're neighbors," I said, noticing Carly's mouth had not closed.

Once Myrsini had gone inside, Carly kicked Totten's bumper one more time. "That's for cheating on your wife, *Dr.* Totten."

"He might not be cheating," I said. "Myrsini specializes in conversation. She has a PhD in Cultural Anthropology, I believe."

Carly laughed angrily. "That's what I'm talking about. Londell has a PhD. So does Tweel, for God's sake. They don't make much more than those of us with Master's degrees. Administrators like

Simkins and this asshole—do you have any idea how much Sim-kins's annual salary was?"

I unlocked my room and turned on the dry heat.

"Remember when human resources was the retired postal worker who tried to get us to join his fantasy football league? I passed by his cube once and noticed one of his drawers was open. One hundred forty-seven thousand dollars a year. Seven times what we make. More than seven. There's Delilah's motive right there."

Carly sat on the bed next to Edward. He rubbed his face against her knee.

"Delilah has money," I said. "Family money."

"How do you think her wealthy family feels about her making what a cashier makes?"

"They don't feel much. They died years ago."

"Why do you keep contradicting me, Tate? You know it was Delilah Bibb."

"Knowing and proving are two separate things."

Carly's gaze landed on the painting of a lighthouse Jaysaree had purchased from a discount department store. She stared at it for a long time. No one's eyes had been on it this long since the original artist.

"Can I offer you a drink? Dark rum? Skim milk?"

"Can I use your computer?"

I turned on my desktop. I disabled my screen reader and pulled out the chair for her.

"I just want to check the status of a story submission."

I gave Edward a scoop of the dry stuff. He wasn't hungry enough to eat it. He followed me to the nightstand to say there were messages. More likely he recalled the single time I put his treats in my sock drawer.

The first message was a hang-up. So was the second. Nobody liked talking to machines anymore. Both calls had come in the early afternoon.

Carly hadn't typed much when she stood up. "Why were you Googling my name?"

A third message was the click of a shy or disappointed caller.

"Why, Tate?"

"Were you checking my computer to see if I had?"

A fourth hang-up. Then a fifth.

"I was typing *Carolina Literary Review*. Your search engine filled in my name."

"I'm sure it didn't mean to."

"What were you looking for?"

That I had searched Monday afternoon for a picture of her to enlarge on my screen, to decide how excited I should be about our stroll through campus, was nothing I felt like sharing.

"I wanted to read one of your stories. I thought I might find one online."

"If you want to read one of my stories, just ask me." If her tone got any sharper, I'd need stitches.

"Understood."

The answering machine continued to announce the hour and minute of my missed calls. For the first time, a shallow breath preceded the click.

"Tate, it's me." Mollie DuFrange waited a few seconds to let me—or herself—figure out why she was calling. "Are you going to be around later?"

I turned down the volume. Carly stepped around me and turned it up.

"We need to talk. About who we talked about earlier. It's kind of urgent. Call me back when you get this."

Carly alternated glances between me and the answering machine. "Who were you talking about, Tate?" Carly turned around to face my computer, seeming to shake her head. "The two of you were investigating me, weren't you?"

"What would we be investigating?"

She didn't like that one enough to answer it. I asked her again, thinking maybe it would grow on her. It didn't.

"I expected this from Mollie. I'm not even surprised that our psycho interim dean is stalking me. But I thought there was something between us, Tate."

"Sure I can't talk you into that drink, sweetheart?"

She spun around quickly. I thought I was going to get slapped, but her hands remained at her side. "Do you know why I write, Tate?"

I sat on the bed and let her tell me.

"My characters never betray me. Heroes, villains, they're all on my side. Real people," she said, "only disappoint you."

"One of us," I said, "has no idea what you're talking about."

She put her hands on my shoulders, leaned forward, and gave me a hard smacker on the lips. "See that? Already it doesn't feel the same."

"Not when you do it like that."

She grabbed her jacket from the back of a chair. Edward began a figure eight around her legs, which she didn't let him finish. Sometimes when an animal likes someone, you can take it as a sign of their essential goodness, but Edward liked anyone who scratched behind his ears. We all do.

"Feel free to waste your time scrutinizing me. I have no interest in wasting mine," she said, slamming the door as hard as its bent edges would allow.

18

CARLY HADN'T BEEN GONE the length of a slow pop song about second chances when the hard knock came. It seemed closer to the doorknob than the peephole. I pictured Carly on her knees, asking my forgiveness. I opened the door with an outstretched hand to help her up.

Her entrance was a blur, nothing but a torso and a short pair of arms. Her hair was darker and shorter. The smart money said she had not been to a salon since I last saw her.

"Mr. Thayer. So nice of you to stop by."

He extended his hand, his knuckles connecting with my groin in a gesture no one has ever mistaken for a handshake.

"I'm not a violent person," he said.

"Agree to disagree," I said from my position on the floor.

Thayer was offering his hand again, much slower this time. I had a clear shot at his face, but the moment seemed to have passed. I sat up without his help.

"That phone number is specifically for acting business, Cowlishaw. Imagine my disappointment upon receiving a call about a stolen file cabinet."

"Not interested in theft cases either, huh? Is there a particular crime you do like to solve?"

Thayer hopped a few inches onto the bed. "Listen, Cowlishaw. I'm sorry about your dean. I'm sure it's been—" He stopped talking when I raised my hand.

"I would have used your number at the station, but didn't think you'd want your partner to know about this."

"Know about what?"

"I should have contacted you myself. And I do apologize for giving the impression this was not acting-related business."

"What the hell are you talking about, Cowlishaw?"

I paused until I myself was sure. "I was very taken with your performance in *Glengarry Glen Ross* last year. I'll be honest, Thayer: I'm not much for musicals, but after seeing you in *Godspell*, I ordered the original cast recording."

"Wow. Thank you. Do you know how hard I had to fight to play Judas? Directors say I'm too sympathetic. They never say why, but I know it's because of my condition."

The room filled with silence and the fresh heartbeat of his dying dreams.

"Are you bullshitting me, Cowlishaw?"

I dismissed the possibility with a laugh. "I used to wish I were an actor. Perhaps that's why I'm so taken when I meet one."

"You didn't mention any of this when we took you in."

I remained on the floor. I thought of relocating to a chair, but let my guest continue being the taller one in the room. "What would the praise have meant from a suspected murderer?"

"Yeah, well." Thayer kicked off his shoes and pulled his feet onto the bed. "I'm sorry about that. You were never a suspect, Cowlishaw. We knew all along it was a suicide."

"You mean your partner knew."

Thayer sighed. He hopped down from the bed, got on his hands and knees, and made kissing sounds. "Come here. Come on. What's your name, Mr. Kitty?"

I told him.

Thayer patted the carpet, making little gerbil noises. Edward stayed put under the chair.

"He's had a rough night," I said. "A pretty blonde stormed out on him when he was just getting to know her."

Thayer faced me. "I think I saw her. She was sobbing in her car."

I looked in the direction of the parking lot. My walls and blind spots were in the way.

"I know my partner can rub some people the wrong way," Thayer said. "Deep down he's a pretty sensitive guy."

Thayer swept his hand from side to side on the carpet. I wished he liked detective work as much as he liked cats and theater. I got the canister of Edward's treats from my dresser drawer. The slightest shifting of its contents sent Edward sprinting in my direction. I gave Thayer the canister.

"Are you familiar with the Parshall Theater?" I asked.

"Sure. Over on Gray Street. Before I made detective, my beat included shooing away bums who made their home in the orchestra pit. I was an undergrad over at State when it got condemned. Big loss for the community."

Edward took a treat from the detective's hand. After another, Edward lay on his side, offered up his belly to rub.

"The theater's former patron was F. Randolph Parshall, whose family founded the college where I work."

Thayer turned in my direction. I paused for the sake of his imagination. I took a little while longer for my own.

"Dr. Parshall is at the point in his life when he has to think about his legacy. At the top of his list is the revitalization of Grayford's theater community."

"I pass by that theater twice a day, Cowlishaw. It's a half-stick of dynamite away from its final resting place."

I gave him a half-smile. "His plan," I said, working it out as I went, "is to use the theater on campus, roughly the same size as the old Parshall downtown. I'm hoping—both of us are—that you will accept a pair of roles in the project. The first involves cleaning up crime on campus. As it is, the school's atmosphere isn't conducive to entertaining."

"What's the other role?" He sounded disappointed by the first.

"You tell me," I said.

Thayer said he didn't follow.

"The theater will need a repertory. Actors, directors, the whole nine. Any interest?"

Thayer didn't speak. His mouth was too small to notice if it hung open.

"As you might have gathered, Dr. Parshall has a limited amount of time to see this happen."

Thayer took a bigger breath than yes or no required. "I'm going to level with you, Cowlishaw. Your compliments, while gratifying, are the first I've received on my acting in a long time." He let out the rest of his breath. "I've kind of made peace with it, you know. I'll always have a passion for acting. Lately, though, I've been venturing further and further down the path of screenwriting. I'm still trying to find my voice, as you could probably tell from the piece last night."

"Sounded like you found mine."

"It doesn't come easily to me," he said. "At least not yet. I love it, though, and I'm not sure how much energy I'll have for it if I'm acting or directing."

"Be our writer-in-residence," I said. "We're looking for one of those, too."

"Really?"

"Absolutely."

Thayer stood up. He backed into the bed and lifted himself onto it. He raised an arm in the air and jumped up and down, higher and higher. It had been years since anyone had been so happy on my bed.

At last I moved into a chair. "About that first role," I said. "I hope you have a little patience for an old man's paranoia. Dr. Parshall still harbors suspicions about the circumstances of our dean's death."

Thayer started to say my name, and I put up a preemptive hand.

"He doesn't dispute the findings of the investigation. He would, however, appreciate some kind of proof one way or the other, something tangible to ease his mind about opening a theater two buildings from the site of a possible murder."

Thayer hopped down from the bed. "That doesn't sound unreasonable. This writer-in-residence gig, how much is that going to pay?"

"Competitive," I said, recalling how Scoot Simkins had described the salary I would earn at his college. He never said the decade in which the salary would have been competitive.

"So what's your role in all this, Cowlishaw?"

I told the truth, or what might have been the truth if my promises weren't thinner than the walls of the Gray Knight. "Parshall was in love with my late grandmother. I'm the closest thing he has to family."

Thayer extended his hand and I shook it. "You did the right thing, by the way, not telling me this while my partner was around. I don't know if jealous is the right word, but he can be a little resentful of my creative endeavors."

I held the handshake an extra second, trying to decide if Thayer was a good, good man, someone I could work with. You can't tell much from a hand. Edward vouched for him. He let him rub his belly, but he was probably responding to the treats.

19

THE ACTOR-DETECTIVE HAD BEEN GONE only a few minutes when another knock came. Again I thought of Carly. Again I was wrong. The almond musk of Mollie DuFrange's imported shampoo registered in my nose before the rest of her registered beneath my blind spots. She wore a short skirt and a top that didn't take her arms under consideration.

"Are you here alone?" she asked.

I gestured to the empty room behind me. She took it as an invitation, and I closed the door behind her. "Where's that husband of yours?"

"Home, I guess. I told him I was going out to sing. Where's your significant other?"

"She heard your message on my machine. She thought you were talking about her."

"I was."

"I know."

Mollie sat down on my bed and peered at the inch of night between the curtains that weren't entirely closed. She rested an elbow on her bare knee and cupped her chin in her hand. "Hi, Edward. It's been awhile."

I offered to close him up in the bathroom. When we were together, she claimed to have severe cat allergies. Her symptoms included mercurial headaches and wary looks in Edward's direction.

"It's okay," she said with a measure of contrition. "I'm not really allergic."

"I know."

Mollie eyed me with surprise, guilt, or contempt, possibly none of the above. I continued to look at her, my most convincing argument that I could see, which was my most convincing argument that she had chosen poorly in deciding to go back to her husband three years ago.

Mollie reached for the messenger bag by her feet. She opened the flap of an orange envelope and let out a breath. "This may hurt initially, but I'm trying to save you from something far worse."

Mollie handed me a book no larger than one of the poetry collections she had shelved on my window sill for a couple of months. She handed me another, this one red and twice as thick. There was a third and a fourth, each a little bigger than the one before it. One of the middle two had a dark cover with the word *Dustbowl* in large white letters. *River Creek Review* took a little more time to glean.

"The font in the tables of contents might be too small for your magnifier. I've got time if you want to scan them into your computer."

"I take it these are the stories of our colleague, Ms. Carly Worth. And I take it you find the content a little disturbing, suspicious even."

Mollie took back the *Dustbowl* and read me the fiction selections from the table of contents. She got out a sheet of paper from the orange envelope. "This is the curriculum vitae of Carly Anne Worth. If you'll recall, Simkins asked me to chair the committee on writing across the curriculum, and I asked everyone to send me their CVs. Never got yours, by the way. Under 'Publications,' Carly Anne Worth lists a story called 'Thumb and Forefinger' from this issue of *Dust Bowl Literary Review*. Did you hear that title among the stories I read you?"

"Perhaps she typed the wrong issue number."

Mollie emptied the messenger bag onto the bed. "This is every issue of *Dustbowl* from the last four years. I subscribe to it, Tate. The other journals I handed you are equally devoid of fiction by Carly Anne Worth, although all are supposed to feature her stories, according to her vitae. I subscribe to half the journals she lists, Tate. I've published poems in a few of them."

I paged idly through a *River Creek Review*. Over the years, I had worked assiduously to ignore what I couldn't see, what I didn't know. Suddenly I felt aware of every miniscule letter swimming in the abyss of my former vision.

"What has she told you about this novel she's allegedly sold?"

"Just that it's about vampires."

I'd rather she wrote about a disgruntled college instructor putting bullets into the skull of an insufferable dean. That was a story we had all imagined.

"On top of this, her CV says she earned an MFA in fiction from Iowa seven years ago. I made some phone calls, Tate. There's no record that she ever went there."

I stacked the journals on the floor. I recalled Delilah's suspicions of Carly. I had assumed she was trying to shine a light on someone other than herself, but it was possible she knew what Mollie knew. Mollie's hand found my leg above the knee. It wasn't a hard leg to find. Most of it was touching hers.

"I just don't want to see you get hurt, Tate." She tilted her head onto my shoulder. "It's ridiculous, I know, but I was a little jealous when I learned you were seeing Carly. Probably because Ben and I have been increasingly . . ." Poet that she was, Mollie sometimes paused for fifteen seconds in the middle of a sentence, searching for the best word. "Dissatisfied with each other."

One of her hands moved from her lap to the bed behind us.

"Do you want to know something really ridiculous?" she said. "For weeks now, I tried to gather the . . ." She paused again. "Temerity to knock on your door. I imagined myself in tears when you opened it, but I'm all cried out about Ben. As Edna St. Vincent Millay says, it kind of went in little ways. I half-hoped you would cry when I told you about Carly, not that I've ever seen you shed a tear."

"You do like tears," I said.

She gave a despondent little laugh. "People are more likely to touch each other when one of them is crying."

Mollie pulled very gently on my shirt until it came untucked. I faced her to find her lips parted. She had just wetted them and took her time wetting mine.

My hand found the back of her head, her hair crunchy with mousse. The warm static of her breath filled my ear. She kicked her shoes in Edward's direction, sending him scurrying toward the bathroom. I ran my fingers along her blouse until I felt the cold tip of a zipper beneath her arm. Finding things with your hands is easier than you realize, and everything on Mollie was exactly where I had left it.

"I've missed you," she told me sleepily an hour later.

"This is the easy part," I said. "It's the day-to-day living that wears you down."

"Listen to you, quoting Chekhov."

"Paraphrasing, actually. You quoted him. To me. Three years ago."

Mollie rolled onto her back. I turned onto my side, getting close enough to see what I hadn't seen in those three years. The accuracy of my memory was vindicated, but part of me always doubted its worth as a substitute for the real thing. Mollie located that part with her fingertips and smiled.

"Ben and I are great at the day-to-day," she said. "The passion is what eludes us. We're more like friends, siblings even."

"The last I heard, you were trying to get pregnant."

She laid her head on my chest. A powerful sigh made it all the way to my ankles. "Thank God I haven't. His idea, not mine."

"Full of ideas, that husband of yours. How's that petition coming?"

"He's . . . territorial," she said. "If Delilah gets her way, she's going to eliminate all content-based learning. No more space classes, no more poetry. I'm not sure what she plans to do with the courses you teach."

"Maybe you can teach them. She let me know I wouldn't be rehired."

"Oh my God. Tate, I'm so sorry. What are you going to do?"

"I have a couple of leads," I said.

She kissed my cheek. "Good for you. I've always thought you'd be happier in a different line of work. I don't know why you never looked into financial planning."

I didn't mean job leads, but I didn't correct her.

"It's the hardest thing," she said, "to think outside the box. God knows I tried with you. But I do believe people can change. I'm more patient than that cruel girl who gritted her teeth when she read you the list of entrées on a dinner menu."

"In your defense," I said, "my eyes and your patience weren't the only mismatch."

She placed her hand in the center of my chest and rose up to look at me. Her wide, dark eyes were helpful in feigning eye contact.

"As I recall, sweetheart, you had much more of a fondness for . . ." I pretended to shop for the perfect word, "things than I did. I don't imagine another job would pay me what you'd like to be worth."

Mollie punctuated a long breath with a smile. "I can learn to live without a lot of *things*. Plus, I'll get half of everything Ben and I have."

Her head settled again on my chest. We lay there for a long time, our shared past filling the room. I turned off the lamp on the nightstand.

"I can't stay," Mollie said. "I'm supposed to be singing."

She kissed me before sliding out of bed. I turned the lamp back on. I watched as her skirt obscured what I already began to miss.

"What did you sing?" I asked. "Better get your story straight."

Sitting on the bed, she kissed my forehead, nose, and chin. "I lied to you the other night, when I said I had been singing recently. It was actually the first time I had sung since college. I was planning ahead, giving myself an excuse to go out at night, somewhere I might tell my husband I was when I was actually here."

"Quite a plan."

She kissed another path up the center of my face, making my lips the last stop. "You're worth it." She collected the journals on the floor. "Maybe I should leave these here, prevent him from asking why I took them with me to sing."

"Tell him you needed the words to one of your poems. You're going to put it to music."

"You're a pretty good liar, Tate."

"You're a pretty bad one." I rolled onto my side. "Care to tell me why you're really here?"

Mollie dropped the journals and lay beside me, her nose pressed to mine. "Cut me a tiny bit of slack, Tate. I just cheated on my husband. I may not look like it, but I'm freaking out a little."

I aimed my gaze at the curtained window, focusing the lower portion of my useful vision on the yellow cover of an old *Dustbowl*. "Forgive me. Things have had a way of sounding untrue the last few days."

Mollie's lips curled into a sympathetic smile. She put on her shoes and gave me a long kiss. "It's you, Tate. It's always been you."

20

IT WAS STILL DARK OUTSIDE WHEN I WOKE. I hit the button on my clock that announced the time in a female's stern voice. I hit it again, hoping she would change her mind.

I brewed a pot of Nicaragua with notes of toffee and green apple. My computer was still on from the night before. I turned on my screen reader and did my own search for info about cremation. None of the frequently asked questions addressed how and when decisions were made to cremate someone without family or a will.

I got directions to the house of Sarah Freyman, nine miles outside city limits. I had never been to that area by foot. I wasn't a fan of taxis. Drivers unfamiliar with my destination liked to ask me if we were there. Half the time we were not there, but all I knew was the address, which I had already given the driver.

I checked my e-mail. Seven students wanted to know if we had class Friday. They were all dated Wednesday. I hadn't known them to think so far ahead. I deleted the lot of them and opened the message from Islanda Purvis, subject heading "paper you assigned." Out of the mildest guilt and a desire to finish my coffee, I opened the attached file.

"The failing business I have chosen to write about," the paper began, "is Parshall College, located in Grayford, North Carolina."

She catalogued the physical degradation of the buildings and landscape, campus crime, the volatile curriculum—her word—and the lack of extracurricular activities that might better promote a sense of community among the student body.

"How a school that charges so much money for tuition can't offer a decent college education, I have no idea. They sure aren't using that money on professors. I know this because there aren't very many of them, and the ones we do have barely do anything. For example, I know Mr. Cowlishaw won't actually read this paper, so I'm just going to keep typing until I reach the bottom of the page, which is how he grades all of our papers, by checking to see if we reached the last line on the page.

"To refer to something Mr. Cowlishaw mentioned in class, something which I already knew because it's common sense, the business world operates on the principle of supply and demand. A college education is in high demand, so Parshall College, located in Grayford, North Carolina, needs to supply a better education in order for more students to pay the insane price they charge. The more students there are, the more money the school will make from tuition. This probably isn't going to happen, so the way I would save Parshall College, located in Grayford, North Carolina, is to beg Sarah Freyman, the richest trustee, for some of the money she probably keeps for herself instead of putting it back into this terrible school. Here are some more words so that the paragraph will end on the last line of the page."

I backed up my screen reader to the last few lines. That a student would know the name of a trustee seemed unlikely, but not impossible. That she knew the trustee's wealth relative to other trustees seemed equally peculiar. I searched the Internet for the name Sarah Freyman with various key words that might connect her to Parshall College. Her name was not an uncommon one. On no web pages did the name appear with the word trustee or the name of the school.

"Dear Islanda," I replied. "Terrific work, particularly the way your words went all the way to the bottom of the page. I have a couple of questions about the source of some of your information. Call my cell phone as soon as you read this so we can resolve this urgent matter."

21

THE FORCEFUL CLACK OF A TALL, full-figured woman in heels passed in front of my door. I opened it in time to catch a whiff of her extra-virginal tailwind. "I take it you had a good time," I called out.

Myrsini threw her head back and let out an incongruously small laugh. She spoke with more breath than one usually finds in a natural, unaffected voice. I was only sixty percent confident she wasn't a man. "Pretentious assholes like that are the reason I left academia."

"Perhaps if you made what he makes, you could have stuck it out."

"Sometimes I miss it, Tate. Not the bullshit, of course. I do miss a room full of people who have paid to listen to me. Now people like 'Big T' over in Room 22 pay me to listen to their tedious stories about nothing and nothing and nothing."

"Big T?"

"That's what he instructed me to call him. They like nicknames, Tate. I have a short chapter on the subject in my book." Myrsini brought her face a few inches from mine. "I'm sure there's a secret name you'd like to be called, Tate Cowlishaw."

"When I think of something, I'll let you know."

Myrsini kissed my nose. "Do that," she whispered.

As she pulled away, I used the cover of my mirrored sunglasses to point my pupils skyward, getting an extended view of what I was eighty percent sure was an Adam's apple. Of all the mistakes I had made with women, this was not one of them.

I knocked a few times on the door of Room 22. I let a minute pass and knocked again. A high, mechanical wheeze somewhere in the room came to a stop. The Big T said something, which I didn't make out. I knocked again.

Totten opened the door until the chain caught. "You are not my Greek goddess."

"And for that I apologize," I said. "She asked me to tell you what wonderful company you were. Mind if I step inside for a moment?"

The door moved a couple of inches in the wrong direction. Totten's voice became pinched, defensive. "I can pay more if I was inappropriate."

"How much did you have in mind?"

"As much as you think is fair. Please consider, however, that she did not do two-thirds of what I requested."

I was thinking about taking his money and splitting it with Myrsini. I was thinking of things I wished I weren't thinking about. "Actually, I'm here on behalf of another woman you know."

The door opened all the way as Jefferson Totten pleaded his ignorance. The towel around his waist resembled a tight miniskirt. Above it he had cultivated a wide field of gray chest hair. I left my sunglasses on and aimed them at his torso, blocking what I didn't wish to see, the one thing my eyes do well.

"I don't know what she told you, but Ms. Myrsini was the only woman I was with last night. I made a few suggestions to the contrary, but those were not to her liking." Totten raised his arms above his head. The towel fell. "If you need to rough me up a bit, I understand. Anywhere but the face. I have an important meeting in half an hour."

I removed my shades, folding the stems and sliding them in my breast pocket.

"Wait a moment. Christ on a crutch, you're no pimp. You're from the college."

Close as we stood, my peripheral vision received a brief synopsis of Myrsini's evening. I handed him his towel. "Interim Dean Bibb sent me. She wanted to make sure you knew where the meeting was being held."

"Tell her I received her e-mail as well as her phone message." He picked up the towel and threw it at the television. "Every time I talk to that woman I miss Scoot a little more."

"You liked working with him, did you?"

"You're goddamn right." Totten faced his reflection in the mirror. The volume of his breathing and his enduring nudity made me wonder in new ways what he found so appealing about our late dean.

"Actually, Interim Dean Bibb had to change the location of this morning's meeting. The room where it was to be held no longer has electricity."

Totten faced me again and sighed. "I fear for the lovely, park-like campus of fair Parshall. Delilah Bibb has not made a positive impression, Dr. Collins."

"Mr. Collins," I said, thinking it best not to correct him entirely.

Totten sat on the bed and pulled on a pair of underwear. "I assume you will forget everything I've said to you in this shabby room."

"I have a terrible memory," I said.

Jefferson Totten clapped me on the back and called me a good man.

We stepped outside. He asked what I drove, and I said my Hyundai was in the shop.

"You need to get yourself a German car, Mr. Collins. Only the Germans understand the meaning of true luxury. Climb into my Mercedes, and allow me to make a brief argument on their behalf."

I told him where to make turns. Enamored as he was of his car's accelerator, he managed to miss most of them. After running his second stop sign, I took the liberty of pointing them out as well.

"Rules, Mr. Collins, are for people who don't know what they're doing. As a steward of the academy, you should be aware of that."

He double-parked the Mercedes across the lot from its uglier cousin, Duncan's Volkswagen. I led us to the former computer lab on the second floor of the student center. The room looked much the same as it used to, long tables arranged in a broken square, minus the chairs and computers. Delilah was not there, as she tended not to visit the second floors of buildings without elevators.

Totten crossed his arms over his sport coat. "This does not bode well."

I excused myself to the hallway, faked a phone call, and returned to the empty room. "She wants you back in the original location."

"Furley Hall, third floor?"

"That's the one."

Totten chuckled unhappily as I led him across the parking lot, past the library to Furley Hall. I bid him adieu between the second and third floors, out of earshot of Delilah's office.

Totten shook my hand with a delicate up and down, as if determining its weight. "It's a shame you're not dean, Mr. Collins. You feel like a man I could work with."

Half a dozen steps led him into the classroom. He closed the door behind him. I heard Delilah's voice, but couldn't make out any words. I took the rest of the stairs and skirted the wall where the floor protested less insistently.

"Go ahead," Delilah said. "I'll be fine."

A pair of footsteps too light to be Jefferson Totten's approached the door. Its hinges were on the inside, preventing me from hiding behind it when it opened. I hastened toward the elevator and pushed the button. It opened as quietly as a fifty-year-old elevator ever does, emitting slightly less noise than a city bus swerving to avoid a head-on collision. The doors hadn't yet closed when someone passed, stopped abruptly, and joined me inside.

"There he is," I said.

"There I was," Londell said.

"Not sticking around for the big presentation?"

"Apparently," he said, "Dr. Totten prefers one-on-one interaction."

The doors closed. I made a correct guess of the button that kept the elevator from moving.

"If you ask me, Cowlishaw, this is some racial shit." Londell gave his sideways laugh that didn't say whether or not he was joking. "Since when do you ride elevators, Cowlishaw?"

"I've been getting too much exercise. How long do you think they'll be in there?"

"Hours, if it's up to Delilah. You need to talk to her?"

I pushed the button that opened the doors. "I think I'll just listen."

"Hey, Cowlishaw. I saw Thayer a little while ago by the dorms. Said you and Dr. Parshall offered him a role in some sort of theater venture. Why ain't I heard about this?"

"It's still in the theoretical stage," I said.

Londell made the terse M sound particular to sassy black maids on 70s sitcoms. "When theory becomes practice, Cowlishaw, I've got two words for you: comedy night."

"From your lips to Dr. Parshall's hearing aid," I said as the doors closed between us.

Delilah was talking when I pressed my ear against the wall beside the door. "As you'll notice in this graph, the mean aptitude of students entering Parshall College has decreased yearly. While not an excuse for the lack of progress under Dean Simkins's leadership, we are profoundly confident . . ."

The rest of Delilah's thoughts were swallowed by Jefferson Totten's enormous, jungle-cat yawn.

"Are you tired, Dr. Totten? I can get you some coffee."

"Not tired, Ms. Bibb. Just bored."

"Dr. Bakker was in charge of the graphs. Perhaps if he were here, he would be able to walk you through the data with the vim you would prefer."

"I doubt the walk will improve with a different escort," said Totten.

Delilah cleared her throat with excessive vim. "Should I begin with formative assessments?"

There was only silence, underscored by the toes of a rodent gaining purchase in the wall. The heavier feet of Jefferson Totten slowly made their way from what must have been the back row. Each step put another crack in the tenuous dam holding back Delilah's sniffles and sobs. Desk legs scraped the floor.

In a voice even softer than his hands, Totten said, "I'm going to close your little computer now. No more PowerPoint, no more charts and graphs. I'll sit in this here desk, and you can sit in your wheelchair, and you and I will have a conversation. How does that sound?"

"It's been a horrible week, Dr. Totten."

"I know it, darlin'. Take my handkerchief and dry your face."

"We weren't able to locate his files. With some additional time, I'm certain we could make a far more compelling argument for our college."

"I'm going to go out on a limb, Dr. Bibb, and guess you did not work closely with Dean Simkins on matters of accreditation."

"I worked very, very closely with him on the new curriculum. Not to mention the exhaustive overhaul of the university's learning outcomes and—"

"Accreditation, Dr. Bibb. Matters of accreditation."

An unruly sob interpolated itself between her words. "I have the checklist of learning objectives and all the accompanying descriptions from the accreditation board's website. If you could please walk me through it and offer the briefest of extensions, I truly am certain you would find everything at Parshall to your satisfaction."

The sound of paper ripping was unmistakable through the poorly insulated wall.

"Dean Simkins and I liked to go off the books," said Totten. "It never seemed fair to hold a school of Parshall's limited resources to the same standards as, say, the state university up the road."

Delilah sniffled. "Our vision is hardly the same as the state university."

"Exactly, Dean Bibb. Exactly." Totten's syllables widened. What might have been a laugh dripped thickly from his lips. "Do you know what I was before I joined the noble cause of administration and accreditation? A philosopher." He pronounced it slowly, a child wrapping his tongue around a species of dinosaur. "Sooner or later, Dean Bibb, we have to recognize the selfishness of our own passions."

"Oh, absolutely. What you'll see in the later slides is a description of our move away from content-based learning. I'm so excited about the benefits our students will begin to see when—"

Totten overwhelmed her with another yawn, louder and less sincere than its precursor. "You lost me again, Dr. Bibb. Save the PowerPoint for conferences and faculty colloquiums. Turn it into a tedious little paper and publish it in one of the pamphlets read only by you and the editor who has to fill two hundred pages a year with inane bullshit."

"Excuse me, Dr. Totten. Your language is—"

"Lose the attitude, honey. The dean of this school has one obligation: to keep this college open for business. Dean Simkins understood that obligation. Year after year, he fulfilled that obligation. In exchange, he was paid a very fair salary by the powers that be."

The wall below my hip thudded with a sound like a miniature jackhammer. I took a step back. My phone was vibrating. A side button killed the sound, only to resurrect it as a piercing bell. I muffled it between my hands, carried it to the elevator, and sealed it up behind the closed doors.

"Of course not," Delilah said when I returned to the wall. "Perhaps it was one of our ghosts. Dean Simkins," she sneered, "tasked one of our lecturers with ridding Parshall of harmful spirits."

"Why do you insist on denigrating the contributions of your late dean? Were it not for his wisdom and selflessness, the accreditation board would have received a recommendation years ago to revoke this school's privilege to confer meaningful degrees on its graduates."

She was no longer crying. When next she spoke, Delilah's voice echoed with the helplessness of someone trapped in a mine shaft. "Tell me what to do. I can do whatever Scoot did."

Two floors down, the building's front door slammed against the inside wall. I listened for the creak of stairs. They never came. I made it to the elevator just in time to situate my phone between the closing doors, causing them to remain open.

"Seventy-five," Totten was saying when my ear found the warm spot on the wall. "Annually, of course."

"Hundred?" Delilah asked.

Totten's laugh, like all his reactions, seemed both offended and intended to offend. "Seventy-five thousand, dear. I assure you, with his generous salary, Scoot managed to live quite comfortably and still afford his contribution to the Jefferson Totten Fund."

"I don't believe you," said Delilah in a shrinking voice that said otherwise. "Scoot would never do that. Never."

"Sometimes the truth is less attractive than we'd prefer, but if we try real hard, we can learn to love it all the same."

My phone rang again between the elevator doors. I kicked it inside. The doors closed, and the elevator began its slow descent to the first floor.

"Parshall College," said Totten, possibly standing, "has been on a ventilator for years. The question you need to ask yourself, and answer sometime before eight o'clock tomorrow morning, is whether you want to be the one who pulls the plug."

"I need to think about it."

"Do that. I trust you'll do your thinking alone."

Totten's footsteps shook the floor. My own weren't without noise as I took the stairs two at a time, holding fast to the hand-rail. On the second floor, I pushed the button for the elevator and waited.

22

"LOOKING FOR THIS?" The anger in Juliet Bibb's voice was accompanied by a measure of anxiety not there when she had hurled a plant over my head.

Another voicemail announced its arrival as I pocketed my phone. Jefferson Totten thundered slowly down the stairs. There was something I had wanted to ask Delilah's daughter. I was trying to remember what it was when she brought her hand across my cheek.

"You sent them, didn't you?"

"You have an unhealthy hatred of botanicals," I said, rubbing my tender jawline.

"The pictures, you jerk."

Totten exited the building more delicately than Juliet had entered it.

"What pictures?"

Juliet Bibb stepped off the elevator and threw her arms around me. Delilah's daughter was shaking. I let her cry until her breathing steadied. I repeated my question.

"Bad pictures." Juliet reached for the purse that had fallen to the floor between us. Her hands continued to tremble.

"Why don't you just tell me about them." I thought I could save us both some trouble.

"My mom," she said, still fumbling with the flap of the envelope.

I took the envelope. "What's your mom doing in the pictures?"

"S-s-s-sexual," she said.

I tapped the top of the envelope, feeling my eyebrows rise. I forced them down. "You mentioned she's been out on dates recently. Do you recognize the . . ." I tried to decide between lover and paramour.

"The m-m-man who died," she said. "S-S-S-Simkins."

I opened the envelope and removed several sheets of standard printer paper. The pictures were in black and white. Large as they were, I could make out Simkins's desk and file cabinets. The person closest to the center had on a tie. Not until I made out the outline of heads, Delilah's much lower than that of the late dean, did I grasp the sexual nature of the photograph. Only the angle seemed to change in subsequent photos. The last sheet contained lines of type.

"Did someone e-mail these to you?"

"Not me."

"To your mom?"

Juliet nodded her orange head. "I check her e-mail whenever she mentions sending me back to college."

I moved my eyes from left to right. "Do you recognize the name of who sent it?"

"It's a fake address. They used a proxy server. I know a little about computers," she said, sounding as though she wished she didn't. The elderly floor quaked a bit as she composed herself enough to continue. "It's from 'motive@youkilledsimkins.com.'"

"Does your mother know about these?"

"It was marked as read in her inbox. They sent it yesterday morning."

It would have arrived before I got to her house, possibly around the time the meeting was cancelled. The faculty had long suspected, with vague indifference and moderate repulsion, that Simkins and his associate dean worked together on matters beyond the academic. Dissenters noted that the two of them seemed disinterested in pleasure, carnal or otherwise. What the pictures seemed to confirm might be less interesting than knowing who took them.

"I was only kidding yesterday." Juliet choked out a sob. "She didn't really kill anyone. Mom would never kill somebody. Would she?"

Juliet Bibb fell into my arms again, the bristles of her crew cut rubbing against the cheek she had slapped.

"There are usually explanations for these things," I said.

Juliet sobbed quietly on my shoulder. We might have been thinking of the same explanation.

"Why don't you go upstairs and talk to your mom. Leave out the part where you saw me."

Juliet got on the elevator. I held the envelope in my hand. I put my foot between the closing doors, remembering what I had wanted to ask her.

"How often does your mom drive your car?"

"She used to never drive it. Now she drives it like all the time. Why?"

"No reason," I said, withdrawing my foot to let the doors close.

23

"TATE, CALL ME," Mollie said in her first message. "Call me soon," she said in her second message. "Sooner than that, if possible. If you're anywhere near campus, I'm teaching in one-oh-six until ten forty-five."

Passing the dorm on my way to Mollie's classroom, someone called my name. He sounded as young as a student, but more enthusiastic.

"Detective," I said, stepping onto the dorm's porch. "Glad to see you're on the job."

"I've been here for an hour, but no one can tell me where to find Ms. Gladstone. She isn't answering her phone."

I had hoped the murder investigation would take precedence over the missing file cabinet, but beggars can't be choosers. "She might be in class. Some of them have been known to go."

I opened the envelope. Thayer started pacing the porch before I could show him naughty pictures of the interim dean.

"I couldn't sleep all night, Cowlishaw. I had a thousand ideas for new plays. Sets, casts, stage directions, you name it."

I handed him the sheet without pictures, the one with the fake e-mail address. "Add this to your list of ideas. How are you with tracing e-mail?"

Thayer read the presumably fake e-mail address three different ways—surprised, pensive, and cheeky—as if directing himself through multiple takes. A pair of female students on their way into the dorm stopped to watch. "Weird," said one of them before going in.

I showed him the pictures. I told him about Simkins's salary and Delilah's new status as the interim dean.

"Looks like possible extortion or blackmail. If she wants to report it, we can investigate."

"Given the nature of the photos, she might not be inclined to share them. I'm reporting it on her behalf."

"Sorry, but with budget cuts, if she doesn't come forward herself, we can't consider her the victim of a crime."

I returned the pages to the envelope. "That must be what happened to Simkins," I said. "He couldn't come forward, so there was no murder."

Thayer pulled a big breath into his little lungs. He let it out slowly with each word. "Ms. Gladstone isn't in class, according to her schedule. Her roommate said she hasn't been back to their room in a couple of days." Thayer moved to the edge of the porch. "What kind of budget does Parshall have in mind for structural repairs, Cowlishaw? I walked around the theater earlier. Nobody's going to pay to see a show in that mess."

"Our students pay forty-five thousand a year for a piece of paper worth far less than theater tickets." I started down the steps toward the library. "I know where Nikki might be."

Thayer remained on the porch, surveying the dilapidated campus. I had witnessed similar hesitation in parents of prospective students. Each spring, the faculty took turns giving campus tours. Like all the students with no other choice, Thayer made his reluctant way into the tangled, unmowed grass.

"Why are all the lights off?" the actor-detective asked inside the library.

"I believe they're on," I said. "The electricity is off."

I led him through the stacks to the dark classroom. Placing my ear against the door of the utility closet, I heard the tiny clicks of fingernails against a laptop keyboard. I knocked lightly on the door.

"It's Mr. Cowlishaw, Nikki. My friend is here to help you find your file cabinet."

Thayer looked at me and at the door. "We spoke on the phone yesterday," he said. "I'm sorry I yelled at you."

The closet was silent. A tide of dim light washed under the door. Remembering that the room didn't lock, I let us in.

Nikki's laptop gave her face a lunar glow. Our jittery shadows suggested candle light. They were scented candles, cranberry or raspberry.

"I remember you," said Nikki. "You were here a couple of years ago when my friend's car stereo got stolen. You never found it. Big surprise."

Thayer pulled a pen and a note pad from his back pocket, policeman-style. "Can you give me a description of the file cabinet? I promise I'll do my best."

Nikki sat up in what appeared to be a plaid sleeping bag. She rearranged the stack of pillows against the wall behind her. "It was a fucking file cabinet."

"What were the dimensions?" Thayer asked.

"I don't know. Three drawers. Like a foot taller than you."

Thayer's head didn't clear the top of the A-V cart. "Metal or wood?"

"Metal."

"And what color was it?" Thayer had the learned patience of a man in his sixth year of a job he never saw himself working.

Nikki went back to her typing. "Black."

"Any identifying marks? Any scratches or dents?"

"A black file cabinet," I said. "Three drawers high."

"That's what I said."

I opened Juliet Bibb's envelope and held one of the pictures in front of her computer screen. "Did it look like that?" I asked.

"Oh my God! That's so gross!" Nikki shielded her eyes with both hands.

"Sorry about that." I used the envelope to cover all but the edge of the picture. "The file cabinet there. Does it look like yours?"

She seemed to peek through her fingers. "I guess so. Was that Dr. Bibb and Dean Simkins?"

"Perhaps you should keep that to yourself," I said.

Thayer squeezed past a pair of candles to have a look. He scribbled in his note pad.

"But it isn't mine," Nikki said. "Mine has something scratched into the top drawer."

"What kind of something?" Thayer asked.

"A drawing, I guess."

"Could you be more specific?"

Nikki closed her laptop and crossed her arms. "A penis, if you must know. This idiot who goes here, Wade Biggins, who acts like he's eleven years old most of the time, he thought he was being funny. None of this matters, anyway. Besides the paper for Miss Worth's class, my senior project was on that flash drive. I asked Dr.

Tweel for an extension on it, and he said no. I'm just going to be here another year." Her voice flickered like the candle against the wall.

"You've given us some solid leads," Thayer said. "We'll do our best."

I walked the actor-detective to the edge of the parking lot. He asked for the envelope, extracted the sheet without pictures, and gave me back the rest.

"I'll see what I can find," he said.

"One more question," I said. "Who decides when to cremate someone with no family or will?"

Thayer pulled on an imaginary goatee. Maybe I just couldn't see it. "After it's been awhile, if the morgue's overcrowded, they'll do a little spring cleaning, so to speak."

"In your expert opinion, would you say twenty-four hours constitutes a long time?"

The actor-detective knew his line, but didn't say it.

24

THE TANG OF DRIED URINE GREETED ME on the first floor of Suddreth Hall. Far as I was from the men's room, the odor might have originated from the unkempt adjunct, who was playing his class an acoustic ballad. I stood in the back of Room 106 and waited for Mollie to reach the end of the poem she was reading her class. An obese boy in the last row was snoring. When the poem was over, I clapped my hands a few inches from the boy's ear. He joined me briefly in applause before returning his head to the crook of his arm.

"Excuse me, class." Mollie led me into the hall with her cold hand. The building was rather warm. "Have you seen Duncan?" she whispered.

"I saw him yesterday. So did you."

"He hasn't shown up for class today. His eight or his nine-thirty."

"His speech at the memorial service," I said, "seemed valedictory in nature."

"His car is in the parking lot, Tate. I called his house. Janice said he never came home."

"Has she called the police?"

"She's scared to. She thinks Duncan might be involved in something he shouldn't be."

"Why don't you call the police?"

Mollie looked left and right. "I don't trust them, okay? I think you know why." She eyed the envelope in my hand. "What's in that?"

"Formative assessments." I shifted it to my other hand. "Since when do you care about Duncan Musgrove?"

"He's one of us, Tate. Like it or not, so was Simkins. There aren't that many of us left to . . . choose from." She snatched the envelope from my other hand. She used it to fan her face. "Maybe Janice knows something and doesn't realize it. Maybe you know where Duncan is. Didn't the two of you used to go out for beers?"

"What makes you think I can find a missing person? Not so long ago, you wouldn't let me go to the grocery store, lest I bring back the wrong brand of chick peas."

"In my defense," Mollie began and swallowed the old arguments before they came up, "you seem much more . . . independent now."

It was a compliment on par with "literate" or "well behaved." Mollie gave me back the envelope. She looked both ways and gave me a long kiss. A shy, teenage smile flickered beneath her perfect triangle of a nose. A round of applause erupted inside the classroom, accompanied by cat calls. The boy in the back kept his head down.

"Don't worry," Mollie whispered. "I'll tell them it's going to be on the test, and they won't remember a thing."

She went back inside, quieting her students with a request to take out a pen and a piece of paper. The instructor across the hall stepped outside to close the door to the commotion.

"I guess you found what you were looking for," Carly said, slamming her classroom door. It echoed like gunfire through the first floor.

25

THE MUSGROVES LIVED FOUR MILES from campus in Hannon Valley, a part of Grayford known for the smaller mall and a proliferation of gas stations. It was nowhere you wanted to run out of gas. I had never ventured to Hannon Valley on foot. The primary deal breaker was an eight-lane intersection with elaborate turn lanes and a series of quick-changing turn arrows, a blind pedestrian's worst enemy. A mile up the road, the street would decrease by two lanes, but I was wasting enough time on an errand whose only purpose was to show Mollie how independent I was.

Traffic in front of me came to a stop. Stopped cars are the good kind, the ones that don't kill you upon contact. Cars in the lanes to my right revved their engines. I started across in a half-jog, waiting by the smoke-belching grill of a tall truck while vehicles in the center lane made left turns. One last occupant of the turn lane honked his horn, braking in time to force me only a foot into the intersection. I pushed off using the hood and performed an unintentionally acrobatic broad jump onto the narrow median, my shoulder colliding with the sign post.

"Why don't you get a cane?" Mollie had asked me years earlier.

"I think those are for blind people," I replied.

"It would make drivers more careful around you, Tate. I worry about you."

I reached the other side of the intersection with the pride of a gambler who's won a five-dollar jackpot. I stopped congratulating myself at the next intersection.

I cut through a pair of parking lots, deciphering the large signs of a fast food barbecue joint and the chain store that rented televisions to people who can't afford to buy them. A gangly, chattering vagrant called out to ask what I was looking for.

"Duncan Musgrove. You seen him?"

The man walked beside me. "What he look like, boss man?"

"Short and stocky. Gray hair. Walks like a penguin." I turned onto a side street narrow enough for stop signs, my strong preference over traffic lights.

"Five dollars," said the probable crackhead. He was tall enough that his breath sailed over my head. The rest of him smelled a lot like the first floor of Suddreth Hall.

"Too rich for my blood."

He tried frantically to renegotiate, but seemed unable to think of other numbers.

Bringing my face a few inches from mailboxes, I discovered that house numbering was irregular. I guessed six times until I guessed correctly.

"I might be awhile," I called out to the lingering crackhead from Duncan's porch.

He got shorter, presumably after sitting down on the curb. "Desert Market," he repeated in the pleasant tone of a salutation.

No one answered multiple knocks. The front door was locked. I made my way around the back of the blue bungalow straight out of the Sears catalog, not unlike the clothing of the man who rented it. He had moved here after one of the four ex-wives got the house he was a few years from owning outright. The back door was also locked. I tried to guess which window was the bedroom. Knocking on the second from the back produced a sound like a sheep trying to hit a high note.

"Janice?"

"Don't kill me," she said.

"I won't," I said. "Can you let me in? It's Tate Cowlishaw."

Janice directed me to a spare key under a fake stone by the back door. Thinking of my new friend out front, I locked the door behind me. The friendliness of crackheads is always a little suspect.

The back door opened into a carpeted laundry room thick with the sour odor of the clothes piled waist-high on the floor. A yellow sheet stapled to the ceiling served as the door to the kitchen. The smell of food, or what used to be edible, told me which room it was before my eyes made their slow inferences. It wasn't the smell of food that had been recently cooked. Recent didn't feel like a word I would be reaching for in the Musgrove home.

A round table against the wall was covered with bright boxes of children's cereal. Between two of them sat a plastic milk carton, half-full. It was warm to the touch. The lid was off. An empty bag of pork rinds leaned against a Styrofoam take-out container. A pan on the stove held the crispy remains of those pancakes Duncan had made for his wife yesterday morning. A mixing bowl contained the rest of the batter.

More take-out boxes were stacked on the Formica counter. Thin black lines like cracks in the Styrofoam were visible on the tops and sides. The cracks moved when I touched the container. I lifted the lid to find a colony of them, glistening with movement.

"I'm in here," Janice shouted, or tried to. She didn't have the breath required to raise her voice.

Neither the thickly carpeted living room nor the dark, wood-paneled hallway was a respite from the odor. If anything, an earthier, feral scent underscored the rotting food. I gagged, trying to recall if Duncan had a dog. It seemed unlikely that a domesticated animal could be responsible for such a smell. The white porcelain of a bathroom caught my eye. I ducked inside it and shut the door.

"Not in there, Mr. Cowlishaw. In here."

"I'll be right in," I said after flushing my morning coffee and a small amount of Malai Kofta.

I pulled my shirt over my nose and stood in the doorway of the master bedroom. I spoke through my buttoned collar. "Janice. It's good to see you again."

Duncan's wife whimpered in the queen-sized bed. She occupied enough of it that only a cat or two could have fit beside her. A ceiling fan above the bed circulated the pungent air, still potent through my shirt.

"Miss DuFrange said you didn't want to call the police. They're generally better at finding people than your average college instructor."

An extensive series of breaths finally controlled her tears enough to allow speech. "Duncan told me not to."

I sat in the corner chair where Duncan must have watched the movie with her earlier in the week. "When was this?"

"Three twenty-eight yesterday afternoon. It was three twenty-two when he kissed me good-bye, and I asked him to wait with me until the minute turned to twenty-seven. March twenty-seventh is our anniversary."

I decided not to ask the chances of his leaving her. "What were his exact words regarding the police?"

"'If anything happens to me,' he said, 'don't call the police.'"

"Was he expecting something to happen to him?"

"I don't know."

I let out a breath and regretted that I would have to replace it. "What about his cell phone?"

"It's in the living room. He didn't take it with him."

"Has anyone else called it?"

Janice shushed me before I could get the question out. "Listen."

All I heard was the slipstream of traffic four blocks away.

"Even the mice know he's gone. They've hardly stirred since he left."

"Our mice on campus aren't so sentimental," I said. "How about you hop up and help me find that cell phone?"

"Oh, I can't do that."

"Sure you can." I stood up and offered her a hand.

She pushed my hand away like an eighth helping of cobbler. "You don't understand, Mr. Cowlishaw."

"Maybe I could roll you to the edge of the bed and . . ." I trailed off, not sure if I was being insensitive.

"It is not possible," she said, trying again to summon the wind to raise her voice. Her frustrated words floated toward me with the odor I now recognized as human waste, pushing its way through the defenseless fibers of my cotton shirt. "Not for two years have my feet felt the floor of my own home. And yes," she said, straining to keep her words together, "I am aware of the smell."

"I hadn't noticed," I said through my shirt.

"Duncan always took care of my . . . needs."

"You must be hungry, Janice. Can I bring you something to eat?"

The pillowcase crackled as she shook her head. "I'm trying to go without," she said, launching into a long sob that more resembled a lioness fighting off sleep.

I noticed a red plastic cup on the night table. I carried it to the bathroom and returned with water. I set it within her reach on the night table, beside an old-fashioned telephone, the kind with a cord. I listened to the dial tone and asked her for Duncan's cell number. I dialed it and followed the ring tone, a Musack version of "Ain't No Mountain High Enough," to the top of the old television in the corner of the living room.

It was a 1960s TV with a wooden exterior and little legs. I asked Janice to hang up the land line. This much she managed. Cheap as Duncan was, his cell phone was older and larger than mine. I read its display with my magnifier. Most of the missed calls were Janice from the land line. Everything prior to yesterday morning had been deleted. The last number that had been called seemed familiar. I mouthed and said it aloud until it resembled a jingle. I pushed send.

"Randallman Dudek," said a girl who didn't sound pleased to be answering a telephone.

I pulled my shirt away from my mouth long enough to speak. "This is Duncan Musgrove," I said and waited to see if that meant anything to her.

"Mr. Musgrove!" She sounded pleased. Her accent was Southern. "Are you calling to reschedule?"

I took my conversation through the kitchen to the laundry room and the gentler fumes of soiled clothes. "I suppose I am." I used my own voice, not confident I could do Duncan.

"Ms. Randallman was disappointed you didn't show up."

"Is that right? Usually it's my presence that disappoints people."

The secretary gave Duncan a big, ingratiating laugh. "Marianne has appointments through lunch, but she can squeeze you in at two."

"Two would be lovely. Could you give me that address again? I think I got lost earlier."

The secretary laughed softly, affording me the patience of a man worth her time. She gave me the downtown address, Grayford's lone skyscraper, a mile from the college. "Anything else you've forgotten?"

"Sure. Who are we suing again?"

This time she only laughed, and I hung up while I was still ahead. I wasn't that far ahead. I slipped Duncan's phone into my left pocket.

"Were you talking to the extortionists?" Janice wanted to know when I returned to the bedroom.

"In a manner of speaking," I said. "Did Duncan ever mention talking to an attorney?"

Janice lay perfectly still beneath the bedclothes. Before, she had the habit of fidgeting, perhaps for circulation, perhaps involuntarily. She was thinking of divorce. I was thinking of Marianne Randallman's ex-husband, Detective Rick Stashauer, wondering if their connections to Parshall College were coincidental.

"I take that as a no," I said.

"Tuesday everything was fine again. We were going to go somewhere together. For the first time in a year and a half, Duncan kissed me like he meant it. He said—"

"I don't think this is a matrimonial attorney, Janice. This is the kind who sues people. Any idea who your husband might want to sue?"

Janice resumed her arm exercises, making a snow angel with narrow wings. "I remember something he said before he fell asleep in my arms Tuesday morning. He called me Big Mama. He hadn't called me that in a long time. He whispered to me, 'Big Mama, make them stop.'"

"Make who stop?"

"He didn't say. He just lay there, letting me hold him until he fell asleep."

Janice asked for a wet wash cloth and the bucket beside the toilet. I brought them to her along with the boxes of cereal.

"It's a lot easier than it seems," she said. "Nobody decides never to get out of bed. You decide one day and then another. After a while, you have no choice."

26

M Y WALKING COMPANION STOOD UP from the
curb to greet me. He asked if I thought it would rain,
if I had tried the new crispy ranch chicken sandwich
at the national burger chain, or if I thought he would be a strong
applicant for entry into Parshall College next fall. It was hard to
say what he was asking since the only words he used were Desert
Market.

"He isn't home," I said.

The vagrant seemed to dispute this with his two favorite words,
this time in declarative form.

I lowered my sunglasses.

"Desert Market." He pulled something from behind his ear and
showed it to me. A cigarette. He pointed to it and pointed to the
house.

"Desert Market lives in the house?" I asked.

My friend gave a huge nod. A smile ran away from his face. It
had better places to be.

"Desert Market isn't home," I said.

He started along the walkway to Casa Musgrove, motioned
for me to follow. He made a left before the porch and continued
around the side. An aluminum ladder rested against the house, ending a few feet below the roof.

"Desert Market," my friend said in the manner of presto.

I climbed a few rungs of the ladder. My friend clapped his
hands. I kept climbing as he returned to the sidewalk. The ladder
led to an outline no larger than a microwave. A bent nail stuck out

a few inches on the right side. On the left side, painted the same canary as the house, I felt a pair of hinges.

I knocked four times. "Desert Market. It's Cowlishaw."

I waited half a minute and pulled on the nail. The panel opened to a square of darkness. The air inside was dusty and thick. In my lungs, it felt like the opposite of air. I reached inside and couldn't feel the floor. The ceiling was a few inches from the top of the opening. I climbed to the ladder's top rung, holding onto the thin panel with both hands, and lowered my feet into the attic.

They touched sooner than I expected. I lost my grip on the flimsy door and hit my head on a support beam. Sitting down, my head remained in close contact with the roof. I estimated the clearance at three and a half feet. I said Duncan's name a couple of times, but my sixth sense told me I was all alone. The only sounds were the creaking ceiling beneath my knees and the murmur of the television in Janice's bedroom. The half-open panel illuminated the corner closest to it and little more. I was turning around, on my way back to that brighter place when my foot sank into a piece of foam several inches thick, the egg-shaped padding found in couches left on the curb. It stretched further in either direction than my arms. I crawled forward, feeling the floor with both hands the way the near-sighted search for their glasses in cartoons.

I came upon a hardcover book sized between a collegiate dictionary and one of those novels about Cold War submarines. An unsharpened pencil bookmarked it two-thirds in. A few inches beyond it sat a metal drum about a foot in diameter. It had no lid. A synthetic smell reminded me of Halloween. I reached inside. There were thin plastic wrappers with sticky residue that came off on my fingers, a scent of maple and cinnamon. Beneath the wrappers were little rectangles of card stock, perforated on the wider ends. The wax on one side suggested scratch-off lottery tickets. I shoved my arm into the trash can and found a pile of coarse hair. It stayed together when I lifted it, as hair does when it's part of a wig.

To the left of the trash can was a bed sheet wadded into a ball. It had ruffles and seams, but seemed too large to be clothing. It smelled of cigarettes. Under it was a thick cord. The left side was taut. I traced it in that direction to a piece of furniture with two drawers. On top of it, barely clearing the ceiling, I felt the once-standard glass face of a television. It had four knobs, two large and two small. The small one on the right turned it on.

Voices arrived before the fuzzy picture. I turned down the

volume. It was a ten-inch black-and-white set, possibly older than me. With the light, I could see the logo of Duncan's hometown Pittsburgh Steelers on the side of the wastebasket. Holding the wig against my jeans, it looked orange or red. The sheet was a dress with a plaid pattern. The hardcover was a large print Bible. To the right of it I noticed a stack of books. Past them was an entire book-shelf two levels high.

I turned the second small knob on the TV to the far left, sharpening the contrast. The additional light danced on the edge of something several feet long, darker the foam on the floor. I crawled toward it. The spoiled food in the kitchen seeped through the ceiling. The length of darkness had a plaid design, a distant relative to the wadded dress. It was a couch cushion. Three of them were arranged in a row. On top of them lay a pair of legs as firm as the ceiling.

I felt the gold stud in Duncan's left ear and the horse head adorning the breast of all his shirts. I was close enough to smell what might not be the kitchen. His arm lay crooked beside his face. In his hand, light from the TV caught the shiny surface of what I knew was not a stapler.

Wary of fingerprints and warier of Grayford's law enforcement, I used one of the plastic wrappers to feel the scabbed blood on his cheek. Hard spots of diminishing size led from the back of his head all the way to the wall. I pushed up his lips far enough to find his teeth intact, confirming as much as I was able that he had done this to himself. I wondered with renewed suspicion what else he and his pistol had done.

In my left pocket, Duncan's phone chimed with the Motown classic to which, I now remembered, Duncan and Janice had danced their first dance as a married couple.

"This is Musgrove," I said.

"Hello there," said Stashauer in a falsely cheerful tone meant to be menacing. "Why don't you save us both a little trouble and tell me where you are."

I put a little sandpaper in my voice and said, "You might not like what you find."

"Is that some sort of threat, Musgrove? I warned you once. That's all you get." Wind from a brisk walk or an open car window put static between his words.

I discovered a handwritten note above Duncan's head. "Don't let them hurt her," it said in neat, uncommonly large letters written in black marker. Writing of such generous proportions was hard to come by.

"Never mind, Musgrove. I'll see you soon."

A police siren swirled in my ear before I hung up and dialed Stashauer's partner.

"How soon can you get to Hannon Valley?"

"I'm meeting a contractor at the college to get some estimates on theater repairs. What's in the Valley?"

"A Caucasian male in his early sixties, recently deceased, gunshot wound to the head." I left out the self-inflicted part.

"Did you call 911?"

"I didn't have their number." I gave Thayer the address and hung up while he was talking.

I wondered if Janice had heard her husband's gunshots, or if she had rationalized the sound as rodent-on-rodent violence. I picked up the dress. Its wide measurements made it clear whose closet it had come from. I reached for the wig, wondering if the brown might be red. The wig and dress added up to the homely Delilah Bibb at Rosewall Glen, seeking a signature for that petition. Duncan might have been trying to secure his pension under a new regime. I still couldn't convince myself that my late colleague had killed Simkins, if only because murderers tended to issue more threats than they received.

Rick Stashauer's enduring interest in the case was its own mystery. Perhaps Ms. Randallman had alerted her ex-husband to the rescheduled appointment. I picked up the note Duncan had left someone, possibly me. Don't let them hurt her. Five words. I understood four of them. Who and how many "them" referred to, beyond Stashauer, I couldn't say.

The TV buzzed in spite of the volume turned all the way down. I could hear my friend on the sidewalk whistling a rhythmless tune that seemed to be missing notes. I sat on the foam floor between the late Desert Market and the Steelers trash can. I tried to think of something sweet and sentimental to say, a eulogy for the man with whom I had shared dozens of beers and five unrewarding years at Parshall College. Nothing came to mind, but it was hard to concentrate with a wailing siren outside the house.

My friend was no longer whistling. Crackheads tend not to linger in the presence of law enforcement. Stashauer yelled something. I might have been well-advised to turn off Duncan's cell phone, recalling now how they were used to pinpoint the location of missing persons. The crackhead stammered an incoherent response.

"Stocky motherfucker with gray hair."

"Five dollars."

"Or I could not kill you. Which house is his, you fucking wastrel?"

Words failed the crackhead. It might have been the other way around.

I took shallow breaths, partly to listen, partly to control my creeping nausea. Conventional wisdom on odors says they weaken over time. The human waste downstairs and Duncan's corpse seemed to contradict this. The downside of smelling things more intensely than other people is smelling things more intensely than other people. I dry heaved into the Steelers trash can. I let go of it on a part of the floor not covered in foam. When the ringing dipped below the humming television, rustling was audible in the tall grass. Much louder came the sound of feet on the ladder.

I switched off the television and found a few boxes by the wall that hid half my body. I went with the upper half. Duncan's phone rang. I gave it a toss in his direction. Stashauer reached the top of the ladder. The phone stopped ringing and started again. A sphere of light skittered across the ceiling and back wall. It touched my leg but didn't like me enough to go all the way.

Stashauer's weight shook the floor. It seemed to tilt a little in his direction. "There's an easy way and a hard way, Musgrove. To be honest, they're both easy for me."

The flashlight dipped and swayed.

"I see you back there. Put your arms in front of you and crawl toward me."

Defiant even in death, Duncan stayed put.

"Time's up, Musgrove. If they had asked me, which they didn't, we would have gone this route Monday night. God knows you didn't do what you were so politely asked to do."

Stashauer counted to three with his trigger finger. He crawled toward us to check his work.

"If anybody asks, which they won't, you fired first." Two more shots found the wall near the exit. "Let's see. Were you right-handed or left?"

Stashauer laughed a little, then harder and harder. "You didn't have to kill yourself, Musgrove. I would have saved you the trouble."

Seconds later, the square of light went away as Stashauer closed the door. I liked the sound of his feet on the ladder, much more than I liked the sound of the ladder being dragged around the house.

27

"How the hell did you get up there?" Thayer yelled.

"I took the elevator. Now I can't find it."

Thayer located the ladder and climbed through the opening. He shined his flashlight into the darkness. Standing upright, he cleared the ceiling by a couple of inches.

I filled him in on what had happened in the minutes between our conversation and his arrival. I wasn't sure if it was a crime to kill a dead man. Perhaps it was attempted murder if the shooter doesn't know the victim is dead.

Thayer cocked his head to one side and looked at me with the pity commanded by a grown man on his hands and knees. I thought he might pat me on the head. "Listen, Cowlishaw. I know your experiences with Rick have been negative, but enough is enough."

I found Duncan's phone beside the couch cushions and handed it to Thayer. "Your partner's number would be the last two. I spoke to Stashauer's ex-wife on Duncan's phone a little while ago. Marianne Randallman was the last person he called."

"Now I know you're wrong. Stash and Marianne haven't spoken since the divorce."

"As far as you know," I said. "At the very least, you must find his proximity to both of Parshall College's recently deceased faculty a little troubling."

"No more so than yours, Cowlishaw." Thayer picked up the plaid dress near his feet. "It's true, is it not, that you don't see very well?"

"My hearing's pretty good," I said.

Thayer picked up the wig and shook it like a pompom. "Look at this," he said hopefully. "Your colleague was a cross dresser. His proclivities must have become known to his wife or family, or he couldn't bear the thought of them knowing. Charade over. Open mouth, insert gun. We see this all the time, Cowlishaw."

"When was the last time you saw it?"

Thayer thought about it. He kept thinking.

I directed him to Duncan's note beside the bookcase. "Who is he talking about when he says 'Don't let them hurt her'?"

"People like this, they often think of themselves as two people. He killed himself to protect his female alter ego. He probably had a name for her. They always do."

My phone buzzed. I took it out of my pocket and answered it.

"Found some info on the cop," said Hoopel.

I raised the volume on my phone. "Let's hear it."

Thayer smacked the side of the television.

"That Will Read for Food thing," Hoopel said. "It's an annual benefit for the Grayford Food Bank. Faculty from the writing program and a couple of local alumni read their work. They raffle off signed books and lunches with the writers. Rick Stashauer was one of the participants four years ago."

"In what capacity?"

"He was one of the readers."

Thayer turned up the volume of a soap opera. Violins swelled above an actress's tearful soliloquy. I crawled toward the television and spoke a little louder.

"And what did Mr. Stashauer read, Hoopel?"

"It doesn't say in the program or the student paper. Each year somebody does a write-up of the event, but it looks like nobody did one that year. I know the faculty advisor for the student paper. He sends us interns. I asked him why nobody covered it that year, and he gave me a funny smile and said to ask somebody in the writing program."

"You've been busy." I shot Thayer a meaningful look. He didn't get the meaning as he didn't see the look.

"It beats moderating reader comments on editorials," said Hoopel. "F that, Mr. Cowlishaw."

"Can I assume you spoke to someone in the writing program?"

"I talked to a graduate assistant. She's the one who gave me the program. She wasn't there that year, but I sweet-talked her into finding someone who was."

"Sweet-talked her, huh?"

"I told her I was investigating a murder."

"How sweet."

"She took me to the office of this bald guy with frizzy hair on the sides. He had on a white cardigan. He looked kind of like a scientist, but apparently he's some kind of playwright."

"Doug Finch," Thayer said without turning around.

"His name was Douglas Finch," said Hoopel. "He started Will Read for Food back in the eighties."

"He's had a couple of his plays produced off Broadway," Thayer said to the television.

"Finch told me the readers were always faculty and well-published alumni. Stashauer was the one time he had made an exception. Never ever again, Finch said and grinned at me with a bunch of chipped teeth. He held his smile for a long time, like he was posing for a picture."

"Or showing you something," said Thayer quietly.

"This next part is off the record, Mr. Cowlishaw. Mr. Finch offered to let Stashauer read at this event. In exchange, Stashauer was going to fix a few DUIs for Mr. Finch."

"That was bad enough," said Thayer in the same lugubrious tone the doctor on TV was using to deliver news of a miscarriage.

Hoopel continued. "So Stashauer read some kind of story about goblins and warlocks. Like half a minute in, people in the audience started laughing. Finch said it was hilarious, which wouldn't have been a problem if Stashauer had set out to write a comedy. Every time somebody laughed, Stashauer paused to stare them down. Apparently, everyone is supposed to read for ten minutes. After about forty minutes, people started leaving. Finch tried interrupting him a couple of times."

"That's when it got bad," Thayer said.

"I don't know if any of this helps, Mr. Cowlishaw. Are you sure you don't want me to pay a visit to his ex-wife?"

"You've been very helpful, Hoopel. I'll be sending some more work your way very shortly."

"Another assignment?"

I took a deep breath a little too close to my late colleague. "Another obituary."

The soap opera went to commercial, a jingle about oil soap set to the tune of the 80s sitcom about a boarding school. Thayer turned down the volume and faced me with his head bowed.

"I'm afraid my partner's less admirable qualities might have rubbed off on me," Thayer said.

"Does that mean you're going to shoot me?"

I couldn't tell if the actor-detective was shaking his head. He was not reaching for his gun. In a voice as small as the rest of him, he said, "I'm covering for him, Cowlishaw. I've done it for years. It's like Hamlet says, 'Lying 'tis easy.'"

Thayer reached above his head. A click turned on a light bulb screwed into the ceiling. He circled Duncan's body. It was brighter and still dead.

"Guy's got a hot plate, coffee maker, bottles of water, a whole cabinet of canned goods."

My own eyes noticed a dark design on the front of Duncan's white shirt. A small constellation of bullet holes circumscribed the embroidered horse. Dead as he had been when they went in, no blood had come out.

"What's this guy's story, Cowlishaw? Did he live in his own attic?"

"He had a preference for stuffy climates. He was a professor for over thirty years."

Thayer was sliding cans across the metal cabinet. It might have been the curiosity of a good detective. It might have been the fidgeting of a man avoiding the truth.

"What was that you were saying about your partner?" I asked.

Thayer closed the cabinet door. After a long moment, he had a seat on the floor, Duncan's body between us. "Stash has always been a big brother to me, Cowlishaw. He's kind of an asshole, but he's saved my life a couple of times."

Outside, a siren got closer and faded into the din of Hannon Valley traffic.

"Stash blamed Finch for the audience's reaction. At the end of the evening, he followed Finch into the men's room. He stood behind him at one of the urinals. When I walked in, he was ordering Finch on his knees to kiss the porcelain. He only got in a couple of kicks before I got him to stop." Thayer pulled a thin book from Duncan's shelf and turned pages. "Worst of all, for me, anyway, is that Doug Finch had been a mentor of mine. I smoothed things over the best I could. Covered things up might be more accurate. All this is to say I owe you an apology, Cowlishaw. Here it is an hour and a half after I saw the coroner's report, clearly forged, and I'm still defending him." Thayer's sigh pushed the odor of decomposition in my direction. "I wonder if I'm not a little co-dependent. It can happen when you've been in life-and-death situations with someone."

"What was that about the coroner's report?"

"Stash forged it. For God's sake, he started to sign his own name and crossed it out." Thayer's voice cracked. "Why? Why would he want to kill this guy? Why would he kill your dean?"

"Maybe someone else wanted him to. Has he ever mentioned a woman named Delilah?"

"I don't think so. He has been seeing someone lately. At least I think he has. I heard him say her name on the phone the other day." Thayer snapped his fingers, trying to think of it.

"Wasn't Carly, was it?" I held a deep breath to cushion the blow.

Thayer kept snapping his fingers. "Sarah. That was it." He examined the wounds in Duncan's chest. "Sarah Freyman, I think."

Below us, Janice Musgrove shouted to the mice that Daddy would be home soon.

I tried to calculate the odds of two Sarah Freymans with links to Parshall College. "Do you know anything else about her?"

"Just that Stash is as happy as I've seen him since the divorce. Why?"

"Sarah Freyman is the name of a trustee of Parshall College. If they're the same person, she's quite a bit older than your partner."

"A May-December romance?"

"More like 'May I be named in your will.' From what I gather, this gal's in her nineties."

We chewed on this for a little while. At last Thayer switched off the overhead light. I got the television and followed him to the pale square of afternoon.

His unmarked car was parked across the street two houses down. Four houses away in the other direction, I heard a man imitating a high hat. The crackhead hadn't showered in the last thirty minutes. I thanked him for his help and went through the bills in my wallet. I only carry ones and fives so I can count my change from purchases without a magnifier. He wouldn't take my five.

"Looks like somebody roughed him up," Thayer said.

We followed the crackhead to Thayer's car. He slapped the hood and pantomimed a punch to his own jaw.

"What does your partner drive?" I asked.

"One of these. A little newer. Why?"

"I think he might have socked our friend one."

The crackhead tapped the hood again, faked another punch. Thayer gave him a round of applause. I gave him five bucks, which he accepted with a bow before exiting stage left.

Thayer saw me noticing the dark spot on the hood of his car. If you stare at something long enough, people give you clues about what it is.

"Grayford's version of an unmarked car," he said. "See where they painted over the parts that said 'Police'?" He indicated additional places on the doors and front panels, not unlike the sloppy paint job on the car belonging to Juliet Bibb. "Budget cuts, Cowlishaw. We drive these things until they're about to die, then auction them off for whatever we can get."

"Who buys them?"

"Whoever wants them. They don't publicize the auctions. Often it's friends and family of people on the force."

"This might be nothing," I said, "but I think our interim dean bought one of these a couple of years ago. Thus far, she's the only one who's profited from Simkins's death." I put air quotes around profited, coming as her post did with its hidden fee of seventy-five thousand dollars.

28

I ASKED THAYER TO FIND OUT what he could about our interim dean. In the interest of being thorough, I gave him Carly's name as well. At this point, neither was going to open up to me. Maybe a badge and the charisma of a trained actor would be more effective.

He let me out on the sidewalk beside Hemsworth Tower. Grayford's skyscraper rose forty stories above downtown, twenty-five higher than the next tallest building. It was named for the late senator no one seemed to like, who nevertheless died in office at age ninety-three, a month after being elected to an eighth term. Marianne Randallman was expecting me at two o'clock.

The throng of people by the elevators meant I wouldn't have one to myself. Bringing one's face a few inches from the panel of buttons requires a certain amount of privacy. For this lone reason, I had once considered learning Braille, but feeling the little bumps beside the buttons didn't seem any more discreet. I found the unmarked door that usually leads to a stairwell. This one did. I started up the first flight and started counting.

I emerged panting on the twenty-eighth floor, hands on my knees. My exhaustion drew the attention of an elderly man in a sweater vest. His white hair appeared fluorescent in the left rim of my blind spots. He had the frail, regal gait of a man who has spent many hours on horseback. He mistook my breathlessness for confusion and asked what I was looking for. I told him and followed his small paces to a brass-handled glass door around the corner.

"Mr. Dudek," said the receptionist I had spoken to over the phone. "Shame on you for coming back."

"The links will wait long enough to show this young man where he can find the best legal counsel in the great state of North Carolina." Mark Dudek, the man who had famously negotiated a nine-figure settlement out of big tobacco twenty years ago, clapped me on the back. "What's your name, son?"

"Musgrove. Duncan Musgrove."

"Mr. Musgrove, this young lady will get you situated. And Sarah, let them know the elevators are broken. I suppose I, too, will have to take the stairs."

The receptionist with the compelling name waited until Mr. Dudek left and said my name, my late colleague's name, with something other than pleasure. "I'll tell Ms. Randallman you're here."

She walked down the hall. No one else was waiting in the foyer. As soon as Sarah turned the corner, I crouched in front of her desk to read the name plate. Sara Freyman, it said. Assistant. I wasn't sure if Sarah Freyman the trustee spelled her first name with or without an H. No one had spelled it for me except Islanda Purvis, and I hadn't asked my screen reader for the exact spelling. It seemed odd that a wealthy trustee would take a job answering phones, but Islanda might only have assumed she was wealthy. I had only assumed she was in her nineties. I stood up, frowning the way a man does when things make less sense than they did minutes earlier.

"Right this way, Mr. Musgrove."

I followed Sara Freyman into a two-room office larger than my residence at the Gray Knight. The first room held a round, wooden table and bookshelves stretching to the ceiling of two walls. On the third wall was a pair of portrait paintings and what I guessed to be Ms. Randallman's diploma. The fourth wall was only windows looking out at the Grayford skyline. As far up as we were, there was only sky.

Marianne Randallman had the firm handshake of a woman who regularly competes against men and regularly wins. "You're much younger than I pictured," she said warily.

"You're too kind," I said. "And dare I say those ads don't do you justice."

My compliment went unacknowledged, unless you counted her implacable stare. Marianne Randallman had a narrow waist and the kind of curves they don't teach in law school. Her hair and voice, mannish and severe, weren't as enticing.

Sara Freyman, lingering in the hall, offered me coffee or tea. I declined, not sure who else she was assisting. She closed the door quietly, unconvincingly.

"I'm going to miss that girl when she's gone," Marianne Randallman said.

I had a seat at the round table in the center of the room. "You won't have to tell her."

"Excuse me?"

"She's right outside the door."

Marianne Randallman furrowed her brow, or so I assumed. "Sara, are you out there?"

The jangle of a charm bracelet faded into the foyer.

Marianne Randallman apologized with what seemed sincere contrition. "I don't know what's gotten into her."

"Perhaps she's nervous about leaving. You did say she was leaving, didn't you?"

"Yes. Headed to Nashville to follow her country music dreams." The derision underlining her words suggested she knew with whom Sara was heading to Nashville. Randallman cleared away the bitterness from her throat. "Speaking of cold feet, I was afraid you had gotten them when you missed your appointment."

I wondered if Duncan's cigarettes had finally caught up with him, but didn't think he would be retroactively eligible for the old tobacco class action. I went with my second guess. "I do confess to some doubts about whether or not I can prove wrongful termination."

"Termination? What happened to the wrongful death?"

"They're not the same thing?"

Her mouth was the black dot at the base of a question mark. Whatever resemblance my mouth had to a dollar sign was rapidly fading.

She slid a sheet of paper across the table. I gave it the perfunctory once-over and accompanying nod. It's the latter in which people are most interested when they hand you something to read.

"Is this not the man you said was murdered?"

"Yes, of course. My short-term memory isn't what it once was."

"Jesus Christ, Mr. Musgrove. They pay you to teach college students?"

"Dr. Musgrove," I said.

"Sara, would you come in here please?"

Seven seconds preceded the opening of the door. The sound of shoes and jewelry did not.

"Sara, could you cue up my conversation with *Dr.* Musgrove from Wednesday morning?"

The assistant of questionable means opened a cabinet that comprised the lower half of the bookcase. A hum came and went in the upper corners of the room. She set a plastic object on the table the shape and weight of a remote control. Years ago, I had read about a blind attorney and thought briefly about going to law school. That it meant another series of buttons to memorize seemed a good reason not to have gone. The original reason, I believe, had been the lack of law schools within walking distance of downtown Grayford.

Sara Freyman exited the office. Her boss sat down again, crossing her muscular arms on the table. The door remained open.

"I hope this jogs your memory, Dr. Musgrove." Randallman pointed the remote control at the bottom half of the bookcase.

"Let's just say we both know someone," said the real Duncan Musgrove.

"Someone referred you?"

"Not exactly." Duncan's voice sounded worn and raw. It also sounded nothing like mine.

"What was the nature of your relationship to the deceased?"

The chirp of a bird was followed by feet on an aluminum ladder.

"Is it your spouse, Mr. Musgrove?"

His breathless words sounded like, "Not yet."

"I don't like guessing, Mr. Musgrove."

"Give me a goddamn chance. I'm trying to get somewhere I can talk."

Randallman reached for the remote control on the table. I reached first. "It's coming back to me," I said.

Randallman stepped slowly into the adjoining room. She opened a desk drawer. There was the cold sound of metal scraping its way to the front of the drawer.

Duncan's breathing was steadier. "Murder is considered wrongful death, isn't it?"

"Are you related to the deceased, or are you the executor of his will? Otherwise, you cannot initiate a lawsuit, no matter how the individual died."

The Marianne Randallman I could see, if not very well, pointed her gun with both arms extended, like she knew how to use it. "Who are you?"

I showed her my hands, dropping the remote on the table.

"You used to be married to one of them," Duncan said.

"Excuse me? One of who?"

"The people who killed him. Randall Simkins." Duncan breathed into the phone, listening for her reaction. I did the same.

"Who are you?" she asked me a second time.

I told her my name, as if it meant something to her.

"Have we met?" her prerecorded counterpart asked Duncan Musgrove.

"I saw it in the paper. I knew your name from the commercials. I like to read the divorce filings. It's my favorite part of the paper next to the crossword. I get a warm feeling when one of my exes gets divorced from whatever fool took her off my hands."

"Give me one reason why I should continue this conversation, Mr. Musgrove."

"Listen, woman, I don't know where else to go. I think I was about to catch them in the act of cleaning the office where he died. That's when your ex showed up. He said he would kill my wife if I didn't . . ." His voice got light and flew away. It took him a moment to find it. "They made me dress up like a goddamn woman to get a signature from the school's trustee. They wanted me to kill two of my colleagues. I'm just a science teacher, goddammit. I'm just a science teacher."

Randallman grabbed the remote control. There was a click and a brief hum in the speakers. There was a second click in the hand not holding the remote.

"You have five seconds to tell me what you're doing here."

"I'm one of the colleagues Duncan didn't kill."

"Where is he? Who told you he was coming here?"

I spoke in a low voice that might disappoint Sara, who had not returned to her desk. "Duncan's dead. According to his phone, you were the last person he called. The last person to call him was your ex-husband. That call came a few minutes after I, as Duncan, rescheduled his appointment with your secretary. You probably prefer personal assistant, don't you, Sara?"

"Sara, call the police."

"Preferably not your boyfriend. You did know she's dating your ex-husband, didn't you?"

"What are you talking about? Sara dates a redheaded boy with tortoise shell glasses. He brings her lunch on his bicycle."

"Poor kid."

"Sara, come in here."

When no footsteps followed the request, Marianne Randallman stepped into the hall. Dim voices were audible behind the doors of other offices. She made a sound that confirmed her secretary's departure and came back in, closing the door behind her.

"I don't believe you. Sara would never . . ."

"You don't seem to have trouble believing the parts about your ex-husband."

For a long moment, she stood beside her chair. "Do I need this?" she asked, holding up the gun in a non-pointing fashion.

I wondered what Sara kept in her desk drawers. "One of us should probably have one. Might as well be you."

Randallman ended up by the windows. She peered outside, as people do before talking about unpleasant things. I turned one ear to the door, listening for the return of Marianne's assistant. There was only the wall-muted tap of a keyboard and what might have been a banjo on computer speakers.

"Rick and I were married for two years, one if you don't count the separation. I had just broken up with another man, one I had actually loved. In my defense, Rick was very charming while we were dating. He can be a sensitive man."

"I've heard that about him."

"Rick didn't get less romantic exactly. More like his romance grew more specific to his personality. That gun, for example, was a Valentine's present." Her huge sigh would have dismantled cobwebs. "He said it was me. That my strong personality overshadowed his gentler qualities. I certainly wasn't going to pat him on the head for his little dragon and wizard stories. Forgive me, Rick, if I have a low tolerance for bullshit. You know who hates bullshit? Judges. Juries. I'm not your fucking 'follow your bliss, go for it, what lovely imagery in your descriptions of a forest of metal trees' favorite college teacher whom you talk about twenty-four-seven."

"Favorite college teacher?"

"Where I went to college, we took tests and wrote research papers. We didn't sit in a circle and share our feelings like a bunch of mealy-mouthed mama's boys at a Montessori summer camp."

"The academy seems to be moving away from content-based learning," I said. "Do you remember the name of this teacher?"

"Perhaps you know her. I understand she teaches at Parshall." Randallman pronounced the school with a faux patrician accent. "What a brain trust that must be at faculty meetings. No offense."

"None taken. Would you remember her name if you heard it?"

"I never knew her name. I never wanted to. According to you, he's moved on to my secretary, which I still don't believe, by the way."

I let her not believe me. "What years was your ex-husband a student at Parshall?"

"He didn't go to Parshall. I always assumed he had her as an undergrad at Coastal State."

If Stashauer was in his forties, he would have been an undergraduate more than twenty years ago. Only the CVs of Duncan, Delilah, and Simkins would have gone back that far. Of those three, Delilah was the only woman, not counting Duncan's cameo in drag at the nursing home. I stood up slowly from the table, showing Marianne Randallman both my hands.

"I've put the gun down, Mr. Cowlishaw."

Marianne Randallman walked me to the waiting room. The desk of her assistant remained unoccupied. Randallman sent me on my way with a firm handshake. When we let go, I was holding a business card.

"If you do know of any relatives of your late dean, whatever the circumstances of his death, tell them to give me a call."

29

MARIANNE RANDALLMAN GREETED another client in the waiting area and walked him to her office. I gave the glass door a little push and let it close in front of me. Marianne Randallman closed her office door. I went around Ms. Freyman's desk, relatively free of bric-a-brac. Given the purse beside the wastebasket and sweater on the back of her chair, her exit a few minutes ago appeared temporary.

I said her name in the stairwell. The word returned in shrinking ripples, unaccompanied by the name's owner. The white paint of the hallway made it easy to see people, but no one was there. An unmarked door was locked. I placed my ear against it and heard nothing. Further down the hall, I followed the powerful flush of a public restroom to a pair of recessed doors. I leaned over the fountain until someone emerged from one of the restrooms. The harsh fumes of Aramis told me which one.

The fountain quieted. The women's room started talking. The accent was Southern, the tone anxious. I placed my ear against the door, carefully so as not to push my way inside.

"How much longer?" Sara asked.

I pushed the door a few inches.

"I know. I just—You promised my fellowship would start—"

The elevator opened and beeped. Footsteps came my way. I bent over the fountain and lapped up water until a door around the corner finished closing.

"I don't want to get in trouble with Ms. Randallman."

The conversation dipped to a volume I couldn't discern. Her

heels clicked toward the door at a volume I understood. They stopped when I entered the restroom. Sara didn't scream. Some women do when I walk into the wrong restroom. Those little white pictograms are the same from the waist up.

"Don't tell me you're not going to wash your hands, Sara."

She backed up to the sinks. "Your name isn't Duncan Musgrove," she said

"Did you figure that out on your own, or did your boyfriend help you?"

"I don't know what you're talking about."

"I wouldn't expect Rick to go with you to Nashville. He's got a thing for an old teacher."

"Who's Rick?" She was a good actress. I would have recommended her to Thayer for the new Parshall theater venture if she weren't going to Nashville, if she weren't covering up a murder, and if the new theater really existed.

"Perhaps he only shows you his sensitive side, but he isn't a nice person like you and me. Ask your boss."

Sara Freyman stepped sideways toward the door. I mirrored her. She tried the other direction. I knew how to go that way, too.

"Tell me about this fellowship, Sara. Has this been approved by the other trustees?"

"I don't know what you're talking about."

"But you don't like what I'm saying, do you? I don't imagine the other trustees appreciate being left out of all these decisions you're making."

"Leave me alone!"

She went left, right, and left again. She barreled toward the door and I wrapped my arms around her. She had a haircut like a mushroom and a body to match. Her sad mouth looked as though the smiling muscles had atrophied from years of disuse. Prison would give her the chance to work out, but probably not those particular muscles.

"You might not go to jail, Sara. You're young, impressionable. Judges like that."

Her arms relaxed. I loosened my grip. Her elbow shifted. She looked me in the eyes. She got tired of looking and gave them a good feel with her thumbs.

Sara made it to the door. "Leave the school alone! You're going to ruin everything."

30

I T TOOK A MINUTE FOR THE temporary blind spots
to give way to the permanent ones. I made it back to
campus in time for the office hours I never kept past the
third week of any semester. Outside the library, a pair of voices
overlapped one another, the way voices do in the middle of a good
time or an argument. One of the voices shouting, "Ouch! Let go!"
seemed more consistent with the latter.

"Dr. Cowlishaw, tell him to let go of me."

"He's not going to help you, Mr. Biggins." This calmer voice
belonged to Benjamin Tweel.

Two empty steps were between them. I stood on the top one,
closer to Tweel. Wade Biggins's head was cocked, nearly flat against
his shoulder. He seemed to have little choice in the matter. Tweel's
hand was on the student's neck in a grip he might have learned
from *Star Trek*.

"I don't know if this is the best way to motivate our students,
Dr. Tweel."

"He was stealing from the library." Tweel gestured with his foot
to a stack of books.

I grabbed the hardcover from the top. Turning pages, I said,
"Wade and I were just conversing about this topic last week. I recommended he check this out."

"See? I told you I was checking them out."

"Don't start with me, Cowlishaw." Tweel spoke with an odd
serenity. "Mr. Biggins did not sign his name in the ledger."

"I forgot. Let go and I'll go back and sign it."

"Mr. Biggins has not checked out a book from the library," said Tweel, "in all his years at this school. Ask him how many times he has failed my class because he refused to support his claims with valid research."

I couldn't help feeling responsible for Tweel's hostility, although in fairness to myself, he had punched me several hours before his singing wife belted out a few numbers in my bed.

"Maybe we could call this a warning, Ben. He didn't mean any harm."

"I can't feel my arm, Dr. Tweel."

Tweel gave solemn instructions before he let go. They were to pick up the books and return each one to its place in the stacks. "I'll supervise," Tweel said.

I handed Wade the stack of books and the three of us went inside.

"I don't know where they go exactly," said Wade.

Dewey Decimal had been another casualty of the library lay-offs. The faculty voted to revert to alphabetical order, but Christine Katzen, the temp in charge of reorganizing the stacks, was promoted to registrar. We took another vote and settled on an eclectic approach.

"Do the best you can," Tweel said.

Mollie's husband turned to me in the darkness. His face seemed to brighten. He gave my shoulder blade a weak little pat.

"Mollie told me what you've been up to," he said in a voice even calmer than the one he had employed on the steps.

"I suppose you were bound to find out."

"Listen, Cowlishaw, you probably think I don't like you very much. To be honest, I don't. But as much as I think Simkins killed himself, I was hasty to judge the motive behind your little investigation. It seems we have different means to the same ends."

I unclenched my fist, realizing he didn't know what I thought he knew. "What end is that?"

"Giving Bibb her walking papers. Look, I know we're at Parshall for different reasons. That's fine. The Academy needs foot soldiers like yourself. Both of us have to do what we can to protect the institution." He smacked his palm with the back of his other hand. "The distribution model is sacred. Disciplines are sacred. What business do we have standing before our students if what we teach them comes not from our heart but a soulless sheet of directives. Soft skills, man. That's what they call them. Do you want to teach soft skills? I don't want to teach soft skills."

"You lost me at distribution model," I said.

"It boils down to this: we need Bibb as our dean like Mars needs igneous rock." A laugh started in his nose and unraveled in his lungs. He noticed I wasn't laughing and cleared his throat. "I believe in the importance of other worlds. There's got to be more than this." He indicated the entirety of the library with both arms. "It would be a damn shame if at the end of my career I hadn't inspired a handful of students to stare up at the nighttime sky and think, yes, I can get there from here."

Wade Biggins held out his empty arms for Tweel to inspect.

Tweel crossed his arms. "How long have you been here, Mr. Biggins?"

"Like three minutes."

"Here at Parshall, Mr. Biggins."

"Eleven years next fall."

He said it proudly, and I clapped him on the back for his years of service to the Parshall community, which is to say his father's tuition payments. Wade's back was as hard and flat as a book, maybe several.

"Eleven years." Tweel's voice reverted to its low, modulated timbre. "How long do presidents of the United States serve, Mr. Biggins?"

"I don't know. Like five or six years?"

Tweel expelled a puff of air through his nose. "Where would you be, Mr. Biggins, if Parshall College didn't offer you refuge from the cruel world beyond these lawns, where failure is not only unrewarded, but punished?"

Wade Biggins didn't answer. In my classes, he sometimes had trouble with questions that contained too many words.

I gave him another back pat, gentler than the first so as not to signal the presence of contraband. "He means he'll see you in class," I said.

Tweel halted the eleventh-year junior with a hand on the shoulder he had previously squeezed. "A day may come, Mr. Biggins, when Parshall is no longer the inviting bosom you've known it to be these many years."

"What does that mean?" He looked to me to translate.

"Dr. Tweel won't let that happen," I said. "He's fighting to keep this bosom warm and inviting."

Tweel looked at me as if I had slept with his wife. He pushed another brief laugh through his nose. "You may go now, Mr. Biggins."

Wade Biggins went. Benjamin Tweel gave me an "after you" with his hand, and I followed the junior through the metal detectors meant to prevent people from stealing books. Even when the power was on, they weren't functional. Simkins had obtained them from the big-box bookstore across town during their liquidation sale.

"How's that petition coming?" I asked Tweel, who resumed his position as sentry on the top step.

He unfolded a piece of paper and rattled it in my direction. "It may prove unnecessary. From what I understand, Delilah has her work cut out for her with this Totten fellow. All the same, I'd be appreciative if you added your name to the vote of no confidence."

"I'd be glad to talk to Dr. Parshall, if it comes to that."

Tweel didn't respond. Perhaps he wanted to be the one who talked to him, present the petition along with his own resumé and take over as dean, be the one who restored the academy to its former glory, the one his wife thought of when she closed herself in a room and crafted words into poems.

I started in the direction of the swimming pool, leaving him to stare at the sky. If he were waiting for the stars, he would be there awhile.

31

THE ODOR OF BACKED-UP SEWAGE had finally overwhelmed the pool's more tranquil odors of mildew and ant spray. In the ceiling, the runaway train continued to circulate unheated air. Loud, continuous sounds are the equivalent of sun in my eyes. It was all I heard until I got to my desk.

"You just need to calm down," Carly told someone.

The cluck and wheeze above her words didn't sound like another loose belt in the duct work. Someone was crying.

"He's a good person," Carly said. "He'll understand."

"I just want to get out of here, you know?" It was a girl's voice, unrecognizable under the burden of tears.

Carly was the one faculty member who regularly received visitors during office hours, usually for matters unrelated to class. She was the big sister for female students, the older, unattainable crush for the boys. I had heard many an account of break-ups and parental disappointment from my adjacent cube. Students brought her baked goods and the occasional vase of flowers. "Why do they like you so much?" Mollie DuFrange wanted to know one morning Carly had received a cupcake with a candle. "All I've ever gotten is the word 'cunt' engraved in the center of my desk."

I took out my cell phone to call Thayer. When I pressed send, the phone sang an unhappy little tune that meant "game over" in old video games. The screen went black. It occurred to me that I had yet to charge it. I called the actor-detective from my desk phone.

"I think your partner was one of Delilah Bibb's students," I said by way of a greeting.

"Mom," said Thayer. "I'm right in the middle of something. Can I call you back?"

"Your partner is there, I assume."

"Absolutely."

"In case he escapes your supervision, you may want to put an officer on a fellow named Jefferson Totten. He's staying at the Gray Knight, Room 22."

"The Gray Knight? Are you sure you want to stay there when you visit?"

"By morning, they're going to give Totten seventy-five thousand or a few well-placed bullets. My money's on the cheaper option."

"I looked into that other one," Thayer said. "The one you spent some time in before? Couldn't find a thing about it."

He was talking about Carly. I listened as Carly continued to comfort her student. The girl's sobs had gotten louder. "That's fine. Worry about Bibb. Put an officer on her," I said.

"I'll make those reservations."

"Room 22," I reminded him before hanging up.

I turned on my computer to check e-mail. Only one student had written to ask if we had class tomorrow. Some things they learned quickly. I opened the browser to review directions to Sara Freyman's house on Norville Run.

"Mr. Cowlishaw?" said Carly's sniffling visitor outside my cube.

"Islanda. Good of you to stop by."

Someone with lighter skin and hair appeared to Islanda's right. "I told her you would go easy on her," said Carly. "Islanda is one of the best students I've ever had."

"One of my best as well."

I offered Islanda a seat. She sat down slowly, wary of the lawn chair.

"I'm really sorry for what I said in my essay. It was disrespectful to you and to your class. If you let me rewrite it, it will be the best paper you've ever graded. I promise." She hugged herself in a too-large Parshall sweatshirt they no longer gave to new freshmen.

"Actually, I found your essay quite engaging, particularly the part about—"

"I'm really sorry, Mr. Cowlishaw. I didn't think you read our papers because you never give them back and this girl on my hall said she got a hundred on one of your assignments and all she e-mailed you was a blank document." Islanda's words ran together in a teary blur.

"That'll do for the apologies," I said. "I'd like to hear more about that idea of yours for revitalizing the college. Where did you come across the name Sara Freyman?"

Two whooshes, a white blur, and the appearance of what might have been Carly's arm were followed by the sound of Islanda blowing her nose. "Who?"

"In your paper, you referred to her as the wealthiest trustee. Where did you hear that?"

"I wasn't serious. I promise to take your class seriously from now on."

"That's fine, Islanda. Where did you hear the name? Who told you she was a trustee?"

Islanda thought about it. She leaned forward with her elbow on her knee and thought about it some more. As quickly as she finished her tests, her hesitation didn't seem like a positive sign. I started to ask if it might have been Dr. Bibb, but as Delilah herself taught us in one of her seminars on designing exams, open-ended questions are a more accurate measure of what a student knows.

"Dr. Tweel," Islanda said tentatively, almost as a question. A moment later, she sat up straight. "Yeah, it was Dr. Tweel."

"When was this?"

Islanda found the poise with which she had delivered her memorized presentation on her uncle's pawn shop earlier in the semester. "He was on the phone. It was a few months ago. I'm an R.A., right? So I had a meeting with the new housing director to go over the spring semester—requests for roommate changes, broken furniture or whatever—and I get there twenty minutes early. I like to make a good impression or whatever. I didn't know Dr. Tweel was the new housing director, and he didn't know I was in the room waiting for him, so he was out in the hall on the phone for a few minutes."

"How did the name Sara Freyman come up?" As soon as I asked, I recalled Tweel volunteering last year to chair a committee on Budgetary Diversity. Its primary task was writing letters to the trustees asking for an increase in the school's operating budget. Tweel was a frequent volunteer for additional duties, padding his vitae for a job at a better school.

"I didn't eavesdrop or whatever, but I remember the word

'trustee,' and Dr. Tweel mentioned F. Randolph Parshall, who I know is one of the trustees because I met him one time on account of I'm a Parshall scholar. He shook my hand and said how much he admired my people for what they had overcome."

"In your paper, you called Ms. Freyman the wealthiest trustee. How did that come up?"

"I think he said something like, 'Most of our money's going to come from Sara Freyman.' He said something about Dr. Parshall maybe dying. Is he still alive?"

"By most definitions," I said. "Do you remember anything else about this conversation? Anything at all?"

"Just that Dr. Tweel was kind of pissed when he saw me waiting for him, but he's always kind of pissed off. All y'all are. Except Miss Worth."

Islanda was waiting for me to speak. I was in the process of forgetting she was there, which is to say I was staring directly at her, rendering her all but invisible.

"Mr. Cowlishaw? Can I write the paper over?"

"Let's hold off for now," I said.

The locomotive in the ceiling pulled into the station, dropping a heavy silence into my lap. The front door of the swimming pool opened and closed. The pair of sounds could have auditioned for a gunshot and accompanying echo.

Islanda was standing. "Do we have class tomorrow?"

I gave a pensive look to the spot where the ceiling met the far wall, giving me a view of Islanda's face, which isn't to say I could read her expression. "You have vision you don't even use because heaven forfend you abandon your little charade of looking people in the eyes," Mollie had once shouted during one of our arguments. Right as she was, a man who can't see a face from five feet away puts little stock in what he *can* see.

I pulled an ungraded student paper from semesters past out of a desk drawer and turned it over. I grabbed a pen and wrote some letters Islanda could mistake for her name. "I'll send you an e-mail as soon as I know."

When Islanda was gone, Carly took her place in the lawn chair. "That was very forgiving of you."

"She did nothing wrong."

"How forgiving are you when someone has?"

I couldn't decide if it was a rhetorical question. I made it one by not answering. I had been right and wrong so many times in the past two days, I couldn't tell if Carly was offering an apology or asking for one.

"I haven't slept since I left your motel room, Tate." Carly let out a breath. It wasn't warm when it reached me. "There are reasons why Delilah isn't going to renew my contract."

"She found out about your publications, or the lack thereof."

Carly slumped forward in the chair. "I suppose it wasn't hard to find that out," she said.

"Somehow you got your hands on some naughty pictures of our dean and the heir apparent. From what I hear, there are laws against blackmail, but you were only trying to protect yourself."

Carly stood up and sat back down. "What pictures? I didn't—" She paused to listen to a pair of feet drumming toward us on the hollow floor.

"You didn't what?" asked Mollie. "Get your MFA from Iowa? Publish any of the stories you claimed to have published? Any other lies you'd like to come clean about, Ms. Worth?"

"You told them? What did I ever do to you?" Carly brushed past her fellow writing instructor. She was a few inches taller than Mollie, but seemed very small as she returned to her cube. In a quiet, tearful voice, she said, "Thank you, Ms. DuFrange, for the most miserable week of my life."

"The truth will set you free, dear," Mollie said around a growing smile.

I stood up as Mollie became the third occupant of my lawn chair inside of five minutes.

"Tate, where are you going?"

"To see a trustee."

"Who, Dr. Parshall?"

"Not that one. Sara Freyman. Poor thing works as a secretary at a law firm. Sweet girl when she isn't poking people in the eyes."

"What are you seeing her about? Do you think she can save your job?"

In truth, I hoped to make my way inside her home before she got there, see what I could find in the way of evidence of a murder plot. If she was home when I got there, I thought I would listen outside a window, maybe wait around and see if any interim deans or detectives showed up. "I have some business matters I want to go over with her."

"You aren't going to walk, are you?" Mollie asked me this with a patronizing half-smile, as though I fancied myself capable of something so audacious as locomotion.

"I always do."

"Students might be stopping by, or I'd offer you a ride."

"I'm on my way out," said Carly. "I'll give you a ride."

I stared at the felt-covered wall between me and the blonde with whom I had slept two nights ago.

The brunette with whom I had slept last night crossed her legs. They were the kind of legs that benefitted from a good crossing. "If you can wait an hour, I'll give you a ride, Tate."

I shut down my computer.

"Really?" Mollie asked. "You can't wait one hour?"

I put on my jacket. I didn't mind waiting any more than I minded walking. It was the passenger seat of Mollie's car, where our prior relationship underwent the most strain, which I was hoping to avoid.

From Carly's cube came the sound of zippers and keys.

Mollie stood up, positioned herself where the door would be if my cubicle were an office. "You know what? I doubt if anybody's going to stop by. Let me just get my things."

Carly looked at me. Mollie looked at Carly. Carly started for the door.

"That settles that," said Mollie, retrieving her sweater from the back of her lawn chair.

I followed Mollie up the crumbling steps that led out of the swimming pool. "I found Duncan, by the way."

"Really? Where?"

"His attic."

"His attic? What was he doing there?"

"Decomposing."

She stopped putting on her sweater, letting the left arm drag the ground. She looked at me sideways. "Are you kidding again?"

"I wasn't kidding before."

"Did you call an ambulance?"

"It was a little late for that."

"Did you call the police?"

"They called him. A detective came over and made sure he was dead. Apparently, it's a service they offer."

We stood on either side of Mollie's SUV. When the doors had not unlocked after half a minute, I worried I was at the wrong vehicle. I couldn't see Mollie through the tinted glass. I was listening for the crunch of gravel somewhere else in the parking lot when the doors unlocked.

She inserted the keys into the ignition, but didn't turn them. "Do you think his death is related to Simkins?"

I noticed Mollie shudder in the driver's seat. "Duncan killed himself," I said. "I don't think you're in danger."

After a classical interlude and some starched banter on public radio, Mollie finally put the car in reverse. I gave her a block's warning and told her to make a left on Fielding. She made it. Two blocks later, I instructed her to make a right on Carlisle. Mollie didn't hide how much she hated driving, groaning when other cars approached, gripping the steering wheel as if it were a life preserver. She wished I could drive and let me know it most times I rode with her. Today, for once, she remained quiet, save the occasional exhalation after a lane change.

"You just missed Olsen," I said, second- and third-guessing myself until the large white steps and pillars of the courthouse confirmed we had gone too far. "You can take Bergen to Weston. It wraps around Massenberg, which becomes Olsen."

"I know where the streets go, Tate."

"It doesn't look like you do."

Mollie pulled into the parking lot of the tall office building on the corner of Chester and Cornelius. Instead of turning around, she pulled into a spot facing the street and turned off the engine.

"Before we go any further," she said, "we need to figure some things out."

"I'm giving you directions. You're not following them."

"I'm talking about you, Tate. About us." The sound of her displeasure was as familiar as the pleasure had been the night before. "I promised myself," she said, "the first time I felt you were taking advantage of me, I would say something."

"I'll take a rain check on this discussion." I opened the door.

"Don't walk away. Please. I want us to be partners, Tate. A team. For that to happen, we need to lay down some basic ground rules about your independence."

I stepped out of the car and closed the door.

Mollie rolled down the window. "Blind people take the bus, Tate. Why can't you?"

Why she found it more independent to pay someone to drive you around than to get there on your own feet I never understood. Either way, no buses went to Norville Run. I walked around her car, noticing a pair of eights painted on the ground behind Mollie's bumper. Why can't all writing be so large? My eyes counted backward to the edge of the parking lot.

Behind me, an older man with a Mediterranean accent told Mollie she was in a reserved parking space.

"Hold on! Wait!" I couldn't tell if she was talking to me or the parking attendant. Her footsteps moved in the opposite direction of mine. Her car door opened and closed.

The parking attendant was apologizing. I was approaching the corner of Chester and Cornelius. Seconds later, a breathless Mollie was doing the same.

Halfway across the street, Mollie stepped in front of me and pressed her cheek against mine. "I want you. That isn't what I'm saying, okay?"

"If we don't cross in six seconds, we can be together for all eternity."

She held my hand the final fifteen feet, a gesture I tried to interpret as girlfriend rather than guide dog. She led me to a wooden bench and kissed me.

A middle-aged white woman carrying grocery bags said, "Well."

Mollie whispered, "Let's go somewhere and . . ." She searched her mind's thesaurus for the best word. "Fuck."

The woman took her groceries to the curb.

"I'm not sure that would solve anything," I said, though part of me liked the idea. That part tried its best to dissuade me from standing up.

The screech of hydraulic brakes came to a stop in front of our bench. The bus opened its doors. I followed the woman with groceries up the steps.

"Tate, where are you going?"

"I told you."

I handed the driver a pair of ones. He pointed to the waist-high contraption between us. It was polite of buses not to have changed in the twenty-five years since I had last taken one. Perhaps I had been too hard on them.

I took a window seat next to the rear door. I hadn't bothered asking the driver which bus I was on, or explaining my situation. Such is the advantage of not caring where you're going.

Mollie raced us across the intersection, running with the awkward gait of a woman in dress shoes. Her headlights winked as she unlocked the doors. She laid on the horn. A car to the left of the bus responded in kind. I waited three blocks and a right turn and tugged the cable to say I wanted off.

"Got your money's worth, didn't you?" asked the ancient driver as I waited for the doors to open.

I let him have that one and smiled. The sidewalk wasn't as witty. I had missed it all the same.

32

I WAS WITHIN TWO BLOCKS of the Gray Knight and stopped by my room to charge the cell phone. Totten's Mercedes remained parked outside Room 22. His curtains were drawn and the lights were on.

"You cannot park here. This is private property," said Sundeep to the only other car on that side of the building.

It was a dark car. I got close enough to see the shield painted on the driver's side door, the parts of it not blocked by the Gogeninis' legs.

"I pay taxes. You work for me. I am telling you not to be here."

"Sir, this isn't my choice." The black officer sounded beleaguered beyond his years, which I wouldn't have guessed to be more than twenty-four.

"You are scaring away business," Jaysaree said. "The mayor of Grayford stood over there in that office and asked what he could do to win our votes. We said stop harassing our customers. He shook our hands. We put his poster in the window." Jaysaree noticed me and pulled me between her and her husband. "He lives here. He saw the poster."

I extended my hand through the window. "You wouldn't be keeping an eye on Room 22, would you?"

The uniformed officer was by himself in the car. "I'm not at liberty to say."

"I think these folks just want to make sure that's all you're interested in. Maybe you could promise not to arrest anyone for what many consider victimless crimes."

"How about all three of you leave me alone and I promise not to arrest you," said the officer before rolling up his window.

I persuaded the Gogeninis to return to the office. They turned their heads as they walked, regarding the squad car as one regards a wild animal tethered to a tree by fraying rope. Once inside, I gave them the short version of why Jefferson Totten might be in danger. The short version kept getting longer.

Sundeep covered his wife's ears with his hands and lowered his voice. "Fuck that man, Tate Cowlishaw. He is nothing but trouble."

Jaysaree pulled her husband's hands away. "Fuck him hard. And I should have known that Bibb woman was up to no good when she gave me the shoulder treatment."

"Cold shoulder," said Sundeep. "Silent treatment."

"I'm still coming up short in the evidence department," I said. "Maybe Mrs. Thopsamoot would like to describe the state of those clothes when Delilah brought them in."

"I will talk to her," Jaysaree said.

Sundeep followed me outside. "What about you, Tate?" he asked in a low voice. "Are you still in danger?"

"I'll be fine."

"That does not answer my question."

"Sure it does. You just don't like the answer."

Sundeep sighed. I started for my room, and he stepped in front of me. "A human being eats a pound of dirt over the course of his lifetime, Tate."

"Are you inviting me to dinner?"

Sundeep put a hand on my shoulder. "Factories that put food in cans are allowed a certain number of rat parts in the food without any punishment. In India, we have cobras. If they bite you, it is deadly. If you leave them alone, they almost never bite."

"I think you've maxed out your quota of metaphors."

"People kill people, Tate. Is that literal enough for you? Some people pay other people for sex in many of these rooms. Some purchase drugs from individuals in this parking lot. What do I do? I look the other way. Since I learned how to do this, I have not been robbed one time."

"Buying that handgun couldn't have hurt."

Sundeep let go of me and scratched the spot in his beard that used to grow in white. I assumed it still did. "You will let me know if you are in danger."

"I'll give you a call," I said.

In my room, I plugged the phone into the wall. Edward lay at the foot of the bed, which hadn't been made. Mollie's scent clung weakly to the pillow. I gave it another sniff and couldn't find her at all.

Edward yawned and stretched his legs. I brought my face an inch from his. He seemed always to be smiling, perhaps because he was always sleeping.

Light rain fell as I reached Battlefield Avenue. I had come too far to go back for my umbrella, which offered little protection from the rain. The same could be said of Grayford's sidewalks, which collected puddles deep enough to drown mice.

Streets on the way were no more than four lanes. I crossed them without trepidation, able as I was to see traffic lights against the dark blue sky. I was making good time, as they say. So was the rain. I was five miles from my destination when the beads in my hair became streams down my cheeks and neck. My shoes got along well with the puddles, inviting them all inside for a nice long visit.

Making my final left onto Norville Run, five miles from the house of Sara Freyman, the puddles finally disappeared. They had no sidewalk to cling to. Neither did I. The side of the road alternated between a weedy ditch and a foot of crumbling hillside between asphalt and guardrail. I shielded my eyes from the high beams of oncoming traffic. The cars coming from behind me, the ones with whom I was competing for the edge of road, were the ones I worried about. I had six seconds from the first hum of engine to jump the guardrail and wait for the slipstream to chill my rain-soaked face.

Rental prices in the outskirts of town must have been more appealing to a frugal-minded trustee. Tweel's estimate of her wealth, like that of his wife's happiness, seemed to be greatly exaggerated. My view of potential dwellings on either side of the road was limited. The city had given up on illumination well before they had abandoned sidewalks. I checked my watch and did the math. At fifteen minutes a mile, allowing for pauses, I should have come upon a house by now. I trusted my eyes to spot one from fifty feet away. I would at least know a driveway if I crossed one. My clothes were covered in mud from my various excursions to the hillside. Shivering, I reconsidered the long-term memory of a ninety-eight-year-old man who believed in ghosts. For all I knew, Parshall might have given me the address of Sara's mother or great grandmother.

It had been a mile since a car had passed. I crossed to the other side. The space for walking was more generous. For a small stretch, I had a bona fide shoulder sprinkled with little rocks.

The shoulder narrowed and widened again. It became an arm. Weeds were waist-high, but sparser and not as tall as the flora to my left and right. The taller plants leaned toward the ground. The sides of the clearing dipped lower than the center. I skirted a puddle as wide as I was tall. The edges where water didn't quite reach were stippled with tire tracks.

The house sat half a mile from the road. "Sat" might have been too charitable a verb. In my obstructed view, it seemed to slouch in the direction of the half-moon to its right. It was three stories with large windows and a turret, possibly attractive in its younger days. In its current state, the house would be lucky to get stand-in work in made-for-cable haunted house flicks.

The bowed porch steps infringed on the trademarked dilapidation of Parshall College's original architect. I pushed the rocking chair by the door and watched it rock. To the right of the door, where a mailbox might hang, there was a rectangle a few shades darker than the paint. In the upper half of the rectangle, a pair of small holes stared at me.

Black numbers on the door matched the address I was looking for. Unfortunately it didn't seem as though anyone had lived here this side of Nixon's first term. Then again, passersby often said the same of Parshall College. I tried the doorknob. The last person to leave had seen fit to lock up on the way out. The knob was made of the cheap brass that corrodes easily, but every inch of it was smooth. Stepping back, I admired the way it caught the moon. Below it, centered on the door, a brass mail slot gave me a bright, flat smile. This, too, was free of blemishes. The hinged cover didn't creak. Caught between it and the brass lip was a thin white envelope.

I got out my magnifier. Dark as it was, it took half a minute to read the name above the address. Readers with low vision are prone to mistakes not always related to poor eyesight. The mind can rush to judgment, see what it wants to see before all evidence has been gathered. For this reason, I took my time with each letter, making certain the name above the address, Sara J. Freyman, was, in fact, spelled with the H eschewed by the secretary on her name plate.

The envelope didn't feel dusty or weathered. The return address held the logo for Carolina Energy. I knocked lightly, testing the thickness of the wood. My feet and shoulders weren't as thick. They certainly weren't as hard. I made my way to the back of the house, checking all eight windows on the way. None was open. The back door was another sturdy affair, also locked, but the top half was composed of glass. No welcome mat welcomed me with a hidden key, nor did I find one under the large stones in the immediate vicinity. I chose one the size of a softball and rapped it against the lowest of four panes on the door, the one closest to the doorknob. It broke as quietly as glass ever does.

"Ms. Freyman," I called to the darkness. "I'm from the power company. I've got your bill."

I unlocked the door and let myself in. Glass clinging to the door shattered near my feet when the door closed behind me.

"Ms. Freyman," I said in a half-hearted, half-throated voice, "we can't restore your power until this bill gets paid."

According to my senses, I was alone in the house. Previously my gift had come in handy only for sparsely attended classes before the start of a holiday weekend. If teaching didn't pan out, I could have a future in breaking and entering, although it's probably better to know if anyone's home before one does the entering.

There was the damp, earthy odor of undisturbed air. I found a light switch under the cabinet closest to the door. It worked. A tea kettle sat on the gas stove. The stove worked, as did the faucet. The dishwasher was empty. Inside a cabinet was a full set of china, pots and pans, drinking glasses. The P on the side of a chipped mug matched the one in the top center of Parshall stationery. The counters had a layer of dust. Items in the cabinets did not.

I outed the kitchen light and ventured down a long, narrow hallway. Moonlight showed me a pair of doorways across from each other. I took the one on the left. It smelled of faint lavender and must. The lights in this room worked, too. So did the adjustable bed. It was unmade, the top half at a forty-five degree angle. Between the bed and a tall dresser sat a walker on its side. A water glass on the nightstand offered me a half-smile. The top half. The contents of a second glass completed the set of teeth. Beneath a 5X magnifying glass was a twice-folded magazine opened to the crossword. It was the kind of celebrity tabloid sold in check-out lanes. The headline was large enough to read with the weaker magnifier. The aging rock star had been seen canoodling with the co-host of the popular singing competition. The couple had since married and divorced.

I turned off the light and made my way down the hall. A stiff white cylinder resembled a lampshade. Objects are what they resemble half to three-quarters of the time. Dim orange light revealed a furnished living room, a painting above the sofa larger than some rugs. Dust mushroomed when I bumped into an overstuffed recliner. On the mat by the front door sat four additional pieces of mail, all of it addressed to Sarah with an H. Someone wanted to know if she was happy with her car insurance. The linens store offered her 20 percent off her next purchase. The nature of the mail was less compelling than the small amount of it. The untarnished mail slot seemed to suggest a recent preference for mail where no one could see it.

I noticed steps in the corner. I switched off the lamp, letting moonlight and memory guide me around furniture. Halfway upstairs, I heard the hum of an engine much closer than the road. Somewhere in the distance, a door opened and closed. Quick footsteps seemed not to need a walker. A key crunched in the lock, and I took the rest of the stairs two at a time.

The front door opened with a protracted squeal. The high tide of light from the living room reached the second floor, helping me notice another set of stairs, this one spiral. A woman spoke quietly. I listened for a second voice, listened for words, but the words and footsteps faded down the long hallway.

The woman spent some time in the kitchen, studying the broken glass and the still-wet footprints of a size ten walking shoe. They led her back to the living room. I left more, albeit lighter prints on the spiral stairs as she started for the second floor. The spiral stairs were metal and not at all quiet. Nothing is when someone is listening. They ended in the center of a round room with a round window and a moonlit view of the woman's car, half-obscured by trees. The car was not black. The woman was not using a wheelchair.

Ten paces completed a lap around the loft. On closer inspection, the walls were octagonal, allowing frames to hang. I noticed a pennant with a Parshall P and a smiling cartoon insect wearing a white top hat. The curve of its smile and wide-set eyes matched those on the stuffed animal that lived under the bed of F. Randolph Parshall. He had slept with it until the nurses labeled it a respiratory hazard. He introduced him to my grandmother and me as Armistead the ant, "Army to his friends," Parshall's mascot in the years the school still fielded an equestrian team.

The lady caller might or might not have reached the second

floor. I heard nothing that couldn't have been the walls sighing against a gentle breeze. Above a rollaway bed with a quilt and no mattress hung a framed newspaper, possibly just the front page. I stood on the edge of the bed and held my loupe against the glass. The header of *The Chanticleer* had not changed in the seventy-five years since the publication of this edition, save the replacement of ink with pixels. I read the headline a few letters at a time. "Grand-daughter of Founder Becomes College's First Woman Graduate." Without my magnifier, I could see the silhouette of her mortar-board. Her hands were clasped demurely in front of the dark gown. The font of the article was too small and the moonlight too weak, but I managed to read the photo's caption. "Sarah Freyman wants to make a difference in the world." She seemed to be squinting at the camera, smiling with her mouth open as if in laughter. It was depressing in the way grainy, black-and-white smiles are, knowing as we do how the joy inevitably ends for every single one of us.

I stepped sideways on the bed, eyeing the next frame. My heel slid a little on the quilt and I caught myself on the wall. I stepped elsewhere, but there was something under the quilt. This time I lost my balance in the opposite direction of the wall. The floor broke my fall.

My female caller had gone back to the living room, but the noise summoned her back to the second floor. I pulled back the quilt, thinking it a good place to hide. Someone else had thought so. How long ago they had thought so I couldn't tell. The body's arm was no warmer than the metal bed frame. What remained of the flesh beneath a cotton garment, possibly a night gown, was hard and delicate at the same time. The smell wasn't as bad as Duncan's more recent state of decay. I poked a finger inside the half-closed mouth. The teeth were missing, which is to say I had already found them.

"You must be Sarah," I said. "You look nothing like your pho-tograph."

I heard someone at the base of the metal stairs. No lights came on. I crouched on the floor beside Parshall's first woman graduate, whose choice to lie on a bed without a mattress, up a staircase less than conducive to a walker, might not have been hers.

There was the click of metal on the handrail, possibly jewelry. The handrail was on the right. It wouldn't be the sound of a wed-ding band. The feet came slowly up the spiral stairs. I dragged Sarah's quilt to the other side of the room, behind the stairs.

"Who's up there?" asked the husband of Mollie DuFrange, whose adenoidal voice I had only mistaken for the fairer sex.

I asked myself all the obvious questions about why he was here. The answers were never as obvious. The moon of his flashlight orbited the ceiling above the stairs. I hadn't counted steps on my way up. Slowly Tweel's head appeared. The flashlight beam skirted the bed, lingering on the toothless smile of the late trustee. The sight of a dead body didn't produce a scream. His breathing didn't quicken. Neither had I been startled, but such discoveries hadn't surprised me since touching the cold cheek of my grandmother, having mistaken her for the bag of art supplies I had brought her the day before. Maybe Tweel had his own story for how he came to regard dead bodies so stoically. Doubting he'd want to share it with me, I unfurled the quilt over the opening in the floor.

Tweel let out a scream worthy of the first victim in a horror movie. I gave a few good kicks to what felt like his face and neck. Kneeling, I managed to grab one of his arms. The other arm took a swing. It hit the curved railing connected to the floor. We were even from before, but I threw in a couple of knees.

Tweel squirmed like a man under a quilt who doesn't want to be there. He descended the stairs, and I lost my grip on his head. I let go of the quilt. Something heavier than a flashlight banged the railing near the bottom stair. Three little explosions like the ones in Duncan's attic came in rapid succession. Bits of the ceiling fell like sleet against the quilt, which continued to cover the staircase.

Telling Tweel who he was shooting at might not make him stop. At this point, who I was probably mattered less than where I was and what I knew. I crouched on the floor by the window as three more shots hit far-apart sections of the ceiling, white crumbs falling in front of my feet.

"I've got a lot more of those. Identify yourself and I might not use them."

I waited for him to use them. There were only clicks and a pair of curse words.

Out the window, another car's tires crunched across what might have once been a gravel driveway. It parked behind Tweel's hybrid. Staying close to the wall, I moved clockwise toward the bed and pulled it over the wounded quilt. Sarah Freyman did her best to protect the ceiling, but four of the next six bullets still connected.

"You're not getting out of there."

I couldn't think of a convincing argument to the contrary. The window was thicker and higher than I liked my windows. Outside, someone from the second car moved briskly toward the house. They would probably take Tweel's side in the matter of my getting out of here alive.

The front door opened, but didn't close.

"Who's down there?" Tweel shouted.

The latest guest to our party remained silent.

"I've got a gun. I will shoot you," Tweel said, but didn't offer the same proof he had offered me.

A single shot hit the low-hanging chandelier on the second floor.

"Stashauer? Is that you? Don't shoot! It's Tweel."

The new guest started up the first set of stairs.

"Come on, man. Don't be like this." Tweel's voice got further away until a door slammed.

Once they reached the second floor, the footsteps didn't continue down the hall. They tapped their way up the spiral staircase. I liked that window more and more. I gave it a pair of useless punches.

The bed springs rattled. The quilt rose in the inches between the bed and floor, a dark hand crawling out the side like a skeptical mouse. I had just positioned my foot above the fingers when I heard my name in the accented, half-whispered voice of my landlord.

I pushed aside the bed and removed the quilt.

Sundeep climbed into the room. "Are you okay, Tate?"

"Better than her," I said.

He checked the pulse of the late trustee.

"I think her blood pressure might also be low," I said. "How did you know I was here?"

"You left the directions in your printer. I called your phone, but you left it on the nightstand." He placed the cell phone in my palm. "You said there was nothing to worry about. This woman is dead, Tate."

"You didn't ask about her."

A door on the second floor creaked like a beginner taking violin lessons. Sundeep crouched beside the stairs, aimed his gun, and fired it. The door closed hard. The patter of little feet could have passed for a well-fed terrier.

"He's out of bullets," I said. "Perhaps he's better with ray guns and photon beams. His expertise is in the field of space tourism."

"You know this individual?"

"You know him, too. A few years ago, he tried to rent the room next to mine."

"Mollie's husband?" Sundeep bowed his head and shook it, or the other way around—the moon wasn't in one of its most generous moods. "You aren't seeing her again, are you?"

"He doesn't know it's me he was shooting at. Help me lift this young lady onto the quilt."

"Where are we taking her?"

"Your backseat. Unless you heard her call shotgun."

We set Sarah down on the second floor. She couldn't have weighed fifty pounds. We made our way to the only closed door. I ran a finger across the keyhole of the large variety found in castles and old jails.

Sundeep came out of the adjacent room I hadn't seen him enter. He handed me a knitting needle.

"Maybe you could just shoot him," I said.

"I am not shooting anyone. Put it in the lock."

I slid the knitting needle into the keyhole and pushed down until it resembled a horseshoe.

"This will buy us some time, but sooner or later, Tate, he is going to be a problem."

"Rick?" Tweel called out, his voice muffled by more than the single door. He seemed to be in a closet or under a bed. "I'm sorry about what I said about your novel. I just—I'm a science fiction guy. I think you're very talented." Tweel was crying, his words mangled as if caught in a yawn. "Tate Cowlishaw is the one you need to worry about. Go shoot him."

33

WE SLID THE LATE TRUSTEE into the backseat of Sundeep's hatchback. Careful though we were, she did not remain in one piece. I followed Sundeep to the rear bumper of Tweel's hybrid. The windows of the house remained black. The room in which my colleague was temporarily sealed was on the other side. Sundeep crouched beside Tweel's tires. He knew a trick for letting the air out. I knew a trick for putting holes in the tires, but I wasn't the one with the gun.

"Now will you admit you are in danger?" Sundeep said as we backed onto Norville Run.

"Okay, I'm in danger. Maybe I could borrow that gun for a little while."

"Absolutely not. With your eyesight, someone is bound to get hurt."

"I think someone getting hurt is the point."

Sundeep cleared his throat with more force than any throat required. "Where are we taking this woman?"

"I was thinking your place."

Sundeep faced me longer than I like my drivers to do in a moving car. "I am not keeping a dead body. You will call the police as soon as we get home."

"Put her in one of the rooms where people have died," I said. In my tenure at the Gray Knight, we had seen half a dozen overdoses and a pair of suicides.

"Put her in your room," Sundeep said.

"I won't be there to watch her."

"Where will you be?"

More traffic appeared as we left the part of town that didn't have street lights. I reached in the backseat, made sure the quilt covered what it needed to.

"Make a left up here on McNultie," I said.

"What is on McNultie?"

"Nothing is on McNultie. On Cedar, you'll find the house where Mollie DuFrange lives."

"Mollie? I thought you said you are not seeing her."

"I said Tweel trying to shoot me had nothing to do with me seeing her. Either way, she should probably know her husband is involved in a murder."

"No. I will not be a party to your adultery. You can call her on the phone, the one I gave you to use and take with you when you go out finding dead bodies."

"The phone died," I said. "That was my fault. If the same thing happens to Mollie, it's going to be partly yours."

Sundeep grunted and sighed. He continued through the next two lights. At the third, he shook his head and made a left.

"You have made some bad choices, Tate. You do not need eyes to see this."

"I'm still alive. I might be setting the bar a little low, but that's something."

"I am talking about love."

We skirted the edge of the state university, where faux gaslights lined the brick sidewalks. From the street, I could see their library still had electricity. The last I had heard, they still had a long list of majors from which students could choose. Through a friend of a friend of a former teacher, Mollie had been hired there to teach a single section of composition four or five years ago. Around that time, she and Tweel bought a house well above their price range in the gentrified neighborhood favored by faculty of her part-time employer. They hoped one day to teach there full-time, even as adjuncts, but each August they returned to their cubicles in the deep end of the swimming pool.

"The advantage of arranged marriage," Sundeep said, "is that you grow with one another, and over time the love arrives."

"You met Jaysaree at a cocktail party after a tennis tournament."

"And we are the exception that proves the rule."

"I think it proves the other rule." I gave him Mollie's house number.

"You are missing my point. Tate, I remember how miserable you were with this woman. Jaysaree and I both liked Carly very much."

"Maybe Mollie and I will do the happily ever after thing in a lovely mountain town. Maybe we'll crash and burn before take-off. Either way, I'd like to warn her that her husband has a new hobby of shooting people."

Sundeep parked on the curb. I told him he could turn around in their driveway, trying to establish which driveway was theirs.

"Someone is pulling into their driveway."

I found the glowing tail lights behind us and opened the door. Getting out, I thanked Sundeep for the assist. He thanked me for the dead body.

The SUV's engine cut off. I knocked on the passenger-side window. Mollie ran around the car and threw her arms around me.

"I've been looking everywhere for you! I tried calling your cell phone. When you didn't answer, I thought . . ." She didn't say what she thought.

"Did you know Ben has a gun?"

Mollie had been about to kiss me. "He bought it last year when students kept keying his car. Why?"

"He tried to shoot me a little while ago. That trustee I went to see turned out to be dead. It didn't seem like Ben was eager to share this with anyone. If your husband didn't kill Simkins, he's definitely connected to whoever did."

Mollie stood there, frozen. A car approached her driveway and kept going. I led Mollie to the house, took her keys, and unlocked the door with the second key I tried.

"I'm going to be sick," Mollie said and hurried for the bath-room.

The busy Oriental rug was even busier with colorful piles. I noticed stacks of books on the glass coffee table on which I had once broken a lead crystal wine glass, prompting a rule to leave all glasses in the kitchen because the end table was too close to the arm of the white sofa. I picked up a paperback the size of a phone book. I had just made out the year and "North Carolina" when Mollie took it from me and set it on the coffee table. She sat me on the sofa and took the cushion beside me. The room's disheveled state and her disregard of the mud on my clothes made it seem as though Mollie really was capable of change.

"I think Ben's having an affair," she said.

I turned this over a few times, trying to recall every conversation I had ever overheard between Benjamin Tweel and Delilah Bibb. Most were about composting and the show about plane crash survivors on a magical island. If the two of them were romantically involved, it explained why Tweel would think Stashauer would want to shoot him. I asked Mollie if she thought it could be Delilah.

"I don't know. I just found out a few hours ago. Those are his things on the floor."

I waited for the thought of Tweel and Bibb to sink in. It had a long way to sink. What about those pictures of Delilah and Simkins? What about Tweel's petition to get Delilah fired? If all of it was an elaborate ruse for my benefit, Tweel punching me was a nice touch. My jaw was still convinced.

"How much of that were you able to see?" Mollie asked.

It took me a moment to realize I was staring, or my eyes were aimed, at the book on the coffee table.

"Enough," I said, my standard answer when anyone asked how much I could see.

Mollie sighed. "I might as well tell you. It wasn't going to be a secret much longer." Her hand found my thigh. It didn't feel the same as it had last night. "I was afraid if I told you, you would try to stop me. You've always been so supportive of my poetry."

She must have meant my attendance at her poetry readings at the used bookstore, during which I calculated in my head the total from my last grocery delivery, making sure I hadn't been overcharged.

"The writing has been on the wall for some time, Tate. There's no longer a place in the academy for people like me. It's a business like any other. If no one's buying what you're selling, well, time to sell something else." She handed me the big paperback and ran her hand across it as if brushing away crumbs. "Like real estate."

"I didn't think anyone was buying that anymore either."

She gave a nervous laugh. "I guess we'll see."

I stood up from the freshly stained sofa. "You're welcome to stay at my place until this blows over. I'd rather we not be here in case Ben makes it home before I arrange for his ride to the police station."

"What evidence do you have, Tate? As I recall, there's no proof that Simkins was even murdered."

"I have the body of a dead trustee."

"You have what?"

"The one whose house you didn't want to drive me to. Maybe she was murdered, maybe she wasn't. There are people who can tell."

Mollie stood up. She stared at the spot where I had been sitting.

"You don't seem particularly surprised by any of this," I said.

"What is the appropriate reaction for finding out, in the span of a few hours, that your husband has committed adultery and murder?" Mollie's words came easily and without deliberation. She was already letting go of the poet inside her.

"Where were you looking for me, anyway? I never gave you the trustee's address."

"I went to the Gray Knight. I figured you had gotten lost and went back to your room."

"What made you think I was in my room if I didn't answer the phone?"

"I told you: I called your cell phone. Do you think I'm lying? I know Carly must have lowered your expectations for honesty, but I am not Carly."

I tried to apologize. Mollie looked away.

"I should be going," I said. "I know a cop you can trust if you think Ben would try to hurt you."

Mollie said nothing.

I started for the door and tripped over a pile of clothes. Crouching to restack them, my fingers dwelled on the glossy, elastic texture of the bright red garment I had difficulty refolding.

"Don't touch that. It's Benjamin's."

"So were you last night. You didn't mind where I put my hands."

From an open suitcase a few feet away, I extracted a ball of socks no larger than an egg. A pair of jeans were much smaller than my own. Benjamin and I were the same height, give or take an inch. The size of the bras underneath the jeans were larger than he needed. I showed one of them to Mollie.

"They're mine." She spoke solemnly, as though it were a body in the suitcase rather than her underwear.

I dropped the bra into the suitcase and stood up. "I assumed you would have told me if you were going somewhere. But like you said, my expectations for honesty might be a tad low."

Mollie sat on the rug with the items she liked well enough to take on her trip. In my mind, I backed away from her and opened the door. I wished her well and walked home in the cool night air.

In reality, I let her kiss me. I kissed her back. When she pulled away, my hand in her hair brought her forward, and we kissed until she pulled away once more.

"I need time, Tate."

"This isn't time," I said, nudging the suitcase with my foot. "It's space."

"That, too."

"How much?"

"I'm leaving Grayford." She rested her forehead on my shoulder, the heat of her words palpable in my chest. "My students have exercises to keep them busy the rest of the semester."

I stared over her shoulder where the North Carolina Realtor's Manual sat on the coffee table. Not seeing things never gets rid of them. "New career, new life. I wish you all the best," I said and reached behind me for the door knob.

Mollie held me by the wrist. It was a tight grip. I didn't try to break it.

"It isn't about Benjamin. It wasn't about him before."

"It's about me," I said.

Mollie shook her head hard. Her black hair levitated like those carnival swings tethered to a carousel. "There will be a time for us, I promise. There won't be anything to worry about, and we can try, really try, the both of us, to be the person each of us needs the other to be."

I wanted to believe her. Sometimes wanting is enough. This wasn't one of those times. I tangled my fingers in her straight black hair, but it wasn't the kind of hair that tangles. I pulled her toward me and kissed her lips one last time. I always liked how they felt more than anything they ever said.

At the end of the block, I could make out a rectangle of light from the house I had just left. She was waiting for me to wave. I held up my hand and pretended one last time that I could see her.

34

LISTENING TO A LOVER SAY NOT YOU, not now, makes a man very tired. So does walking twenty-plus miles a day, no matter how used to it you are. To those who walk everywhere, I recommend living in a motel room of around three hundred square feet, where the bed is never far away.

I locked my door, turned out the lights, and thought I would leave them both that way for a long time. Someone outside thought otherwise. A hard knock went unanswered. I untied my shoes. The knock became a pounding.

Edward went to the door to protect me. More likely he waited for the food with which he associated every knock on the door.

"Tate, it's Sundeep. Open up." My landlord pounded one more time before using his key. He turned on the light. "Tate, she is gone."

"I know."

"The woman's body. Someone has taken it. I left it in the car for five minutes, and when I returned it was not there."

I took a deep breath and tried to decide whether I cared enough to sigh. Sundeep was handing me my shoes.

"Tell the squad car out back, the one watching Totten's room."

"It isn't there."

"Call another officer."

"No. No more officers. I do not like that a dead body was stolen from my car. I do not like that I had it in my possession to begin with."

Sundeep handed me my shoes. I dropped the shoes on the

floor. He handed them to me a second time, and I tossed them against the pole and hangers I occasionally referred to as a closet.

"Fine. Let us pretend someone did not steal a dead body from my car. The next time you are trapped inside a room, I will pretend I do not know you." Holding open the door, he said, "You had better set aside those filthy clothes. Jaysaree will have to clean them herself."

"What happened to Mrs. Thopsamoot?"

"Jaysaree was rebuffed. Is that the correct word? An hour ago, she walked across the street to ask about your colleague, and Mrs. Thopsamoot said she had nothing to say."

"Had nothing to say, or didn't want to say it?"

"It is possible," Sundeep said, "she is still angry with us for buying the second washing machine to clean our own linens. We used to provide her with quite a bit of business."

Sundeep turned off the lights on his way out. Edward remained by the door as it opened and closed. He knew better than to go outside. That made one of us.

I peeled off my filthy clothes and placed them in a paper bag.

Across the street, the sidewalk glowed with neon signs of open stores. Businesses in the bad part of town stay open later than their gentrified counterparts. The word "Videos" had burned out so that the sign read simply "AND MORE!" This might or might not have predated the decision to stop renting videos.

Two doors down, in front of Cleaner Than Cleaners, someone only an inch or two taller than a very short detective I knew smoked a cheap cigarette. They smell no better than the expensive ones, but a sensitive nose comes to know the difference. I smiled like someone who doesn't feel like smiling.

"How are you with mud?" I asked.

"I used to see you all the time. She do your laundry over there, don't she?" Mrs. Thopsamoot head-butted the air in the direction of the Gray Knight.

"Twenty-five a month."

Mrs. Thopsamoot flicked her cigarette onto the sidewalk. She ground it with her whole body, doing the twist for a count of three. "Why they want to take my customer?"

"You get new customers all the time. What about that redheaded woman in the wheelchair a couple of days ago."

"Jaysaree ask about her. I don't remember." Mrs. Thopsamoot sounded a little too pleased not to remember.

"She's my boss," I said. "I believe she killed someone to get the job."

Mrs. Thopsamoot turned her body sideways to look at me. "What evidence you have? I serve jury duty one time. They had no evidence. We don't convict."

"Maybe you could help me out with that."

She crossed her arms.

"If you don't remember her, maybe you remember what she brought in."

"She paying customer. She go to jail, what good it do me?"

I lifted my muddy clothes above her head. "I'm a paying customer."

Mrs. Thopsamoot took the bag, gauged its weight, and handed it back to me. "You just one customer. Lady in wheelchair just one customer. Tie ball game. You tell Jaysaree she bring back sheets and towels, and I tell you about stain on wheelchair lady's dress."

"That sounds fair."

She directed me inside with her entire arm. "Tell you in private. I am Christian woman."

I followed her into the tight, humid space. The floor this side of the counter was empty, save a possibly artificial tree in the corner.

Mrs. Thopsamoot took my clothes out of the bag. "You want tonight or tomorrow?"

"A little late to pick them up tonight, isn't it?"

She set the wet contents of my pockets on the counter. "Many men at Gray Knight need clothes clean fast. Can't go home to wife smelling like whore. They main reason I stay open all night." She made a few marks on a slip of paper and slid it across the counter. "You pay tomorrow. Bring Jaysaree with you. Tell her I give discount, cheaper than before. I am not bad person. I am business woman."

"That you are."

I stuffed the sodden trash in my back pocket. Mrs. Thopsamoot put her elbows where the trash had been and motioned me closer.

"Silk dress," she whispered. Her elbows slid backward on the counter, her feet returning to the floor.

I stayed put in the middle of the counter. "What was on the silk dress?"

"Oh, you don't want to know. Very bad."

"That's kind of the important part," I said.

"I am Christian woman."

"What does the Bible say about murder?"

Mrs. Thopsamoot looked behind her. She looked behind me. She propped herself on the counter and whispered, "Big white stains."

My mouth opened. I hadn't asked it to. "What kind of white stains?"

Mrs. Thopsamoot cupped a hand around her mouth. She motioned me closer, and I gave her my ear.

"Man stains," she said.

I thought of and tried not to think of those pictures Carly had e-mailed Delilah. I connected them to the silk dress and the hardened spots on the floor beside Simkins's chair, on the opposite side where I had found the blood.

"Now you have evidence?"

I nodded. It's the easiest way to lie.

"Your clothes be ready by noon," said Mrs. Thopsamoot. "Clean like new. Like stain never there."

35

THE FORMER VIDEO STORE SOLD their wine on a former bread rack along the back wall. Unintelligible voices, faint and possibly Hispanic, emanated from the former librarian's tinny black-and-white television behind the counter. Each year Galen was at Parshall, he proposed a course in film studies to the curriculum committee, Delilah Bibb and Dean Simkins, who suggested revisions until the course overview had replaced the word "film" with "audio-visual," replacing the films with the morning news, the capstone filmmaking project with a PowerPoint presentation.

I asked my former colleague for a recommendation. This is the best way to give yourself options when you can't see what they are.

Galen had on a purple button-up shirt tucked into chinos a couple of sizes too short. His silver tie matched his ponytail. "You might think they overdid the oak," he said, crouching to pull a red from the bottom row, "but you would be quite wrong. The vanilla arrives just in time. I opened a bottle when I heard Simkins finally took my advice."

"What advice was that?

"To go to Hell."

I carried the bottle to the register. Galen took a moment to watch his movie, laughing heartily at a weeping Latino boy. For once, my confusion at a foreign film had nothing to do with my inability to read subtitles.

Galen swiped my debit card. "Which one of you finally grew the balls to off that fat bastard?"

"The police labeled it a suicide," I said.

Galen laughed at me as if I were a Latino boy crying softly. "What do you call it, Mr. Cowlishaw?"

"I call it an opportunity for change. Let me know when that full-time wine consultant position becomes available."

Galen handed me the receipt to sign. I estimated where the line might be. They never care where you put your signature.

"With your business background, Mr. Cowlishaw, you should open your own store. Being laid off was the best thing that ever happened to me. Now I'm my own boss. I get to watch movies all day. I set my own hours—sixteen a day, but if the economy turns around, I might hire another part-timer. So what if I clear eight or nine hundred a month after taxes. And can't afford insurance. And sold all my belongings that wouldn't fit in the two rooms in the back of the store, which aren't as drafty as they used to be once I patched the holes where the rats got in." Galen sighed not quite as heavily as a bus coming to a stop. "Paper or plastic?"

Taking hold of the plastic handles, I wondered how much baggers at grocery stores cleared after taxes. Cashiers probably made more, but I would have difficulty with the register.

"I'll tell you how I always wanted to do it," he said.

"Find a job?"

"Kill Simkins. There's a second-floor window in the library parallel to his office. Fifty-foot shot. Rifle out the window of a library, Oswald-style. It wouldn't take a trained marksman. Mrs. Garten, bless her heart, used to say she could do it were it not for her arthritis. Of all the shitty things Simkins did to faculty and students, laying off that sweet old woman six months before she would have received her pension was just about the shittiest. Why are you looking for a job, anyway?"

I explained the exciting opportunity with which Delilah had presented me.

"That's probably who killed him."

"That is an idea," I said.

"She had plenty of motive. Who didn't, right? But from what I hear, she moved right into his old job, complete with that ridiculous salary. She probably got tired of bobbing for apples behind his desk, if you know what I mean. I'm not judging anyone, but for God's sake at least pull down the blinds."

"When did you see them?"

"When didn't I see them. Like I said, that window on the second floor. By the way, did you ever meet her daughter?"

"Briefly."

"Who did she remind you of? In the eyes and chin, a little in the ears?"

My hand was on the door. I took it off.

"The asshole had no other relatives. I don't know what he was worth, but if Delilah Junior was his daughter, she should receive whatever he left behind. This was before your time, but Mrs. Garten and I used to wonder why on Earth Delilah Bibb would leave a tenure-track job at Appalachian State, where she was chair of the education department, to join Falstaff's army for less than half her old salary. Just a theory," he said. "Like gravity and evolution."

I asked Galen if he recalled any faculty having taught at Coastal State.

"Nobody I know of. Speaking of dead people," he said, "what happened at the Knight a little while ago?"

"What do you mean?"

"A cop pulled a body from the backseat of Sundeep's car."

"Black officer in a squad car?"

"Tall white guy in street clothes. He was driving one of those cars with the shield painted over. It had one of those removable lights on the roof. He removed it when he drove away."

"I'll let you know if I hear anything."

"Let me know your thoughts on that cabernet."

"Will do."

Outside, I turned the opposite direction of the Gray Knight. At the end of the block, I turned the opposite direction of downtown. A girl seated in an alley asked if I wanted a date. She had a lisp consistent with missing teeth. I kept walking and she yelled something in Spanish or Italian. Her words reminded me of the foreign film, and I wondered about becoming a translator, the kind who work over the phone and don't have to read. Then I remembered that I didn't know any foreign languages. I didn't even know braille.

The money I had in the bank would float me for a couple of months. The Gogeninis would let me slide on the rent. They might never ask for another dime. People like helping the blind. The government offers supplemental income to poor people with bad eyesight. I took it for a year. It was hardly enough to afford the finer things like pride or a decent cabernet.

I cut through the parking lot of the boarded-up tobacco store that had once roasted their own coffee. After closing, it became a parking lot for the civic center, where touring rock stars from the

70s and 80s played their old hits without a band, calling it "An Evening with so and so." This was repurposing, I told my students, a way to breathe life into a product consumers had already purchased or no longer wanted. I passed through the tree-lined neighborhood regarded as run-down when blacks lived there. When whites in their thirties moved in, it became up-and-coming. I tried swapping adjectives on my own predicament, tried to think of a new purpose for myself, wondering what the old one was.

I had been walking long enough to reach the edge of the college from the opposite direction I usually came. Techno music thumped in the house across the street. I cocked my head back and held my blind spots aloft while the half-moon filled the lower corner of my eyes. The stars never came into focus. You can't hold a magnifier up to the sky.

The library remained unlocked. I felt my way behind the front desk into Galen's old office. I thought he might have left a corkscrew in his desk, but there was only his name plate, snapped in half. Mrs. Garten's drawers held a plastic fork and a pair of paper clips. I decided to try the desks of my colleagues in the pool. Those who graded papers with more rigor than me claimed they went down better with alcohol. I was already outside, between the library and Furley Hall, when I heard a sound like a drawer of silverware colliding with aluminum blinds. It came from the library's second floor, behind the window parallel to the office of our late dean.

I set my cabernet beside a few bags of colored sugar. One by one, I threw the bags at the library window. The crashing sound was now a squeak. I found a smashed beer can and flung it at the second floor. The sounds ceased. A minute later, the window opened.

"Dr. Cowlishaw."

"Wade Biggins. What are you doing up there?"

"Stealing shit. What are you doing down there?"

"Looking for a corkscrew. You got one?"

"Not with me. Can you help me carry something downstairs?"

I hadn't had a reason to venture upstairs in years. Moonlight gleamed on the empty bookshelves. The four leather chairs and the round wooden table they had surrounded were all gone. Ditto the sofa that had sat beneath the sun-faded mural of the school's founders with their stern expressions, as if posing for portraits on currency.

"Over here," Wade said.

I traced his voice to the study carrels, or where they used to be, on the other side of the last bookshelf. The floor was gritty with accumulated dust. I doubted it had been cleaned since the librarians, who were required to clean the floors and bathrooms, received their final paychecks.

"The bottom came off the telescope when I was trying to get it to fit down one of the other aisles. I could have just gone around. I'm so fucking stupid."

"Don't be so hard on yourself, Wade. I didn't even know there was a telescope up here."

"The guy at the pawn shop said he could only give me ten bucks for it. I usually sell shit online, but with big things like this you end up losing money on shipping. I wasn't even going to take it, but fucking Tweel this afternoon, you know? I found him using this a couple of times, so fuck him."

It seemed like the inexpensive, half-plastic sort found in toy stores. As little as I could see through the lens, it seemed weak compared to the telescopes Tweel kept by various windows in his house. I asked Wade where he had found it.

"The middle window."

I raised the mini-blinds, confirming the view I had recently seen in photographs. Whether Tweel's aim was as effective with a gun as it was with a camera I couldn't say. The broken glass of Simkins's window was certainly consistent with shots fired. From this vantage, if Simkins was seated at his desk, the bullet wounds would have been on his left temple rather than the top of his head.

Loose parts of the telescope hit the floor. They seemed to multiply upon impact. "Fuck this, Dr. Cowlishaw. I'm wasting more time than this thing is worth."

I rejoined Parshall's oldest junior by the telescope. "Good for you, Wade. You remembered how to do a cost-benefit analysis. If you had actually shown up for the exam, you might have earned the C that I ended up giving you."

"I don't know about all that," he said. "Like ninety-nine percent of these books are just sitting around my house. Most of them aren't worth anything. The ones that are, nobody wants."

After some more tinkering, he got the base back together, and we carried it back to his house along with my wine. The broken telescope weighed a little more than the mummified corpse of the school's first female graduate. Wade's driveway led to the house with the thumping techno beat. Inside, the bass was palpable in my ribs.

"You like it loud," I yelled.

"Do what?"

White carpet and white furniture glowed in the black light. A mirrorball hung from a ceiling fan. My nose found it before my eyes had the chance. Most obstacles come at ground level, so I usually keep my eyes straight ahead.

Wade turned down the volume from 747 to Cessna. The vibrations emptied from my chest. I felt as though I had gotten over a bad cold. Wade switched on the light above the mirrorball. He moved a coffee table from the wall to in front of the sofa.

"This place used to be packed with so many freshman tits you could have opened a tit store, Dr. Cowlishaw. All I had to do was turn on the music. A minute later, they were knocking on the door. I was the pied piper of pussy."

I handed him my wine bottle. "Everyone goes through a slump, Wade."

He opened a drawer in the kitchen. "Yeah, it's called my thirties. This one chick, Dr. Cowlishaw, she called me a pedophile. I don't know, man. I used to be able to make girls laugh. Now it's like I'm the joke."

Wade brought the wine into the living room with a pair of glasses. He had been struggling with the corkscrew for a couple of minutes. He examined the bottle from arm's length, twisted off the lid, and filled a pair of glasses to the rim. We clinked them together without making a toast.

I rolled the cabernet around my tongue. They had overdone it with the oak. I checked the roof of my mouth for splinters. "If you don't mind my asking, Wade, how do you afford a place like this on the proceeds from used library books?"

"My dad cut off my spending money a couple of years ago, but he still pays my rent as long as I'm in school. Is it true Dr. Bibb's going to expel people who have been here longer than seven years?"

"She's throwing me out, Wade. I've only been here five."

"I hated Simkins. Every time he put me on probation, my dad gave me less money. The asshole kept changing the curriculum so that I would never graduate, but he was really good at cashing my dad's checks. Not once did he mention expelling me."

I noticed the books around the room, stacks of them waist-high along three walls. The fourth wall, directly in front of us, was taken up by a white screen from ceiling to floor.

"I just wish school wasn't so boring," he said. "How is reading and writing papers and taking tests supposed to prepare me for a job?"

"What kind of job do you want, Wade?"

"I don't know. Why can't somebody just pay me to sleep in and watch movies all day?"

"It sounds like somebody does, Wade."

Wade topped off our cabernet. "Sometimes movies are too long. I mean, you have to sit there for like two hours. It's like sitting through class. Lately I've been more into these videos on the Internet that are like two or three minutes long."

Wade set his glass on the coffee table and stood beside the white wall. A blue screen the size of a laptop computer came on. Cords knocked against one another as the white wall became the blue screen.

"You've got to check some of these videos out, Dr. Cowlishaw. There's this one with a bunch of retarded kids in a mosh pit."

Wade outed the lights and started the video. I didn't mention the debate among faculty on whether or not Wade himself was on the spectrum of mental retardation. Wade did what I assumed to be his impression of the video's participants. When the clip was over, he clicked a few times on his laptop. He typed a few words. We watched an impassioned speech by a mayoral candidate interrupted by a loud, sighing fart. We watched a montage of minor league batters taking fastballs to the groin.

"Check this one out, Dr. Cowlishaw. It's Dr. Bakker doing stand-up. Somebody puts up a new one every week."

A mouthful of cabernet settled warmly in my chest. Wade and I shared laughs at Londell's stories of underachieving students, one of which might have centered around Wade. My host started another video and sat down.

"I don't like these as much," he said, "when he just does impressions."

Londell did his Cosby and Barack Obama. From where I sat, the picture on his cell phone camera was rather blurry. The audio was as crisp as a wet potato chip, but was strong enough to pick up chatter from neighboring tables. I could hear my own voice, if not quite every word, talking to Thayer about his screenplay. The whispered words of Benjamin Tweel, only a few feet from Londell's phone, occasionally overwhelmed the ones onstage.

"What's your little boy toy doing here?" Tweel asked. "As

I understand it, he's going to be meeting Miss Worth in a little while."

Someone shushed him.

"I'm more excited to put a bullet in his head than I was Simkins," whispered Tweel. Whether it was loud enough for his wife to hear I wasn't sure.

Londell shouted, "I'm comin', Elizabeth. This is the big one!"

A loud, possibly pot-induced laugh from the adjunct who didn't bathe covered more whispering. Wade Biggins shifted in his seat. The video was five minutes old. Were he not in his own house, he doubtless would have left, as he often did when classes went on this long.

Applause followed Londell back to the table. I heard myself offer him a quick compliment before my departure. Moments later, the emcee announced the next performer, Oral Tradition's very own hostess, Ms. Sara Freyman.

Wade got up. I held him in place by his crewneck collar.

"But it's over, Dr. Cowlishaw."

I reached for the wine bottle and filled his glass. I filled my own and took a big swallow. I was wrong about the oak. The vanilla arrived just in time.

"As some of you know," said Sara Freyman, "I'm going to be following my dreams to Nashville real soon. Tonight I want to dedicate a song to the lady who's helping to make that possible. She's been taking singing lessons from me, and y'all got to hear her earlier tonight. Miss Mollie DuFrange. How did she do, everybody?"

The audience clapped politely. Someone close to the cell phone hooted loudly. The screen went black before Sara got to sing.

36

WADE TRIED TO GET ME TO STAY for footage of a fellow throwing turtles across a lake. I took a rain check and made my way to the foyer. My foot clipped the corner of a metal cabinet.

"That's my bad," Wade said. "This is a new arrival. I haven't found room for it yet."

"Where did you get this?" I asked of the black file cabinet, three drawers high.

"From a closet on the second floor of the library."

I ran my thumb along the top drawer. Deep scratches formed the crude curvature of a penis. "This wouldn't be your art work, would it?"

Wade examined the engraving and chuckled. "Maybe. Sometimes when I'm nervous I draw dicks on things."

"When did you steal this?"

"Earlier tonight. It's the weirdest thing. Two days ago I found one just like it in the janitor's closet of the dorm."

"Do you still have that one?"

Wade led me into a second living room and turned on the light above a pool table. He lined up the cue ball and broke the rack. He asked if I wanted to shoot a game.

"The file cabinet, Wade."

"Right. Sorry."

Between air hockey and foosball tables, both covered with books, sat a file cabinet identical to the one in the hall, minus Wade's artistic contribution.

"Check this out." Wade turned it around to the left side.

I ran my thumb along the holes. Three-inch dents radiated from the spot where each bullet went in. It was too late to match these to the bullets in Simkins's head, but I knew of a few other places Tweel had fired his gun. This and the whispered confession on YouTube ought to be enough for an arrest.

"I'll give you twenty bucks for this, Wade."

"It's yours, Dr. Cowlishaw. No charge. Without your classes, I'd still be a sophomore."

I told him I'd be back for it. The techno beat returned when I reached the sidewalk. I pulled out my phone. I was getting the hang of this walking and talking. I'd have to add it to my resume under "skills."

"Are you alone?" I asked Thayer in lieu of a greeting.

"I tend to be at this hour." He made me hold while he finished writing a line of dialogue. "What do you need?"

"I need you to arrest someone for the murder of Randall 'Scoot' Simkins."

I told him everything I knew, including where he could find the erstwhile scholar of space tourism.

"I'll send a car," he said.

"Perhaps you should be inside it. The officer you put on the Gray Knight went AWOL. This was around the time an eyewitness saw your sensitive partner help himself to a dead body that didn't belong to him."

Thayer let out a long, perforated scream. "Do you have any idea how hard it is to carve writing time into a detective's schedule?"

"Seems like I'm doing the detecting. All I'm asking you to do is read someone his rights."

Thayer gave me a big sigh befitting a man of the stage. I gave him the address of the late Sarah Freyman. After a long silence and a few keystrokes, Thayer asked me to hold on while he got a pen. I threw in the Cedar Street address in case Space Boy proved stronger than a knitting needle.

Maybe I should have asked for an officer to pay Mollie a precautionary visit. Who was to say what Tweel would do with that gun once he got his hands on more bullets? I swallowed my concern and pocketed the phone. My worry, I admitted to myself, was only hope that Mollie wasn't already long gone. I thought instead of her voice teacher, Sara Freyman, who seemed a more logical candidate for the role of Tweel's mistress. How the two of them were connected to Stashauer and his former teacher I couldn't say. Nor did I see a motive for any of the lost lives, Simkins and Duncan and Sarah Freyman the elder, beyond Delilah's new salary, which didn't seem worth killing for after it was split four ways.

I was only a block from Wade's house when a white sedan pulled beside me, well short of the stop sign. The passenger-side window came down.

"Do you need a ride?" Carly's question sounded sadder than it needed to. It was closer to the tone people use to ask how your parents died.

"How far to New York?" I said.

If she was smiling, I couldn't see it. I opened the door and got in. Instead of pulling away, she killed the engine.

"I waited for you at the Gray Knight. As soon as you got home, your landlord went in, and then you left. You bought a bottle of wine and I followed you at a distance. I almost shouted your name, but you were walking so purposefully, like you knew exactly where you were going and wanted so badly to get there."

"I was looking for a corkscrew. Turned out I didn't need one."

"There are things I need to tell you," she said, her voice somewhere on the floorboard.

"I probably don't need to hear them."

"I want you to hear them."

She removed her hands from the steering wheel and looked at them. The volume of her weeping rose only slightly above her shallow breaths.

"So you told a few fibs on your CV," I said. "We all embellish. On mine I included a second-place finish in an eighth-grade spelling bee. Maybe I didn't include the year. Maybe instead of spelling bee I called it a contest for linguistic retention."

Carly brought her hands to her face. I touched her arm. She had on a thin sweater that didn't prevent her from shivering.

"I've never even been published," she said.

Her words came out wet. I looked inside the glove compartment for napkins or tissues. I found one in the door and handed it to her.

Carly blew her nose. "I was rejected by Iowa. I was rejected, in fact, by twenty-two writing programs, some of them multiple times."

"I take it your novel is fiction in more ways than one."

"I haven't even written a novel. I made up the book deal a few minutes before the meeting. I figured it would give me an excuse to leave town before the truth got out and obliterated any chance I had of ever finding another teaching job. That was when I thought Simkins was the only one who knew." Carly raised her head to stare out the windshield at the street in which no cars had come or gone since she shifted into park.

"I think I know where your files are, if you still want them."

Carly said nothing. Her teeth chattered. I placed my hand on hers.

"I don't think a reasonable person would say you profited from your deceit. Your salary certainly refutes that."

I gave Carly my other hand, but hers continued to tremble.

"I suppose you'll have an easier time finding work than Tweel," I said.

I tried giving back her hand, but Carly wanted me to keep it. She faced me for the first time since I got in the car.

"Tweel killed Simkins," I said. "He was the one who arranged for us to meet outside the dean's office Tuesday night. I don't think he liked the questions I was asking, or that both of us had seen Simkins's dead body. I believe Tweel had been cleaning up the office Monday night when you and I stumbled upon Duncan trying to get in. We left. Duncan stayed behind to receive some threats from Detective Stashauer. I'm not sure how he's connected, or if Delilah's involved at all."

Carly stared at me for a long time. If she blinked, I missed it. "Did you just say Tweel killed Simkins?"

"I said some other things, too. Do you need me to repeat them?"

"What makes you think Tweel killed him?"

I dictated the web address for the video of Londell's most recent set at Oral Tradition's. We watched Tweel's confession on her fancy phone.

"It's not overly surprising, as angry as Tweel has always—"
Carly shushed me.

"Tate, I don't think it was Tweel." Carly said this with disbelief and incipient joy. She touched the screen in two places, rewinding the video and turning up the volume much higher than it had been on Wade's laptop.

"I don't think Duncan's going to do it," Tweel whispered, his sigh just reaching Londell's phone. "This whole thing is beginning to feel like a failure of the imagination."

"You're a failure of my imagination," whispered the voice that had whispered much nicer things in my ear. "I can't thank you enough, Benjamin, for making me finish the job. At least sex with you prepared me for something."

"It was a bad angle," whispered Tweel to his wife. "I wasn't expecting him to be asleep."

"You're just lucky he could sleep through gun shots. And that I thought little enough of your aim to wait outside his fucking office."

"He was shot?" Carly asked.

"What did you think when you saw the body," I said, "that he hit his head?"

"All I saw were his legs. I thought he had a heart attack or something, so I called 911."

I took out my phone and dialed Thayer.

"Since when do you have a cell phone?" Carly asked.

"Men who discover dead bodies have to make a lot of phone calls."

Thayer's voicemail picked up. I told him to save room in the car for a dark-haired poet in her thirties with terrific aim from close range. I returned the phone to my pocket and pulled out the clump of wet papers Mrs. Thopsamoot had removed from my soiled clothes. The sheets tore in several places as I separated them.

"Can you read this?"

Carly turned on the dome light. She struggled to decipher Mollie's handwriting on the note she had passed me in Monday's meeting. "Simkins won't be here. I think that's what it says. The words are small and super messy."

"Of course they are. She didn't expect me to read it. When I asked how Simkins had died, she knew I had been in his office. That's how I ended up at the police station."

In my hand was the note with much larger, much neater words asking me to meet Carly outside Simkins's office. I slid my magnifier over the first letter of the late dean's name, the bottom curve looping around itself to form a curly-queue. I held my loupe over the first word on the other note. The writing was small, but it isn't as hard to see things when you know they're there.

"I'm so sorry I doubted you, Tate. I never will again. Never ever."

"I'll put you down as a reference on all my job applications."

"Don't be such a pessimist." She leaned over the emergency

brake, smiling before she kissed me. "All's well that ends well, Tate Cowlishaw."

"That depends on your definition of well, Carly Worth."

Carly turned off the car five seconds after she had started it. "One more confession," she said. "My name isn't Carly Worth."

"Don't tell me it's Sara Freyman."

Her laugh was small and not entirely fake. "It's Carla," she said. "Carla Butterworth. That's why I'm sure very little came up when you searched my name. Frankly not much comes up when you search who I really am."

"And who are you, really?"

"Nobody." Her voice retreated once more to the floorboard. "There's a story about this writer named Kathy Smith. She had written this wonderful novel. Everyone who read it fell in love with it, but no agents or publishers would read it. She started submitting it as Kathryn Smythe, and sure enough, within a month, she had an agent and offers from four publishers. She sold the novel for six figures. What's in a name, right? Sadly things haven't turned out the same for Carly Worth."

"A Butter," I said.

"Excuse me?"

"A note on Simkins's desk said 'A Butter.' That's one fewer thing that doesn't make sense."

We drove across town past the state university, onto McNultie, then Cedar. The driveway was empty and the windows dark. I felt no better, knowing I wasn't the only thing from which Mollie was running away.

"Where to now?" Carly asked.

"Let's hang around, make sure Tweel doesn't show up without a police escort."

We parked on the street four houses down. The only car engines were blocks away, so faint they might have been a strong breeze. After a time, Carly reached into the backseat. She opened her laptop, clicked a few times, and handed it to me.

"This is the first chapter of a novel I began two nights ago. I think it's the best thing I've ever written. Then again, what do I know?"

I stared at the screen, moving my pupils from left to right.

"Sorry, I forgot." Carly took back the computer and read to me. She reached for my hand, our fingers lacing together.

The novel was a mystery set on the campus of a small, dilapidated college. A blonde librarian named Charlene enters the chancellor's office to find him slumped over his desk.

"A certain trustee will be disappointed by the lack of vampires."

Carly cleared her throat. "I hate vampires. It just seemed like something people would believe since everything has vampires in it."

She closed her laptop. I listened for cars or footsteps. There was only the half-throated chirp of the first bird in the neighborhood to wake up.

"What is it like, reading everything with your ears."

"Like listening," I said.

"What do you see when you look at me?"

My thumb and forefinger found her chin and guided her face within inches of mine. Her blonde hair curled around her ears, a few strands parallel to her cheek. She had a small nose and small eyes beneath light eyebrows. It was a face. It was a pretty face. If there were more effectual words for describing faces, I had been out of the practice of describing faces long enough that I no longer knew them.

"You don't like to talk about it, do you?" She ran a finger down the bridge of my nose. "Maybe that's why we're drawn to each other. You'd rather conceal that part of yourself every hour of every day than let people see who you really are."

My vibrating phone saved me the trouble of changing the subject.

"I wish I had known you were sending me to an empty house," Thayer said. "I would have brought my computer and finished the scene I was working on."

"I'm on Cedar. Nobody's here either."

"I know. I went there first. The door was unlocked, so I had a look around. There was nothing but furniture and appliances. I'm leaving the haunted house now, Cowlishaw. Any other ideas?"

"Maybe they're at your partner's house."

There was the sound over the phone of a car door closing. The ignition beeped. The sound of the motor never came.

"I don't think Stash is home," Thayer said.

"Where is he?"

"The backseat of my car, pointing his service revolver at my head."

37

THE PARTNERS EXCHANGED NO WORDS before the line went dead. I told Carly the quickest route to Norville Run. All my calls to Thayer went directly to voicemail. Carly had just spotted the late trustee's overgrown driveway when my phone buzzed.

"Help! Please help!"

The words weren't surprising. That they came from a young woman rather confused me. "Where's Thayer?"

"You said to call you if anything bad happened." Juliet Bibb steadied her voice. "My mom's got a gun, Mr. Cowlishaw."

"What's she doing with it?"

"I don't know. She just left the house. We had a big fight."

"There are no cars here," Carly said.

"I asked Mom about the pictures, Mr. Cowlishaw. She didn't want to talk about it. I asked her if she killed the dean, and she slapped me."

"I think your mom was romantically involved with the dean," I said.

"Gee, do you think?"

"Where do you think she went?"

"I don't fucking know. Why do you think I called you?"

"She isn't with me," I said, motioning for Carly to turn around. No cars were in the vicinity. No lights were on. "By the way, I like you better when you're crying."

"Fuck you," Juliet said, but took my advice on the tears.

"What did your mother say before she left?"

Delilah's daughter took jagged breaths. "She called me an ungrateful little twat."

"That doesn't sound like your mom."

At the mouth of the driveway, Carly pointed left and right with her arms, turning up her palms. I shrugged my shoulders.

"I asked her who my father was. All she ever told me before was that he was a cold man. I was made from her love and no one else's, she used to say, but I always thought it was weird she wanted to move back to Grayford. She hated coming back to visit my grandparents, and Parshall, you know, is such a shitty school. I asked her if that dean was my dad. She just looked at me. Her face got dark pink. I asked her again. She tried to slap me again, but I grabbed her by the wrist. I looked her in the eyes and confessed that I had been faking my illness so I wouldn't have to go to college anymore. She tried to slap me with her other hand, but I moved out of the way and told her I wished she were dead."

"How long has she had this gun?" I asked.

"It was my grandfather's. He used to take us to the firing range when we visited. What do you think she's going to do?" Juliet's question became a high keening, like the pinched-off neck of a balloon leaking air. "I grabbed Mom's chair on her way to the garage. That's when she took the gun out of her purse. She was crying. Not normal crying. Silent sobs, you know?"

I checked my watch. I didn't know what Delilah was going to do. I wasn't sure what she had or had not done already. I thought I knew, however, where she might be.

By the time we reached campus, I had appealed Mollie's conviction, wondering if we could have misheard her in the video. Second-guessing comes naturally to a man who needs a magnifier for twenty-four-point font. Students who don't know an answer on my quizzes like to guess all of the above. Once in a while, they're right.

Carly spotted Delilah's car, her daughter's retired cruiser, in the parking lot behind the library. Duncan's Volkswagen remained in its final resting place. Of the other vehicles, none was Tweel's hybrid, Mollie's SUV, or the Mercedes Benz of Jefferson Totten, with whom Delilah had a meeting scheduled for this morning.

You can take old wooden stairs quietly or quickly. We opted for the former, leaving ourselves the option of surprise. Slowly as we climbed, the steps were no louder than a string quartet in a capacious auditorium.

Carly peeked around the doorway on the third floor. "Her door's open," she whispered.

I stepped around her. She wrapped her arms around my waist, looking up at me. She was mouthing words, a form of communication as useless to me as tiny cursive. I shook my head.

"I said be careful," she whispered.

Two big strides brought me to Delilah's doorway. I waved. After a count of five, I stepped inside to confirm she wasn't there.

My steps toward the classroom were careful ones, as they tend to be when moving toward a woman with a gun who doesn't much like me, a woman whose aim might well have benefitted from childhood trips to the firing range. I poked my head inside an inch at a time. Delilah's red hair stood out against the pale wall furthest from the door. From twenty feet away, her hair color was no help in seeing if she had used the gun on herself. I sensed a heartbeat and breathing lungs, but a single bullet might not have finished the job.

"Just the woman I was looking for," I said.

Delilah's gasp froze me in my tracks. The click of her gun, a sound with which I had become overly familiar, sent me backward a few feet.

"You don't belong here, Mr. Cowlishaw." She was facing the windows. I tried to read her flat tone, somewhere between determined and resigned.

"That's not very nice, Dean Bibb. Scoot used to say everybody belongs at Parshall."

"Dean Simkins," she said, "was a selfish, egotistical, morally bankrupt son of a bitch."

I slid the sentimental approach back into its holster.

"Your daughter's worried you're going to do something with that gun," I said.

Delilah turned her chair around to face me. "If you could see where I'm pointing this pistol, you would be the one who was worried."

Quick footsteps in the hall didn't give the floor a chance to creak. "Don't shoot!" Carly ran into me, nearly knocking me over.

Delilah's high, warbling laugh died before it reached the ceiling. "Young love. How sweet."

I stepped slowly from behind Carly, positioning myself in front of her. Her legs shook.

"Perhaps I should have taken a bullet for Scoot. Perhaps then he would have made love to me instead of unzipping his trousers to let me suck his penis for the last two decades. But that's me: self-less to a fault. Everyone's needs always come before my own: Scoot, Juliet, every single one of my oblivious students."

On cue, several coeds traversed the lawn outside the building, laughing the way they do when traveling in packs.

"Those little piss ants don't realize I give two hours of my life to each of their papers. I used to dream of rolling across the rose garden of the White House, accepting an award for my contributions to higher education. I would ask former students with whom I had kept in close touch over the years to introduce me."

Carly was reaching into her purse. Suddenly the purse was on the other side of the room, its relocation coinciding with a gunshot.

"Do you know how many students I've heard from after my class has ended? Not counting the prank calls and the baseless appeals for a grade change, the grand total is zero."

"Someone thinks you're a wonderful person," I said. "He sent you that lovely house plant, remember?" I had thought it was Stashauer until learning Delilah had not taught at Coastal State. I still didn't know which of us had.

"Yes, well. When I'm feeling down, I try to remind myself how I'd like to feel."

"Scoot must have loved you," I said. "About twenty years ago, give or take nine months."

Something a little higher than Delilah's wheelchair clicked into place. Carly covered her ears.

"He was a leader, a visionary," Delilah said. "That's what I tried to tell myself all these years, but do you know what attracted me to Randall 'Scoot' Simkins? He bought me a drink. So yes, maybe I sympathize with these students who feel unwanted when every other college has rejected them."

"That's what makes you such a great educator," said Carly in a shaky voice. "Your empathy."

"Your lies are more believable on paper, Miss Butterworth. Sit down, both of you."

We sat in the desks we always chose in meetings.

"Take out your notebooks and pens. You can tell my daughter . . ." Delilah stifled a sob, "everything I've said when this is over."

We had no notebooks, but she seemed flexible on that one.

"We met at the annual Mid-Atlantic Teach for the Stars Conference in Cumberland, Maryland. That afternoon I had attended a panel on the double-entry notebook as pedagogical tool. Scoot hadn't noticed me in the audience. I always sat in the back row. Believe it or not, Mr. Cowlishaw, I spent many years trying to deny my handicap, trying to be heard and not seen. I had a little trick for hotel bars. Once I was comfortable at a table, I would fold up my chair and tell the waiter, one who hadn't watched me come in, that some previous patron had abandoned their wheelchair, which the waiter would carry away. I was in my late twenties, finishing my dissertation, and despite having never had sexual intercourse, I was, if I may toot my own horn, rather comely. I had on a black sleeveless dress. I used to get compliments on my arms. God knows I never got compliments on my legs." She spoke with the calm and purposeful demeanor of a woman who knew exactly how her story would end.

"I'd like to hear more about that conference." I spoke with the unconvincing interest of a man trying to delay the story's ending.

"Both of you will have the chance to leave," said Delilah, "after I put a bullet between the eyes of Jefferson Totten. Until then, do not interrupt me. I have no compunction about shooting you in the kneecaps."

A bird belted out a song Delilah didn't care for. The echo of her gun whistled a tune not dissimilar to the bird's. I was partial to the original artist.

"Where was I?"

"At the table in the bar," I said.

"Right. Scoot was at the next table with the other members of his panel. He was making toasts to himself. I don't know how many drinks he had consumed, but no one else at his table was interested in another. When they left, his eye caught mine. More likely his eye caught the conference lanyard around my neck. He bought me a sloe gin fizz and ordered another for himself. He talked and I listened. We drank. He asked if I'd be interested in seeing some of his other papers. He had them upstairs in his room. 'Meet you there in ten minutes,' I said, and when he left the bar, I asked a different waiter if anyone had come across a wheelchair."

Delilah paused to listen to the birds. They were further away than she could shoot them.

"Let's take things slowly. Those were Scoot's words as soon as he answered the door to find a woman in a wheelchair. He took off his clothes. 'You can leave yours on if you want,' he said. 'I'll go first,' he said, 'and we'll take turns.' I waited my turn. I waited twenty years."

"Juliet is under the impression that Simkins was the cold man you said was her father."

"I followed him from conference to conference. He always welcomed me into his room with a stupid grin and an open zipper. It became clear I wasn't going to get pregnant doing what we were doing. Juliet's father was a cold man. Frozen, in fact. I selected him from a three-ring binder. Years later, in town to attend my mother's funeral, I bumped into Scoot at a restaurant, and he offered me a job. I should have guessed what he was and was not offering, but love makes idiots of us all, doesn't it?"

The front door of the building opened and closed. A pair of hard-soled shoes clacked up the stairs. Delilah turned her chair toward the door.

"We'll leave you to your meeting," I said, standing up.

"Sit down. I am not done with my story."

"We get the gist," Carly said.

The heavy footsteps reached the second floor.

"This is the good part," she said. "The part where I realize how foolish I was, thinking Scoot Simkins would someday acknowledge something between us, whatever it was, and become a father to my ill-mannered daughter. He would steer her in the right direction as he had steered this God-forsaken ship for so many years. Inwardly I always questioned how he kept this place afloat. As spectacularly disorganized as he was, he certainly had the magic touch, didn't he? I'll wait a moment and let Dr. Totten explain the secret behind Scoot's magic."

Totten reached the carpeted hallway of the third floor. He moved tentatively toward the classroom. In my interactions with the man, Jefferson Totten had been anything but tentative.

"In here," Delilah trilled.

Two steps into the room, I recognized the difference between hard-soled shoes and stiletto heels. Carly was motioning toward the door. Her windmilling arms summoned to my nose the faintest hint of olive oil and Bijan perfume.

"What a hovel this place is." As pleased as Myrsini sounded to say this, she probably hadn't noticed the gun that was, in all likelihood, pointed in her direction. "Tate, you need to get away from here. I can tell by looking at the ceiling that there is asbestos in the tile."

"Who the hell are you?" Delilah asked.

"Myrsini taught here for a couple of years," I said.

"Before your time," said my neighbor. "When there was a sociology department."

"She gets nostalgic sometimes, wanders in to remember the good times."

Myrsini gave her Adam's apple a workout with a vigorous laugh. "Fat chance. I am here to let you know Jefferson Totten won't be making it to today's meeting."

Delilah spoke with gritted teeth. "How do you know Jefferson Totten?"

"Carnally," said Myrsini. "Where he is going, I suspect that knowledge will not be hard to come by. He offered me a thousand dollars to pass along an address to a Delilah Bibb—that's you with the cute little pistol, isn't it?—where he wants you to send the materials. I will not be giving you that address. I will not be taking his money. I am here because I think you are disgusting. I am old enough to choose what I do, Ms. Bibb. These children with their stolen innocence and broken wills." These words Myrsini bit off hard, spat them out, and ground them on the floor with her sharp heels.

"What children?" Delilah's confusion tamped down some of her anger.

"I do not care if you admit anything. That is for judge and jury."

"Are you accusing me of some sort of crime?" Delilah located the anger she had temporarily misplaced. Her finger located the part of the gun that made that clicking sound.

"Where is Dr. Totten?" I asked.

"Downtown," said Myrsini with a measure of pride. "He requested my presence for the second night in a row. When I got there, it was not me he wanted. He had pictures on his phone of little girls and boys. He asked if I knew where he might find any of them. These were not ambiguous pictures. I told him I would be right back. I had a productive chat with my friend, Officer Joseph, whose cruiser happened to be parked at the motel. Some of my colleagues in the pleasure industry, they say, 'Myrsini, who are you to judge? What makes you the moral center?' I taught in higher education for seven years. I know what exploitation looks like."

The room was quieter than an 8 A.M. class. We were waiting for the reaction of the woman with the gun. It seemed the most important reaction.

"Oh, do not cry," said Myrsini. "That pedophile is not worth the salt in those tears."

Delilah spoke in a voice so quiet I flattered myself into thinking I was the only one able to hear it. "I want to die."

Myrsini's heels cut a slow drum beat across the room. She sat in the desk closest to Delilah's chair. "You don't want to die, sweetheart. You just need some better clothes."

"I made him miserable," Delilah said. "I wouldn't let go of him, and his only escape was taking his own life."

Delilah was guilty, it seemed, only of falling in love with an asshole. She had wanted me to find his killer, hoping for someone she might blame other than herself.

Carly stood above Delilah and reached for the hand not holding the gun. "There's a petition signed by the faculty expressing a vote of no confidence in your leadership."

I looked sideways at Carly, my peripheral vision fixed on the gun pointed at her.

"I didn't sign it," Carly said. "Neither did Tate. I'm sure everyone who did would change their minds in light of what's happened."

"It's too late," Delilah said. "Dr. Parshall has already made his opinion quite clear."

"You've spoken to him?" I asked.

"I haven't even tried," Delilah said. "His nursing home has called twice in the last few hours, specifically asking me not to visit him anymore."

"When was your last visit?" I asked, thinking Duncan in drag was the real Delilah non grata.

"I told you. I haven't. I didn't think he even knew my name. It's not like Scoot ever introduced us. God forbid the trustees ever meet the woman doing the majority of work on the curriculum."

Someone's phone was vibrating. Delilah and Myrsini reached into their purses.

"This is them again," Delilah said. "This is she. Excuse me? I refuse to be spoken to in this tone. No, I most certainly did not just run through the lobby. Because I'm paralyzed from the waist down."

38

DELILAH ORDERED CARLY AND ME into her car. It was a polite request, an offer to drive, but she still had a gun, even if she wasn't pointing it. Getting in, I asked her if the car happened to come from a police auction.

"It did. A few years ago, I was looking for an inexpensive car for my daughter. Miss DuFrange told me about the auction. She was sucking up to get her Advanced Poetry Seminar back into the curriculum."

On the way to Rosewall Glen, I explained to the interim dean why she might be forming a search committee for three faculty positions. With each detail, her hand pushed a little harder on the gear controlling the accelerator.

"If Tweel and DuFrange think they can blackmail me into resigning, they have another thing coming. Those two don't know the first thing about running a school."

She was still listing her own qualifications as we approached the front door of the retirement home. Near the front desk, I heard the voices of the black receptionist, Nurse Margaret, and the security guard they called whenever an embroidered pillow went missing. He put on a pair of glasses and got a couple of inches from the guest book. He was older than many of the residents. I offered him my magnifier.

"I'm Delilah Bibb." The name's rightful owner parked her chair between Margaret and the receptionist and showed them her driver's license.

"Where's the other Delilah Bibb?" I asked.

The receptionist put her hand on the shoulder of the security guard. "Clayton chased her into the parking lot."

"Did she make it to Dr. Parshall's room?" I asked, taking a few steps in that direction.

"He was receiving his bath when I stopped her from going in," said Margaret.

"Is he still getting his bath?"

Margaret smirked. "I'm sure he wishes his baths lasted longer, but this is an assisted care facility, not a massage parlor."

The receptionist made an M sound.

I pushed through the double doors to the residents' rooms. Margaret called after me, saying visiting hours didn't resume for another two hours. The security guard gave chase. He didn't have much of it to give.

From the mouth of the hall leading to Parshall's room, I heard the stentorian voice of a professional reader. Sometimes you can discern the genre of book from the narrator's tone. This one italicized words with a halting menace. In the reader's defense, there are few ways to enunciate the words "undead" and "spirits" in consecutive order.

I shouted Parshall's name until he made the guttural sound of a soldier waking after an explosion, or a ninety-eight-year-old man after a nap.

"Is that you, Nick?"

"It's me." I walked over to his chair and examined the bathroom. I wasn't sure what I was looking for. "What are you reading?" I shouted.

He slapped at the cassette player until one of his fingers landed on the stop button. "I'm not eating anything. There was some sort of confusion with my breakfast."

"No, I asked what . . . never mind. What kind of confusion?"

"It was a new nurse. A red-haired woman. No sooner had she brought me the tray than Margaret showed up to take it away. Ten minutes later, this red-haired nurse came back with another tray. She just sat there, waiting for me to eat. I took a bite of bacon. She told me to try the eggs. As soon as I got some on my fork, Margaret had one of the colored fellows take away my tray."

"Are you hungry? I can find you another breakfast."

"Don't bother, Nick. I think I know what's going on."

"What's that?"

"It's happened a few times," he began, choking up a little. "I can't remember if I've eaten or not. I think I keep imagining things."

I had a seat on the ottoman. "What kind of things?"

"A few minutes ago, I saw that red-haired nurse outside my window. Or thought I did. She was floating there, Nick. Ghostlike." Parshall ejected the cassette from the tape player and flung it onto the bed. "I don't know anymore, Nick."

He kept talking. He hadn't seen me step into the hallway. The security guard saw me just fine. He was doubled over, winded from the high-speed chase. He asked me nicely but not very loudly to stop right there.

"Dr. Parshall needs to go to the bathroom," I said, heading for the side door. "See that he gets there right away."

The gently sloping path to the flower garden hugged the building, windows getting further and further from the ground. In front of each window, a birdhouse rested on top of a pole, another of Katherine Cowlishaw's lasting contributions. The poles in front of Parshall's room rose more than twenty feet in the air. I stepped into the hedges and shook the first two poles that went to his room. I turned the corner to shake the other two. When I reached for the one leading to the window beside his bed, it wasn't there.

A solid piece of metal clanked against the building. It was nothing I had touched. Somewhere above the ground came the sound of labored breathing. My shin found something hard. My hand found the muddy end of the missing pole, angled toward the building.

With some effort, I picked up the pole and heard something heavy hit the ground. Hedges crackled around the corner, beneath the room across the hall from Parshall's. Swinging a twenty-foot pole is a slow endeavor. I hit bushes and then the building. A fist hit my jaw. The punch felt familiar, if not familiar enough to avoid a second one to my other jaw.

I sat down in the bushes. A second later, he or she was upon me. I aimed my gaze skyward, providing the best view I had ever had of Benjamin Tweel's angular face. He had a mouth no larger than a grape. Coarse hair from his red wig covered my eyes. I brought my forehead forward into his nose. I traded him places in the bushes. I held his wrists, my knees on either side of him, pinning him to the ground by his dress. He tried my move with the forehead, but I wasn't close enough. He appeared to be nodding in strong agreement.

"Where's your better half, Benjamin?"

"Fuck you." His voice was even higher with a broken, bleeding nose.

"It's nothing to be ashamed of, Ben. This happens all the time. A man likes to dress up in women's clothing. His wife finds out, and the marriage is no longer tenable."

Tweel's little mouth opened. He breathed through it, but didn't speak.

"Unless," I said, putting one of my knees in his groin, "you were dressing up like Delilah Bibb so she would be blamed for whatever you were doing here. What were you doing here, Ben? Help me understand why you would want to be dean so badly that you'd commit homicide?"

Tweel's head turned sharply toward the corner of the building. Ten feet away, an old man's wheezing breaths struggled to become words.

"Let go of that woman," the security guard finally managed to say.

"This is the woman you chased into the parking lot," I said. "She was trying to kill Dr. Parshall."

"I don't know about all that, but you're on top of her, and she's the one who's bleeding."

"She isn't even a woman," I said.

Suddenly Tweel felt like talking again. "Get him off me! Please get him off me!" he cried in a crimped falsetto not much different from his conversational voice.

"This here in my hand is a Taser." The elderly guard pronounced the word carefully, as though he had been corrected the first time he said it. "I'm going to use it in a count of five."

He counted faster than he ran. On four, I eased away from the bleeding damsel, one knee and then the other. Tweel rushed to the side of his white-haired knight.

"Is this your purse, ma'am?"

Tweel thanked the old man, no longer bothering with his falsetto. There was the sound of the purse's zipper. The next few clicks didn't sound like lipstick.

"You don't know how long I've wanted to do this, Cowlishaw."

The guard started to say something. Tweel shoved him into a tree.

"It's a little pathetic," Tweel said, "putting a bullet in a man who can't even see you holding the gun."

"At least we agree on something, Ben."

"Look up in the sky, Cowlishaw. The way you do when you're actually looking at something."

I fixed my eyes above the trees. Tweel got larger, step by crunchy step. The black barrel of my fate came into focus beneath the plunging neckline of a dress that looked much better on Benjamin's wife. I changed my mind about seeing the gun and stared straight ahead. Tweel didn't change his. Dead leaves beneath his feet sounded a little like wet snow. The gun sounded a lot like a gun.

39

MY HEART THUNDERED AWAY. I felt it with my hand. I ran the same hand through my hair on both sides. The gun went off again and a third time. I checked the same parts in the same order. I looked up at the trees in time to see Tweel falling sideways.

"Tate, are you okay?" Carly shouted twenty feet above me.

"He missed," I said.

"He was about to shoot you," said Delilah from a different window. "So I shot first. Plus, he was trying to take my job. Plus he and Mollie killed Scoot."

"Sounds fair," I said.

I knelt beside Tweel's dead body. They were getting easier to find. She had shot him once between the eyes and twice in the heart. I checked his wrist. Tweel's pulse was halfway to Neptune.

I helped the guard to his feet.

"Maybe it's time I move into one of those rooms up there," he said.

A number of people were gathered outside Dr. Parshall's room. Most of them were talking. Nurse Margaret was talking the loudest. She stood outside the room across from Parshall's, turning back nurses, orderlies, and a few residents in wheelchairs. It was my grandmother's old room, the room from whose window Delilah must have shot Tweel. Margaret's hands were in the center of my chest when Parshall told her I could come in.

"Well," Margaret said, "let's have a little party in the room nurses aren't allowed inside."

"If you didn't have to have everything so goddamn clean," said Parshall. "Dust promotes fellowship with the spirit world."

Margaret chuckled under her breath. Delilah was in the corner, speaking quietly, tearfully, to her daughter on the phone. Carly was admiring my grandmother's unfinished mural of Machu Picchu, Lake Geneva, and the Taj Mahal, three places she never got the chance to visit.

"They wanted to move somebody into her room, Nick. That was when I made an offer on this place. The food was getting terrible, anyway."

I had assumed the dispute was over the room housing his library. "It might have been cheaper to pay for the room," I said.

"Never rent when you can own, Nick. Didn't they teach you that in business school?" Dr. Parshall grabbed my hand and squeezed it weakly. "She talks about you all the time. Come by some evening and the three of us will have dinner."

"I'll do that."

Margaret pushed Parshall's chair into his room. Delilah followed them. I told Carly I would be a minute and closed the door.

My grandmother's bed had not been made in the years since she died. Beneath the sterile scent of any other room, I thought I found a whiff of acrylic paint and a drop or two of the rose oil she liked to dab behind her ears. I ran a hand across the mural and felt the texture of her brush strokes. I laid my other hand on the cold pillow case until it became warm.

Across the hall, Margaret was helping Parshall back into his bed. Carly was explaining who the man was who had tried to kill him.

"And who is Annie Oakley over there?" asked Dr. Parshall.

"Delilah Bibb has acted as interim dean in the wake of Simkins's death," I said.

"In that case, she and I have a lot to discuss," said Parshall.

"Another time," said Margaret. "You've had a very trying morning, Dr. Parshall."

"I haven't even had breakfast," he said. "Aren't I supposed to take some of my pills with breakfast?"

Margaret put a hand on her hip. She held it there as she exited his room.

"First things first," said Parshall, raising his voice as much as he was able. "These two will be promoted to tenure-track positions. As long as we are clear on that, we can move forward."

Delilah's head was level with Parshall's pillow. "I would like to think all promotions and hires will be merit-based," she said without looking in our direction.

"Exactly. Mr. Cowlishaw is a preeminent scholar of the occult. Miss Worth is about to publish her first novel."

"About my novel," Carly said.

"They've pushed back the publication date a little bit," I said.

Dr. Parshall expressed his disgust with the state of publishing. Delilah made her own sound of disapproval, unrelated to publishing.

Carly and I passed the nurse's station, where the security guard was still being examined. Further down the hall, I got out my phone to call Thayer. It rang and rang. There was no voicemail. Thinking I had misdialed, I scrolled through the list of numbers I had called and guessed which one was his.

"Well, if it isn't Mr. Biggins," said the newest trustee of Parshall College, in a better mood than when I had last spoken to him.

I dug through the bin of voices for the Southern accent I had used for our previous conversation. "Mr. Skipwith. I just called to offer my condolences on the death of your fellow trustee."

"Such a shame," said Skipwith, his mood improving with each word. "They both lived into their nineties. We should all be so lucky."

"Excuse me. Did you say they?"

"Listen, Mr. Biggins, I truly hate to cut this short, but I'm en route to an important meeting that will insure you never bother me again."

"Mr. Skipwith. Right here," said a voice somewhere in the vicinity of the trustee's phone. I had last heard it behind a flashlight and revolver in Duncan Musgrove's attic.

"There's my ride. Good day to you, Mr. Biggins."

Skipwith hung up before Wade's fictional father could make sense of what he had just heard. I lingered near the sensor of the automatic doors that led outside, the doors sliding back and forth behind me. Carly said my name. I uttered the plural pronoun Skipwith had used to refer to the dead trustees. Only one trustee was dead. If Tweel had not been stopped, there would have been two.

I was out of breath when I reached Parshall's room. Delilah was speaking loudly, the words accreditation and assessment mingling seamlessly with the odor of disinfectant.

"Sorry to interrupt," I said. "Dr. Parshall, didn't you say decisions of the trustees had to pass by a majority vote?"

Parshall finished a long cough into a tissue. "That's right."

"Suppose a vote ends up as a tie. What happens then?"

"For God's sake," said Delilah. "I'll rehire you. Are you satisfied?"

"A tie isn't possible, Nick. Sarah Freyman and I each have a vote, and the Skipwith boy gets half a vote."

"If Sarah should pass away, God forbid, who gets her vote?"

"Sarah never had children, so her share of the college and accompanying vote would go to the closest Freyman relative. This relative, like the Skipwith boy, would also have half a vote."

"Suppose two half votes opposed your full vote."

"Well, that would be a tie. The vote would then go to the faculty."

"Would the faculty vote need to be unanimous?"

"No, a simple majority."

I did the math. If Duncan, being dead, no longer counted as current faculty, the signatures Tweel had collected constituted a majority. It didn't seem like Skipwith in all his indifference would make a trip to Grayford to vote on the appointment of a new dean.

Outside, I ran toward the little golf cart marked Security. "Do you think this thing takes keys?"

"It seems to," Carly said. "They're in the ignition." She turned them and drove us seven miles per hour to the exit. "Where to?"

I directed her left on Lexington, right on Thurman, right on San Martin. Countless vehicles passed us on the left, holding down their horns.

"There should be a high-rise on the corner of Chester and Cornelius. Pull into the parking lot. Look for spot number eighty-eight."

"Somebody's in it," Carly said.

"I thought there might be."

We parked behind Mollie's SUV and jogged toward the building's entrance. A man with a thick voice and thicker body, judging from his lumbering footsteps, called after us.

"You can't park there," said the parking attendant.

I held the door for Carly and let it close behind me. Above the elevator call button hung a list of businesses and their respective floors. I asked Carly to look for a realtor. Her finger made its way down the list.

"Zerbe and Farnsworth," she said.

"Any others?"

"I think it's the only one."

The parking attendant made his way into the lobby. We made our way into an elevator as the doors began to close. We got off on the fourteenth floor, Carly leading the way until we came to the office.

The receptionist was a tall kid in a double-breasted suit. He made sure we noticed him, standing up to block our path as we rounded his desk.

"We're with Mollie DuFrange," I said. "Which room is she in?"

The kid stepped sideways, making himself even with the framed picture of an American flag. "End of the hall," he said, sounding as though we had hurt his feelings.

There were two doors at the end of the hall. The one on the right was open. The room held a pair of small tables and a humming refrigerator. I knocked "shave and a haircut" on the door on the left. Finding it unlocked, we went on in.

It was a rectangular room with a rectangular table. Seated around it were five to seven people. I didn't have time to listen for a definitive count. Once I entered the room, after Sara Freyman the younger said, "It's him, Miss DuFrange," there wasn't much to hear.

I extended my hand to the individual at the head of the table, whose shade of hair was the only one dark enough to be Mollie's. "I don't believe we've met, sweetheart. Francis W. Biggins. A little bit about myself: my son is a student at Parshall College, so you might imagine how I have a vested interest in this meeting."

"We've met." The disappointed bearer of this news was Theo Skipwith, seated to the left and one seat down from the dark-haired female who had not yet shaken my hand. Her reticence was beginning to remind me of Greta Garbo.

"Theo, you rascal. Of course I remember you. Let's go around the table now. Who are my other new friends?" I paired my broad accent with broader gestures involving both arms. "First, let me introduce you to my secretary, Charlene. Say howdy, Charlene."

"Howdy, y'all."

One by one, they introduced themselves. Between Mollie and Skipwith sat Sara Freyman. To Skipwith's left sat Stashauer. He called himself Richard, perhaps to match his formal attire.

"I believe we've met as well," said Richard. It took him a while to let go of my hand.

"We have met, haven't we? One of those little rooms in the back of the adult bookstore. Weren't you holding a mop?"

The man across from Stashauer liked this. He was the only one who liked anything I had said. His patience suggested a man who didn't do a lot of waiting. He had beige skin and a bald pate. He held out his calloused hand before I could offer mine.

The bald man had a Middle Eastern accent. "Kavasmaneck. Cyrus Kavasmaneck."

"And what is it you do, Mr. Kavasmaneck?"

"Until you got here, Mr. Biggins, I was buying your son's school."

"Good for you," I said. "I tell my boy, the future depends on education."

Kavasmaneck laughed again. "I'm afraid I am rather more interested in the school's land than its buildings, which will have to come down."

"That's rather disappointing to hear," I said.

"You have our sympathy," said Skipwith. "Now if you might be so kind as to let these interested parties—*financially* interested parties—return to the business at hand."

"It sounds like a fun party," I said. "What if I were to invite myself to the party?"

"This party has a cover charge," said Stashauer with a clenched jaw.

"I see. What if I were to, say, offer more for the school than Mr. Kavasmaneck."

"I don't think you have that kind of money," said Mollie with a nervous laugh.

"Hold on," said Skipwith. "Let's at least hear the man out."

Mollie stood up from the table. "Mr. Biggins, would you please join me in the hall?"

"Absolutely. First let me have a brief word with my secretary. Mr. Skipwith, you don't mind if Charlene borrows your laptop? Excellent. Thank you."

The pale screen was some sort of document. I performed the keyboard command for creating a new file. I typed brief instructions. Carly read them to herself and patted my hand.

"Be right back," Mollie said and closed the door behind us. "I don't know what you think you're doing, but you need to be gone. Right now," she said in a stage whisper.

"I'm not sure you're in a position to make demands," I said, maintaining my volume as well as my accent.

"Mollie?" asked a man in an open office several doors down. "Everything going okay?"

"Absolutely, Mr. Zerbe. Thanks for asking."

"ABC," said Mr. Zerbe.

"ABC," Mollie said.

She pulled me into the room with the refrigerator. Across the hall, behind the office door, Cyrus Kavasmaneck's reaction to Londell's act suggested a future for *Sanford and Son* reruns in Middle Eastern markets.

"I don't know what you think you know, Tate, but you've got to—"

"Ben's dead," I said. "F. Randolph Parshall is still living. I don't know if either of those details puts a crimp in your plans, but I thought I would let you know."

Mollie inhaled a deep, almost noiseless breath that seemed somehow to symbolize her seven-year marriage. She let it out. "It doesn't. But thank you for passing that along."

"I doubt that quote-unquote petition would stand up under scrutiny. Those signatures were gathered under false pretenses."

"Every signature has already been notarized, actually. And who's going to scrutinize them, Tate? You? Since when do you give a shit about this school? About anything at all?"

"You seemed to like my initiative until it opposed your own."

"Your intentions, as always, are a bit less lucrative than mine."

Across the hall, someone applauded as Sara Freyman took the stage on Skipwith's laptop.

"That's me," said the live version of her prerecorded counterpart.

"What's her relation, by the way?" I asked. "To the other Sarah."

"Great-great niece. She was named after her aunt, not that she knows it. She's here to sign paperwork for a fellowship that will pay her ten thousand a year for the next five years."

"That hardly seems fair, compared to the commission you must be getting."

"My commission," Mollie said, "wouldn't pay off my mortgage. But Sara's share of the sale of the college, to which she doesn't even know she's entitled, well, that's enough to make a gal happy for the rest of her life."

"How could she not know?"

Mollie smiled for the first time since my arrival. "I never thought I'd be grateful for my time at Parshall College, Tate, but all that practice confusing cretinous minds with big words finally paid off."

"What did you say to confuse the detective in there into breaking so many laws?"

"He was in my composition class the year I taught at State. He couldn't get into the writing program, so they put him in my class and told me to be encouraging."

"So you're the favorite teacher." I manufactured a smile. "I can see how you might fall for him, Mollie. He's a sensitive man."

Mollie bowed her head. She reached for my hands. "I had sex with him once. It was rape by most definitions." Her voice was so low it seemed she didn't want to hear it. "He never left me alone. Ben wanted to get a restraining order, but what would that do? He is the law."

"You had a better idea. Seduce him into covering up Simkins's murder."

"He used to write me these creepy letters from the desk of his wife's secretary while his wife was working late. He wrote one of them on the secretary's personal stationery. Ben thought the name sounded familiar. He did the genealogy, found out she was the next in line. We were only going to influence her vote, try to get Simkins fired, until I learned she had no clue what she was going to inherit."

"She seemed to know a thing or two when I visited her boss."

"Stashauer put a tap on Duncan's phone. After he called the law firm, I told Sara to be on the lookout for a disgruntled professor wanting to file a lawsuit that could jeopardize her fellowship."

"And the death of that great-great aunt?"

"Ben said she was dead when he found her, but I have my doubts."

"Why blackmail Delilah? She couldn't have stopped you."

"Probably not, but we had those pictures lying around. Ben had been using them to get cost-of-living raises from Simkins each of the last three years. I like to think we were the reason he wasn't going to be able to make his annual payment to Jefferson Totten. We were doing Scoot a favor, putting him out of his misery before scandal destroyed his reputation, such as it was."

"Were you doing me a favor, trying to put me out of my misery?"

"You know that wasn't my idea."

Mollie leaned into me. Her lips felt stiff. It might have been all the talk about dead bodies. Her thumbs rubbed little circles into the backs of my hands. I used to think I could feel things others couldn't, but Mollie's hands felt no different now that I knew what they were capable of.

"Come with me, Tate. I'm going to the Caribbean. You can have Ben's share."

"I wouldn't want to come between you and Richard."

"Give me a break. The idiot thinks I'm going to move in with him."

"I don't know, Mollie. I've never been overly fond of handouts."

The conference room across the hall opened. Carly spoke my name without Charlene's accent. She stumbled with a gasp into the break room. Stashauer was behind her. He held her by the neck of her sweater, her midriff exposed. He threw her into me. The two of us tumbled sideways into the kitchen counter.

"Do you know what this bitch was doing?" Stashauer stood over us on the carpeted floor. His large hand pulled me up by my jaw.

"Stop it!" Mollie smacked the arm of her former student. "Whatever they've done can be undone. Just keep them here. I'll fix everything."

The break room door closed. The conference room opened. Mollie's apology and brief laugh were the last things we heard before there were two closed doors between us.

Stashauer pulled out a gun and a piece of chewing gum. I asked if I could have a piece.

"No, you may not."

"The force is going to miss you when you're gone," I said.

"I'm not going anywhere. You're the one who's going to be gone when I put a bullet in your head."

"I just assumed you'd be joining Mollie in the Caribbean."

"What the hell are you talking about?"

"I'm sorry, Rick. I shouldn't have said anything."

He closed the gap between us. I smelled his spearmint breath. The barrel of his gun found an uncomfortable home under my chin. "Spill it, Cowlishaw."

My jaw opened the quarter-inch permitted by his gun. "Maybe she meant it to be a surprise. Do you have a birthday coming up?"

The gun barrel made real headway into my chin. "No, I don't." The fridge kicked off.

Stashauer shoved me onto the floor beside Carly. "Spill it!"

"You really should hear it from Mollie."

Stashauer backed away from us, still pointing the gun. He fired it at the spot of wall between our heads. The gun had a silencer. The bullet did not.

Stashauer went into the conference room holding the gun, or so I assumed by the shriek of Parshall College's newest, most oblivious trustee. I stepped into the hall. The sharply dressed receptionist spotted me and asked what was going on.

"We're negotiating," I said, rubbing my chin where the gun had left a dent.

The receptionist returned to his desk.

"You know how to reach me," said Mr. Kavasmaneck, parting ways with his considerable patience. "Give me a call when these criminal matters are resolved."

A second chair after Kavasmaneck's wheeled backward from the table. "I also must confess to a great deal of confusion," said Skipwith.

"Sit down, both of you." Stashauer's voice went left. "When were you going to tell me about the Caribbean?"

"I don't know what you're talking about," Mollie said.

"Don't lie to me, Mollie!"

The receptionist was talking to someone other than me. His inflection rose and fell, settling rapidly into the same umbrage he had taken when Carly and I breezed past him. The footsteps came softer than fast footsteps tended to. The receptionist sat down again, talking to himself.

"There he is," I said, though I had a good idea who it was. "Where have you been?"

"In the trunk of my partner's car," Thayer said. "Pardon me if I'm not my freshest. I was sharing the space with an old woman's corpse."

"How did you know where we were?"

"I asked questions. A cop with a gun and a head wound gets quick answers."

We shut up and listened to the escalating voices of Mollie and her erstwhile suitor.

"Give me that," Mollie said.

"Those weren't Benjamin's plane tickets, were they?"

"Of course they were."

Thayer pulled a gun from a holster on his back.

"Where did you find that?" I asked.

"My partner left me for dead. I'm sure he didn't think I'd use it."

Stashauer's voice broke a little. "I'm the reason you know her. She's my ex-wife's secretary. Mine. Not yours. You'd only have the commission if it weren't for her ten million. And don't forget I was the one who took care of Musgrove."

In a frightened little voice that wouldn't have reached the first row of the Grand Ole Opry, Sara Freyman asked what was going on. "Miss DuFrange, you said the second you heard me sing that I was good enough to win the fellowship."

"Yes, Rick, thank you for quote-unquote taking care of everything. Your attention to detail throughout this process has been nothing short of mind-blowing. If you weren't so careless, maybe your atrocious novels would approach the vicinity of halfway readable."

"You said I was good. You said I was the best writing student you ever had."

Thayer stepped toward the conference room.

"Give them another minute," I said. "They might tell us where they stashed Lindbergh's kid."

The talking stopped. The frantic repetition of elongated N sounds didn't seem like a search for the right words.

Thayer returned his gun to its holster and turned the door knob.

"Take the gun out of her mouth, Stash."

Mollie coughed. A body, presumably hers, collided with the wall I was leaning against.

"You're not supposed to be here." Stashauer sounded more surprised than angry.

"The newer models of squad cars have trunk releases. You could have let me have the newer model," Thayer said, "but you've never been the most generous partner."

"You weren't breathing. I checked."

"I'm a good actor. You'd know that if you ever came to one of my plays."

I considered going in, but Thayer would be the one closest to the door. Stashauer would probably shoot me well before I saw him.

"I suppose one of us isn't leaving this room alive," said Thayer.

"One of us has a gun," said Stashauer. "That's pretty easy math."

"That hardly seems fair. How about if we arm wrestle?"

Stashauer laughed with every corner of his lungs.

"You know you can beat me, Stash. I'd just like one last chance to show you what a little person is capable of when he puts his mind to it."

Stashauer laughed again. It might have been the same laugh's second act. "Okay," he said. "You two, move."

Carly said my name. The door of the break room opened a few inches. I pulled it shut. Carly opened it again. I smelled Mollie's almond shampoo, though it was Carly saying my name.

"Tate, behind you!"

The break room door swung open. With my eyes fixed uselessly on Carly's, I noticed her pointing to the floor. The door of the conference room opened no more than a foot. Out of it crawled Mollie on her elbows.

Carly stepped past me, grabbing Mollie's arm as she stood. Mollie slapped her in the doorway of an open office.

"Mollie," said Mr. Zerbe. "What is going on?"

Mollie kicked off her heels and ran. She had a hand on the door handle when she turned around, saw me coming, and waited for me to reach her. "Come with me," she whispered. "It will be different. I need you now. It'll be different because I need you."

I wanted to believe her. Part of me always did.

Stashauer cackled at the end of the hall. "You never had a chance, little man."

Carly stood behind me.

I took Mollie's hand. Our fingers locked. Our lips came within an inch of touching. My finger made a barrier between them.

Mollie aimed her gaze over my shoulder. "You don't even know her, Tate. There's still time. For us."

The cackling down the hall grew louder until a pair of gunshots brought it to a close. "Did you just shoot me?"

"You'll live," Thayer said in the beleaguered voice that preceded the clink of handcuffs.

Mollie pulled against my hand. I wrapped both arms around her and held on tight. She bucked and screamed. A minute later, her body went slack in my arms. She was crying. They didn't seem like real tears until I felt them on my shoulder.

40

WE DROPPED THAYER OFF in the parking lot behind the library. He gave me his left hand to shake. His right held a wad of paper towels against his crown. He needed stitches, but refused medical attention until he had taken a victory lap around the theater.

"When are you going to tell him?" Carly asked, parking the golf cart in front of the former sub shop.

"Who knows? Maybe Parshall will go for it. There are three faculty members no longer in need of their salaries. If not, I'll blame it on a ninety-eight-year-old's faulty memory."

Mid-morning sun warmed our backs as we knocked on Wade Biggins's door. I had promised Carly her folder from Simkins's file cabinet. On the third knock, the door finally opened.

Wade said our names and yawned. "I'm sorry I slept through class, Miss Worth."

I told him classes were cancelled until Monday.

"Really? Sweet."

I made my way into the foyer. "Just to warn you, Wade, some cops are going to be coming by in a little while."

"Shit. Where am I going to hide everything?"

"Just hide your marijuana, and you should be fine. They're interested in that file cabinet with the bullet wounds." I tapped the front of the other file cabinet on which he had carved his favorite section of Michelangelo's *David*. "Perhaps you can return this one to its rightful owner before they get here."

"Who does it belong to?"

I explained the journey Simkins's file cabinet had made from Simkins's office to the janitor's closet in the dorm. When it disappeared, Stashauer searched the dorm, finding a file cabinet he assumed was Simkins's. He moved it to the library, of whose contents Tweel had become so protective, tripping the breaker switch to dissuade visitors.

"Nikki Gladstone?" A wide grin parted Wade's overstuffed cheeks. He rubbed his hands together and slid the base of a nearby hand cart under Nikki's file cabinet.

"Sure you don't want to put on some clothes first?" Carly asked.

Wade stepped backward through his front door in his white bathrobe and slippers. "No way, Miss Worth. You chicks love it when guys do nice things for you. I want to be ready when she, you know, thanks me."

I led Carly around the minarets of library books into Wade's billiard room.

"Wow. Wade might have a future after all," she said.

"As a thief?"

"As a furniture mover. He's put everything in the exact position Simkins had it in his office."

I aimed my eyes at the crown molding, if there was any, and turned in a slow circle. Stand-up cabinets and bookshelves lined two walls. Behind the desk sat Simkins's chair. To the right of the desk was the black file cabinet. Carly pulled open the top drawer.

"Here it is," she said, equal parts embarrassment and relief.

I made myself comfortable in Simkins's chair while Carly paged through the contents of the yellow folder. After a time, she sat on a stack of encyclopedias and tore the pages of her fictional life into two-inch pieces.

I rested my elbows on the desk of the late dean. Unloved as he was, excepting the mixed memories of Delilah Bibb, Simkins's legacy, other than the faint heartbeat of the school he had kept alive through artificial respiration, did not extend beyond the items on his desk. I held my magnifier against the coupon for a free small fry with the purchase of a large soft drink. It had expired a week before he had. I had been outside his office once when a concerned parent asked if Simkins had any family. "Every one of these students," he had replied. The parent, who was there to protest her daughter's grade, told him to go fuck himself.

I lifted the lid of Simkins's candy dish. I took two of his circus peanuts and replaced the lid. Carly stood above his trash can, watching the brief blizzard of her alter ego settle in the bottom. I gave Carly one of the peanuts, held mine aloft, and proposed a toast.

"Where did you get these?"

"They're a little stale, but I think they come out of the bag that way."

Carly yanked my wrist before I could take a bite. "Don't eat that!"

I looked her in the black dots that passed for eyes in my blind spots. I brought the candy toward my nose. She shook my wrist until the peanut dropped onto the floor.

The scent on my fingers was familiar, if not particularly strong. If I hadn't smelled it recently, among the perfumes in Carly's medicine cabinet, I might not have remembered it.

Carly grabbed the candy dish and threw it hard into the plastic trash can. She looked at me, saying nothing. Finally, she collapsed into a hundred books that dominoed across the floor.

So there it was, the answer to the one unanswered question: how Scoot Simkins, who so impressively stayed awake through most of his own meetings, managed to sleep through all those bullets hitting his file cabinet. He was already dead.

"I went back to his office." These were Carly's half-formed words from the floor. "Two hours before the meeting, I went back. I hadn't slept. I bought a bag of candy to replace these. That's when I found him and called the police."

Her poisoned candy had scarcely preceded Tweel's and Mollie's gunfire, judging by the blood. "I didn't even know he still ate them," I said.

"He ate several the last time I was in his office." Carly took a long moment to compose herself. "That's when he told me he had been looking over my CV." Her voice crawled around the floor like a flightless bird.

"Your Internet search for cremation. You worried there might be traces of the poison in the remains."

"I had to use your computer. I was being watched by that detective. I knew it was him in the black car, Tate. I remembered him from Monday morning."

"If only he had known you were on the same team."

"I'm not like them. I tried to take it back. You have to believe me."

"Why didn't you just quit?"

"I tried. I offered to leave right away or finish the semester, his choice. Simkins just stared at me across this desk with those sunken eyes. He told me I had committed the worst kind of fraud, the kind that compromises the foundation of the academy. He said it was a serious crime and said I had left him no choice but to turn me in. I was in tears. I told him I would do whatever it took. He pushed his chair away from his desk. He rolled around to the other side. He put his arm around me. That's what I thought he was doing. Then I saw him unzipping his pants. I turned away. He chuckled and told me to take the weekend to think about it. The things I'd be doing in prison wouldn't be half as pleasant, he told me. Now I wonder if what I did was even a crime."

"The fraud or the murder?"

She didn't answer.

I stood up. Simkins's chair didn't seem like the place to be. I cleared a spot on the floor and sat beside Carly.

"This doesn't have to change anything between us, Tate." She wiped her eyes one at a time. "You could just forget everything, couldn't you?"

I looked into her sad dark pupils. There was remorse in the infinite flecks of gold in her green irises, in the tiny creases around her mouth and eyes. I couldn't see any of it, but most things you can hear in a voice. I searched her face, my memory filling in what I couldn't see. It's a hell of a trade, memory for vision. Which side got the raw deal I was never sure.

A hard, impersonal knock came on the front door. Another followed five seconds later.

"Grayford P.D."

Carly looked into the hall and back at me.

The door opened. Footsteps made their way into the living room.

"Detective Thayer said you'd be expecting us."

Carly let out a breath. She balled her hands into little fists and held them between us, wrists together. I pushed them down and found the Post-it in the center of the desk on which Simkins had written "a Butter." I tore it in half and tore it a second time. I tore it a third time and dropped the pieces onto the candy and broken glass.

41

THE PHONE ON MY DESK RANG. I have two phones and two desks, but the one on the desk closest to the door isn't plugged in. The second desk is never occupied, but people think more of a man who pays someone to answer his phone.

"This is Cowlishaw."

"Tate, you have a customer coming. A woman in her fifties." Jaysaree sounded giddy. She got excited when people came to see me, professionally or otherwise.

"Client," I corrected her. "Thank you."

Most people go first to the office in spite of the sign in the window of the room beside mine. Inside, the room looks a little more like a business. Sundeep put the bed and dresser in storage, and I got a great deal on two desks that had belonged to former faculty at Parshall College.

My client knocked, as they tend to do. I got up to let her in. A large woman filled the doorway, blocking more of the July sun than the cheap curtains. She handed me a thin stack of mail.

"The woman in the office asked me to bring this to you."

"Sorry. My secretary has been out all week with the flu."

"Yes, I hear that's going around."

I led her to my desk and offered her the chair not occupied by Edward. She stood there, petting him for a while.

"What's your name? Hmmm? What's your name?"

I told her his name. Edward wasn't going to.

"You're a handsome one, aren't you? Yes, you are." She went on talking to the cat, as women of a certain means will do when visiting a private investigator in the bad part of town.

"Do you want to tell him *your* name?" I asked.

She laughed nervously.

I checked my watch. I started to repeat my question, but clients seemed to appreciate patience. Until I could afford advertising more effective than business cards and Internet classifieds, I had to rely on word of mouth.

For nearly a minute, she stared at my painting of Grandfather Mountain. At last she swallowed a big woman's breath and handed me a 9 x 12 envelope.

I opened it and pretended to read the first page. I made a knowing sound. This is a good sound to make when the person across from you might pay you to know things.

"You'll see in those statements various charges to restaurants and hotels. Mitchell is my husband. Her name is in the e-mails."

"How long has the affair been going on?"

"Two years. Maybe longer."

"What would you like me to do about it?"

"Catch the bastard in the act." Nerves finally gave way to the indignation that had brought her here.

As far as the courts were concerned, she had already caught him, but it didn't behoove me to question the value a job had to a client. It had value to me. I gave her an estimate of that value, and the woman wrote me a check.

"Do you think you can help me?"

"I see no reason why not."

This is what I always say. In many ways, detective work is a lot like teaching college. Sometimes the students got what they paid for, and sometimes they didn't. The payment was the consistent part.

Once she was gone, I held my magnifier over the box on the check where the dollar amount is written in numbers. They were the right numbers. I went through my mail Jaysaree made my client bring me. It was all junk except for a postcard of the Statue of Liberty. I turned it over. "Love, Carla" read the large letters that didn't require my magnifier.

We had tried to ignore what we both knew, look past it, look off to the side, but it was always there. Before leaving town, she promised to someday make us both forget, or find a way to make it not matter. I set the postcard on top of the others in my desk drawer, all of them containing the same two words.

244

I checked my watch again and phoned the taxicab company that offered minivans. I groaned at the estimate, but had no choice. At least I had been where I was going enough times that when the driver asked if we were there I would know we were. I had him park by the entrance while I went inside.

Dr. Parshall had on his bright blue academic regalia, segments of gold and white rope draped across his neck. Nurse Margaret wheeled him into the hall. He called her bad names while she straightened his mortarboard.

"He's all yours," she said, unlocking my grandmother's old room.

"That won't be necessary, Margaret," Parshall said.

"I thought you wanted to say a few words," I said.

"I'll say them right here," he said in a voice diminished by more than age. "I know there aren't any assholes where you are, Katherine, because they're all down here."

Greeting us in the parking lot behind the library, Londell extended his hand and introduced himself to his former employer. In a month, he would begin his new job in the history department at one of the state universities in Delaware. He had given me the news rather solemnly over beers at Oral Tradition's, the tone of a man with inoperable tumors.

"Londell Bakker." Parshall said the name as though it were associated with unspeakable atrocities. "Who named you that?"

"My mother did, sir."

Parshall grunted and shook his hand. Through gritted teeth, he said, "Thank you for your service to Parshall College."

From the echoes of chatter in the ceiling, the theater seemed about half full. Many students from out of town had decided not to return to Grayford in the middle of summer to receive their diplomas. Some parents, according to one of Hoopel's stories in *The Chanticleer*, refused to honor their children's achievements under these circumstances.

Hoopel shook my hand in the lobby of the Boss Hog's Rib Shack Theater. His girlfriend, the graduate assistant he had sweet-talked into giving him Stashauer's resumé, took a picture of Dr. Parshall. Hoopel bent over the old man's wheelchair.

"Dr. Parshall, do you mind if I ask you a few questions?"

Dr. Parshall took Hoopel's hand. "Thank you for your service to Parshall College."

I parked his chair between the stage and the first row. He

wanted to be the first to congratulate each student after Dean Bibb handed them their diplomas. Seated in the aisle of the front row were Marianne Randallman and Mark Dudek, the individuals most responsible for the highest graduation rate in Parshall's 130 years.

Delilah's PowerPoint presentation never found an audience in the accreditation board. Simkins's annual payments, dating back eleven years, had only purchased probation in one-year increments. Actual accreditation required the approval of board members other than Jefferson Totten. "Unsalvageable" had been the board's assessment of the state of Parshall's academics. When students learned that their degrees, already of questionable worth, no longer awaited them at the end of their four-to-eleven-year journeys, they joined together in a class action lawsuit against the college.

Theo Skipwith voted right away to settle out of court. Sara Freyman, upon learning her inheritance from the namesake she had never met held no monetary value—in fact, her stake in the school could cost her what property she owned—took the legal advice of her former boss and also cast her half-vote to settle. F. Randolph Parshall, knowing his beloved school would have to shutter its doors no matter what, agreed to sell the school if Randallman agreed not to come after his ownership in Rosewall Glen. She agreed, seeing an outside chance to go after the nursing home when she sued the school for the wrongful death of Duncan Musgrove, whose suicide, Randallman had planned to argue, could have been prevented under better working conditions. Fortunately, at least for Dr. Parshall, Janice Musgrove passed away two months after her husband's suicide. She died of a broken heart, according to her obituary. More likely her heart gave out after years of morbid obesity, but Hoopel was entitled to some creative license. It was his final obituary before his promotion to reporter.

Proceeds from the sale of the school's land, after legal fees, were distributed among the student body. All students with at least half the credit required for a bachelor's degree would receive their diplomas. Students with less than half the requisite credits would receive a stipend for tuition not to exceed four years at one of the state universities. Only one student eligible to graduate, Islanda Purvis, turned down her diploma and opted for additional education. Everyone else accepted their parchment from Delilah Bibb in the final act of her tenure as dean. After shaking the hand of the lone trustee in attendance, Parshall's final graduates paused by the front row to collect the additional cash settlement from their attorney, an amount equivalent to one semester of room and board.

246

Delilah delivered the commencement address from the stage, having placed a plank of plywood over the steps to permit wheelchair access. She spoke with passion if not energy. Her speech included portions of screeds she had written for a blog lambasting the state of higher education, a joint venture of her and her daughter.

"I'm doubtful that a single quote-unquote graduate who has walked across this stage today has any knowledge he or she will find useful in the real world. Tell me: What exactly are you prepared to do?"

Half-hearted boos congregated in the cracked ceiling. "How dare she?" said a mother in the row behind me. I recognized the woman's voice in the lobby after the ceremony, sharing her outrage with *The Chanticleer*'s newest reporter.

"Dr. Cowlishaw! I did it!"

Wade Biggins threw his arms around my waist, lifted me a foot off the ground, and spun me around in a carousel hug.

"Congratulations, Wade."

"Now I can do whatever I want."

"Anything at all, Wade."

Someone with white hair and a suit to match sidled up to Wade Biggins somewhat warily.

"Hey, Dad, this is Dr. Cowlishaw. He's the only teacher who ever gave me an A."

I had not missed the accent by a great deal. Mr. Biggins was, however, more reserved than I had imagined, saying a quiet, rather embarrassed *thank you* as he weakly shook my hand.

Twenty minutes after Delilah's final words—"I wish you all so much more than luck"—the theater was empty, save one man onstage. Thayer projected his voice to the last row. He had obtained permission from Cyrus Kavasmaneck to stage all the productions he wished in the three months before the building was scheduled to be demolished. The actor-detective was unexpectedly grateful for how things had turned out. He was turning the events into a screenplay, the treatment for which had already gotten him a phone call from an agent based out of Los Angeles.

"Was that the ending you had hoped for?" I asked.

"More or less," Thayer said. "In my version, Bibb kills herself onstage."

I found Dr. Parshall in the lobby, staring at the bust of his great grandfather.

"That would look great in front of your library window," I said.

If he nodded or shook his head, I didn't see it.

"How about one last trip around the quad?"

I pushed his chair along the crumbling sidewalks. With each bump, Parshall sank a little lower in his chair. I stopped frequently to pull him up by his armpits. When the theater was in front of us again, I asked if he wanted to go inside any of the other buildings.

He shook his head.

I phoned the taxi and we waited in the parking lot.

"Goddammit, anyway," he said. "I hope the spirits that toppled this institution continue to haunt whatever takes its place."

"Yes, sir."

I angled his chair to give him a view of the library and dorm.

"There's that poltergeist, Nick. Above the theater. Do you see it?"

"I see it," I said.